Sugar and Dust

D1713270

Ella Rachel Kerr

To the girls who taught me to be brave. I love you.

CONTENTS

AUTHOR'S NOTE

The inspiration for this novel was taken from my time spent in rural Tanzania. While this is a work of fiction, the light and fire of the characters are based off people who I have met and cooked and laughed with, both in Africa and in my American home. Any character cannot be traced back to one individual, but instead is a patchwork quilt, made up of many people I have known and loved. The setting of this story is in East Africa, however; it is important to realize that this work of fiction delves into one storyline, and no specific region, group of people, or country can be painted with a wide brush and assumed to be similar. This world is a beautifully diverse place, and we must understand that a story gives us a glimpse into a place, but does not define any person or place. Only love can do that.

Furthermore, I write from a perspective of people whose skin I have never lived in. I recognize that I am writing this novel from a place of privilege that I was born into: one of those privileges being I have a platform to stand up, tell a story and have the chance for my voice to be heard. Not everyone has that privilege, but my prayer is one day, everyone will. Difficult and current issues are discussed within this book. If these issues ignite an interest or tug at your heart, I encourage you to do some research. Knowledge is the first step in making this world a better place.

SUGAR AND DUST

ACKNOWLEDGMENTS

I want to say thank you to every person who was courageous enough to show me a piece of their soul and inspire me to write. To the wonderful women in Tanzania who taught me how to laugh until it hurt and what bravery tastes like. To my amazing mother, who encouraged me to keep writing, when I didn't want to. To my father who was the business brain behind this operation. To Remi, for dealing with late night editing and constant storytelling. To Chessa, for being the art of the book. To Lizzy for being my soul sister both in Africa and everywhere in the whole world. To Gabby, Grace, Corinne, Emily and Taina, for holding me steady while I spilled my heart (both over the phone and onto these pages.) This book wouldn't be possible without you. I love you.

SUGAR AND DUST

1

Dear Mom-

I had a dream that you were here in Africa. You were carrying a bucket of water on your head, swaying your hips side to side, not spilling a single drop. It felt so real, it made me think that maybe I had seen you do it before, like my dream was a memory. The nurses say I have a fever, and they tell me dreams that vivid are normal when your blood is on fire. It doesn't feel normal to me.

I messed everything up, Mom. I didn't mean to hurt anyone, truly I didn't. I was always trying to do the right thing. Is this how you felt? Is this why you left? So bleary eyed in the face of right and wrong that you crumbled up into dust?

This letter is to say that I forgive you, even though I know you will never read it. I forgive you because I know that the world doesn't always clarify right and wrong until it's too late. I forgive you because I think I am going to need someone to forgive me, too.

I love you,
Isa

2

This is what I knew of tragedy: run as far and as fast as you possibly can. The plane touched down on red African dust exactly five months and two weeks after the death of my mother. My shoulders were sore from hunching under the weight of her loss, and my legs burned with the fire of the restless. My heart slowed down the longer I stayed on that plane. The burning subsided in my limbs and peace dripped into my veins the further I travelled from the place that I had known her. I did not stop to consider the fact that perhaps Africa had known her, too.

I smelled Tanzania before I saw her. She was warm bodies and smoke and sweet milk. I closed my eyes and willed the scent to seep into my pores and melt into my hair. This smell was not familiar and that was all I wanted in those days: the conscious act of not being reminded. With closed eyes I listened to those around me murmur and stir as the wheels of the plane hit the tarmac. I tried to pick out phrases or syllables I had encountered in my Swahili book that rested in my lap. The language blended and flowed together too quickly for me to distinguish one word from another. I was comforted by such newness.

One by one, the passengers filed down the aisle of the plane and along a narrow staircase onto tired pavement. I bunched my skirt in my hand and pulled it up above my ankles to make my descent easier. It was not humid, but it was hot. My legs sweat and stuck together underneath the skirt. My suitcase lay sleepily on the tarmac, tipped up against another bag, thrown haphazardly from the plane. I grabbed it and began to follow the crowd as they filtered into the night with hugs and songs and whispers from the airport. And this is how I arrived in Africa: with four long skirts in a suitcase, a pocket Swahili dictionary, a broken heart, and a fourteen-month job contract at the nearby school. I swept a mass of curly hair into a bun on top of my head and ensured everything I owned was accounted for. Seeing my life in a suitcase lodged a heaviness in my throat.

"IsaBEL! IsaBEL, where are you, my DEAR?" It felt strange, to hear the familiarity of my own name in a place so foreign. "ISABEL! I know it is one of you!" the voice continued to ring through the colorful crowd under the night sky.

Underneath the street lamp that illuminated the tarmac stood a tall, thin woman wrapped in colorful pieces of fabric. She was so long and lean she seemed like a tree, waving her willowy arms towards me as I began to walk closer. A large purple cloth encircled her entire body from her ankles all the way up past her chest, and was pinned with a safety pin at her shoulder. Smaller, thinner squares of patterned fabrics were tied around her shoulders and neck. The pictures in my dictionary were strikingly similar to the woman before me: this is how the women from the local tribe dressed.

In my long skirt, I picked up my pace, my large suitcase rumbling behind me over the uneven pavement.

"It's me!" I called out to the woman, feeling strangely like a child who had found her way home, "It's me, I am Isabel!"

The tall woman clapped her hands excitedly and neon plastic bracelets clicked around her wrist. She reached out both of her hands and clasped them firmly around my wrist.

"Welcome to Tanzania!" she sang, her smile lighting up her entire thin frame. "My name is Nylie. I work at Amani Manor, too, and I wanted to greet you when you first arrived in Africa!" She flicked her eyes towards me and I noticed a distinct difference in the color of her eyes: one a deep blue black and the other a coffee tan. It drew me in closer and I could not look away.

The woman and I matched each other in height, both lanky legs that stretched too high, and long arms that reached too long. But my sweaty skirt felt uncomfortable and athletic shoes on my feet were clunky and awkward in the heat. I was suddenly self-conscious of the mass of curly hair on top of my head as I spoke to this confident woman with a cleanly shaven head and perfectly drawn eyebrows over her distinctly different eyes.

Nylie continued to hold my hand as she talked, "Richard here does not speak English so well, so I wanted to come help him greet you the moment you arrived!" Nylie gestured with her head to a man standing quietly to her side. He, too, was dressed in large cloths, but in various hues of red, instead of the purples that Nylie wore. He smiled shyly in my direction.

I attempted a formal Swahili greeting, but it caught in my throat the way nervous words do. Richard smiled at the attempt and offered his response in soft Swahili.

"Listen to your Swahili, Madam!" Nylie exclaimed, and finally released my hand. The three of us began walking from beneath the street lamp into the starlit night where I could see a few cars parked in the distance. "You will love Tanzania so soon, God willing!" Nylie led the charge into the dark with her rubber sandals.

Richard was the driver for Amani Manor, the school where I would live and work for the next fourteen months. He unlocked a dusty red jeep parked in the lot and heaved my suitcase into the backseat with Nylie. His hands brushed together, gently, slowly, before sticking the key in the ignition and twisting for several minutes before the engine rumbled and yawned. I sat in the passenger's seat, dust sticking to my sweaty skin.

Nylie continued to chat as we drove along for a few minutes on a paved road with no signs and no markings. Then, the jeep took a sharp turn off of the highway and into the dust. For a moment, I wondered if we had made a wrong turn, but Richard kept the car steadily rumbling down the rocky path, avoiding termite mounds and large rocks. I had heard stories, everyone had, about people who go into a foreign country and don't return. Perhaps this was how it happened: a jet lagged American, a gregarious young woman and a driver tumble into the night, never to be seen again.

My father's wife, Theresa, had concerns about how clear headed I was to embark on this journey. In her mind, I was a tired twenty-five-year-old with a heavy heart who could stumble into the savannah and never find her way back out. Theresa sat me down one day on the couch in my father's house and held both of my hands. She told me that she loved me and she knew I needed to go, but to promise her I would come back home, if not for her then for my father. I nodded solemnly and swore to her I would. My eyes burned and my lips quivered as I held her gaze. Hot tears burned rivers down my cheeks. Theresa reached out and squeezed my shoulder. But I was not crying because I would miss her, or my father, or out of fear of the unknown. I cried because I knew my own mother would never have made me promise her something like that.

The car continued into the dark and my suspicion about our final destination grew. My face flushed and sweat dripped down my chest as I reached for the air conditioner and turned the knob to high. Before Richard could stop me, oceans of dust rushed out of the air vents and onto my face and hair and into my lap. I hurriedly turned the fan back off. Nylie laughed loudly in the back, and stuck her face between Richard and me, "Welcome to Africa, my dear!"

I laughed, too, at the strangeness of the situation. Covered with dust in a car with people I did not know in a continent that I did not belong. That's all humor is, after all. A juxtaposition of unmatchable things.

Just then, Richard slowed down the car even further. In the dark I could make out houses now, small and square with rounded mud corners. In the distance, specks of light radiated, some from fires outside of the homes, some from the eerie blue glow of solar light bulbs. Voices drifted in the air, people laughing, a baby crying, distant singing. My heart lowered gently from my throat to my chest as we came into the village. The voices grew louder and the fires seemed brighter, and soon shrieking children surrounded the car: screaming and waving and laughing as the jeep rumbled down the road.

"This is our home," Nylie said, a smile in her voice. A particularly brave child attempted to hold on to the back of the jeep as it slowly meandered its way through the village. "And now, it's your home, too."

3

Goosebumps sprouted from my skin like houses from the dust: unnoticeable at first, until they covered the entire brown land. Richard steered the tired car past a watchman who waited at the wooden gate of the school and moved slowly to unlatch the metal hook. The driveway to Amani Manor was lined with rose-colored begonias that grew like vines up the wire fence. The school was painted a friendly shade of yellow, and the classrooms formed a square around a central courtyard. In the middle of the courtyard was a single flagpole, ringing listlessly as the metal snaps hit the pole.

"Amani Manor, we love you!" Nylie sang as Richard put the car into park. He quickly walked around to the back seat and set my suitcase in the dust. Nylie pulled a key from around her neck and unlocked the large wooden door closest to the entrance of the school. She struggled to force it open.

I felt a small pinch on my arm and spun around to see what African insect had surely stung or bit or feasted on my arm. But there was no insect; no menacing creature at my elbow. Instead, there was a small boy with fabric tied around his shoulders, who watched with bright eyes for my reaction.

I bit my lip to keep from laughing and knelt down to be closer to the brave toddler, "Hey," I said, and then remembered my words, "*Mambo!*"

The child clapped dusty hands and shrieked with laughter, then ran away on bare feet. Behind him, three other children had followed, all giggling loudly; giddy with the idea that the light skinned woman had spoken and her skin felt just the same as theirs.

Nylie muttered under her breath and clicked her tongue in the children's direction, which made them laugh even louder. With that, she forced the door open and the lights of the room crackled awake. "This is your room, Madam Isabel," Nylie announced, and walked into the classroom that had been altered for the purpose of living.

In the corner was wedged a twin-sized bed on an intricate mahogany bed frame. Above the mattress hung a mosquito net heavy with dust. There was a dresser in the same dark wood with a few knobs missing, and a mirror leaned against the wall. A sink rested in the corner and a few colorful cloths and drawings hung on the wall.

I sat down on the bed and looked around. The light gave the room a greenish hue in the dark and I felt instantly lonely.

"It's okay for you?" Nylie asked, and sat down next to me. She twisted her wrists and watched her bracelets topple down her forearm.

"Yes, it's perfect for me. Thank you."

"You don't fear sleeping alone?" Nylie asked. She continued to watch the plastic shine against the iridescent light.

"No. I think I prefer it."

Nylie sighed, "I think I prefer it, too, but preferring something means you are lucky enough for choices. I don't think I am lucky enough to prefer yet."

I nodded and melted deeper into the mattress under the weight of her words. I did not yet understand decisions as privilege. I had not yet seen what a human would do for the right to choose.

The room was suddenly filled with a low humming; a static crinkle filled the air then the single light bulb fluttered off.

I sat up quickly, "What happened?" I asked, suddenly aware of the noises that accompany the dark. The stillness felt unbearable as I held my breath and waited for the lights to turn back on.

Nylie sighed a big, heavy sigh that was more dreamy than frustrated. "Oh, the power is cut, my dear," she said. I wondered if she had closed her eyes and was dreaming about sleeping alone.

"Well, when will it be back on?" I kicked my feet around the base of my bed to search for the shoes I had slid off of my feet. As if there was somewhere I needed to go. As if my shoes could bring back the light.

"Oh, I'm not sure. Maybe late this evening. Maybe for a few days." She was not distressed in the slightest.

"And why is the power cut?" the darkness seemed suffocating.

Nylie laughed again, unaware of my discomfort. "Sometimes the power is cut because of a bad storm. And sometimes the power is cut because of bad luck. But today? The power is probably cut because the election is occurring."

I waited for her to explain more.

"Well, if the electric company prefers one candidate, then they will cut the power when the other candidate is speaking on the radio. Then no one will hear what he is saying."

"Is that allowed?" I asked. My eyes began to adjust to the light. The moon outside shone navy light into my room. The outline of homes and specks of fire emerged in my window.

Nylie seemed uninterested with our conversation, "I don't know if it's allowed! I have bigger problems than deciding if the electric company is good or bad. Like now, I must convince Richard to drive me back to my home because it is so dark out."

She stood and I heard her slide plastic sandals back onto her feet. "You will be okay here for tonight? Tomorrow we can talk more at school and answer all of the questions you may have. But it's hard to answer questions in the dark."

I nodded quickly, although Nylie surely could not have seen my gesture.

"I am happy you have arrived, Isabel!" Nylie said and pressed the key to the room into my hand.

Her plastic sandals slapped the cement floor and the blue light seeped into the room as she opened the door.

"We are all happy you have arrived."

I had not felt this type of alone in many, many years. It welled up in my chest and sent tears down my cheeks, but not from the sadness. Instead, they were tears like running in the wind: exhilarated tears. Powerful tears. Freedom tears.

I used the last bit of my cell phone battery as a flashlight as I fished a clean t-shirt out of my suitcase and stripped the sweaty skirt down around my ankles. I found the baby wipes Theresa had packed and wiped down my entire salty body.

The sounds of a rural world I did not know screamed in my ears, as I lay wide awake on the mattress. The deep rumbling groans of cows. The crows of a night rooster. Babies cried and dogs yipped and crickets numbed my pulsing in my brain.

My mind wandered to the child who had pinched my elbow and wondered what his home looked like. Who was sleeping with Nylie in her bed tonight? Perhaps a younger sister, a boyfriend, an aging mother?

I closed my eyes and recalled the last time I shared a bed with Ivy Supeet. I was nine years old in my maternal grandmother's home in New Orleans. My father had sent me out there for the month of July to be with my mother, and I had agreed to go. Ivy didn't get out of bed that summer. I cooked her ramen noodles with nine-year-old hands and carried hot bowls upstairs to her room. Sitting on her bed, I begged her to eat the noodles, and then begged her to open her eyes, and then begged my father to not make me go back to New Orleans anymore. He never made me go back, not even for the funeral. Sometimes, I wish he had.

4

The whispers sounded like bird wings. They were light and airy and fluttered against the thin wooden door. Yellow light streamed into the window through a threadbare curtain. There was no panic in my chest when I woke up that morning, as there often is the first night in the new space. I had slept hard and dreamless. My eyes fluttered open to my first encounter with African light.

I stirred in my bed. Sweat dripped off of my forehead and between my thighs. As the bed creaked with my movement, the whispers outside were silent, only to be replaced with unsuccessfully suppressed giggles of girls. What time was it? My phone battery was dead. I sat up in bed and searched the room for a clock. The room was cheerier in the daylight, albeit still entirely made of cement and tin. The paint peeled yellow on the walls and the sink looked tired in the corner. Out my window I could see a handful of girls in powder blue shirts and navy skirts attempting to make their way through the dust and short bushes towards the school. I wanted a shower. I wanted a whole pot of coffee to pour down my throat while it was still too hot.

I unzipped my suitcase and pulled out a burgundy skirt that hit mid shin and a fresh white t-shirt. The scent of Theresa's laundry detergent flooded my senses. I pulled the elastic out of my hair and attempted to contain the frizz and curls in a tight braid at the back of my head. Next, I tried the sink. It spit and sputtered, but after a few nervous moments, it gently released a clear stream. After washing my face, brushing my teeth and smoothing my hair back, I slid on sandals and zipped up my suitcase tightly. The thought of a scorpion crawling into my clothes tightened my chest and I cautiously shook out a sweater before tying it around my waist, and taking one last look in the mirror. Today, I decided, was the first day of everything I wanted.

Upon opening my door, I was met by six whispering girls sitting on the cement in navy skirts with cleanly shaven heads. Their brown eyes widened at the sight of me. Someone whispered under her breath "One, two, three!"

"Good morning, Madam! Welcome to Amani Manor, Madam!" the girls sang out in a clearly rehearsed greeting.

Their nervousness mirrored mine.

"Good morning to you!" I sang out cheerfully, faking confidence that did not live in my bones.

I closed the door behind me as I stepped outside. The girls stood, shy and giggling, and gathered their notebooks, dusted off the backs of their skirts, and ran away. All except for one. She was taking longer to gather her belongings, and I realized it was because a baby was tied to her back in the same pattered fabric that Nylie had worn yesterday.

"Who is this little one?" I asked the girl, who looked up at me from behind curly eyelashes.

"This is Samwel, Madam," she stood and brushed the back of her skirt as the others had done.

"Is he your brother?" I asked, warmed by the idea a sister would care for a sibling in such a way.

"No, Madam, Samwel is my son."

I searched the girl's face and attempted to picture her slim frame recently pregnant. She was a teenager, perhaps fifteen or sixteen. The girl was darker than her peers and her irises were a milky brown. Her eyes stayed fixed on mine as she waited for me to react to this news.

"Well, Samwel is sure lucky to have you as a mother," I declared, with the same artificial confidence I had found to say good morning.

The girl smiled briefly and ran in the direction of her schoolmates, the baby bouncing on her adolescent back.

"Good morning, Madam!" rang a familiar voice. Nylie appeared walking down the dusty driveway, wrapped head to toe in a different thick fabric, burgundy this time, with accents of yellow and black. Thin silver chains clinked around her ankles.

"Hi, Nylie," I walked towards the thin woman as she fished a key from around her neck and unlocked the office door.

"How did you sleep, like a baby or like a rock?" she asked me as we walked into the dusty office.

I laughed. "Well I suppose I slept like a baby," I told her, suppressing a sneeze as the dust settled.

Nylie paused, a wide grin on her small face. "So, you wet the bed then?" She laughed loudly and I followed suit, surprised at the nature of the joke. I quietly wondered how I was to distinguish jokes from language barriers in the future.

Inside the office sat a large oak desk with an American style office chair and gray file cabinet. A Tanzanian flag hung faded and tired on the wall. The back of the office opened to a large kitchen table with four chairs, a mini fridge, a small electric burner and a dripping sink. The wall was furnished with cabinets stocked with jams and jellies and packs of noodles.

Nylie began an energetic tour of the space, "This is where you will sit, Isabel." She gestured to the dusty desk with several adaptors and converters, made specifically for plugging American appliances into Tanzanian outlets. "And in here is your work." She opened the file cabinet that held stacks and stacks of spiral notebooks labeled "Expenses 2015, Expenses 2014, Contracts 2013."

I felt my head pulse, my senses were overwhelmed and I rubbed my forehead, "And you, Nylie? What is it you do here?" I hoped to hear her say she was the secretary or the translator or the office assistant: someone who would stand by me every step of the day and answer my questions and calm my fears at they arose.

Nylie continued her tour, "Oh, I just bring water to the school. On the back of my donkey. Every day, 7 a.m. I will be here with the water for the day!"

She saw my brow furrow as I quickened my step to keep up with the lively tour, "I just have a lot of ideas, and I know a lot of things, so I stay at the Manor, even after the water is delivered."

There was nothing to do but laugh at her enthusiasm and I followed right at her ankles as she continued the tour.

It was strange to think familiar working thoughts in such an unfamiliar place. In my past life, my American life, I had worked in finance. In high heels and a dress skirt, I had sat at a desk organizing budgets and writing expense reports. That is, until my mother died. Her death created a paralysis in me so strong that even the tears refused to fall. I lived outside of my body that refused to sleep, refused to drive me to work, even refused to swallow or even speak my mother's name.

After Ivy's funeral in New Orleans, while I stood red eyed and resistant in my Denver apartment, I told my father I needed to leave, to find something grounding and meaningful. Life those days felt strange and plastic. Food tasted artificial and the cubicle walls of my once stimulating job suffocated me. I stopped going to work. I stopped answering my phone. When my father sat me down and asked me what I needed to keep moving forward, I told him I craved perspective. This was mostly true. The complete truth was I no longer wanted to wake up in the same bed and the same world without my mother.

Mink Kelly, the founder of the school, was the mother-in-law of my father's colleague. My father heard his colleague mention Amani Manor, how they were looking for someone to migrate down to the dust for a year to organize financial records of a school in the rural land.

I bet my father tried to turn and walk away. I bet he tried to shake the words out of his mouth and winced when he heard the words come out of his own mouth, "My daughter Isabel would be interested."

5

"I met a girl with a baby this morning," I told Nylie as we walked the campus together. Nylie pointed out the grasses the donkeys liked to eat and where to "burn the rubbish," as she swung her thin arms at her sides.

She paused her tour to answer me, "Yes, that is Loveness. Her mother usually takes care of the baby while she is at school but her mother was sick today so she had to bring Samwel with her."

"That is her own baby, though? Is Loveness married?"

"No, my dear, that was not a baby or a husband Loveness wanted. She was very angry at the beginning of that baby's life. Very angry. Because that baby came from, you know… the *rape*." Nylie whispered this last word as if to make the reality softer. It didn't work. The word, it seemed, was more taboo then the action itself.

Nylie tried to change the topic when she noticed the furrow in my brow.

"She is a good student and she thought the baby would prevent her from continuing school at Amani Manor. But her mother is a very strong woman. Her mother watches that baby every day so Loveness can learn." Nylie rattled on a potentially happy ending to the story she found herself telling. The bracelets clicked around her wrists as she talked.

I nodded and followed Nylie underneath the banana trees and considered the world where people awaited their fates like prizes from a gumball machine. It didn't matter what you did to prepare, you turned the handle and took whatever came out. We walked towards the kitchen where three cooks bustled in a smoky cinderblock kitchen, hurriedly making meals for the students. The light was thicker here; I could feel the sun on my skin like a heavy blanket, orange and yellow and sighing.

"Where is Samwel's father?" I asked, and considered all of the fifteen-year-olds who did not have a mother as strong as Loveness's, who were forced to create new lives outside of the classroom.

Nylie shrugged. "I don't know. He wasn't from this village or from this tribe. He came one night, then ran away. We don't know who he is."

"And the police can't find him?"

Nylie laughed, with an edge of cynicism, even condescension. "The police don't come to the tribal lands, Isabel. Nobody comes to the tribal lands."

The students were beginning to filter in through the gate now, bright eyed and shy at the newcomer with the long hair and the light skin. The brave girls came tiptoeing close in plastic shoes with white knee-high socks and whispered, "Good morning, Madam." A few came with small gifts: plastic bracelets like Nylie's, or intricately beaded Tanzanian flags on a string. A particularly small girl pulled at my skirt and handed over a plastic bag of okra that must've weighed nearly as much as she did. I knelt down close to her walnut cheeks.

"Thank you," I said, and she reached out to touch the blonde hair on my arms. She cried when she touched it, and ran away holding her skirt around her waist so it wouldn't fall down her thin hips. Nylie laughed loudly.

The garden was located behind the kitchen where the three large cooks stirred enormous pots with long wooden spoons. One cook sat on a rock outside the kitchen, sifting rice in a large, flat, woven bowl. She picked out rocks or bugs from the grains of white rice. Two gardeners bent over deep green rows of vegetables.

"You may take any food from here that you like," Nylie said, smiling. Tomatoes and eggplant hung heavy from vines, and shiny green mangoes clung in clusters of three. "But no mangoes yet. You must wait until the mangoes are the color of the sun."

Our tour continued out past the garden where a wooden stand-alone structure hovered on a cement platform.

"The shower is here," Nylie explained. "But you must know that the cobras like to hide underneath the concrete. So, if you see a cobra, you just scream the name of Richard the guard and he will come running to kill the snake."

I waited for Nylie to laugh at another ridiculous joke, but she did not. The cobras were no joke.

"Also," Nylie said as we turned and made our way back to the yellow school building, now teeming with life, "If you see a small ant with wings, but its stomach has small red stripes on it? Do not squish it! Just blow it off your skin." She mimicked blowing an ant into the wind. "Because those are Nairobi flies. And their guts will burn you!"

"Nylie, don't scare the poor girl, not yet anyway." A woman's voice came from behind me. A slim, clean-cut woman with chocolate skin in a business blazer and a long brown skirt reached out to shake my hand. "My name is Marie," she told me confidently, "I am the head teacher here at Amani Manor, and you must be Isabel."

I nodded and shook the woman's hand quickly. I was intimidated by her poise at a moment when I felt smeared with dust and newness and jet lag.

"Nice to meet you Miss…"

"Head teacher. You may call me Marie."

Marie had a deep smooth voice with hints of British-accented syllables.

I smiled and felt my lips crack, "Nice to meet you, Marie."

"And where are you from, Isabel? You don't look American to me." We walked past a large girl who rang a metal bell with a rock. The harsh clanging sent the girls sprinting in black plastic shoes to their classrooms.

"I am American. My mother is half black."

Marie walked with her hands behind her back, gazing at her perfectly shined shoes. "And the other half?" she asked.

"Oh! The other half is white." I felt my face flush. This world did not hold white as the default.

Marie nodded, seemingly satisfied with my answers. As we reached the courtyard, she stopped and looked at me, squinting slightly into the sun. Students began to sing within a classroom, their small voices echoing against the concrete walls. Another teacher had instructed the girls to move their desks. Metal chairs screeched as they dragged them across the floor.

"Now, before we begin this school year, and so everyone has their priorities in line, I ask you, Isabel, why are you here?"

Marie crossed her arms across her chest. Not in a challenging way, but in the way a leader does when comfortable with hard questions.

The wind-swept particles of dust against my bare legs, burning my calves. My stomach growled gently, a complaint from lack of food since the airplane ride. I was here because I could not continue *there*. That was the true answer. I was here because my body no longer felt like my own in America and I wanted there to be a reason for that feeling. If I did not feel like myself, if I made mistakes or could not find the right words, if life was simply too much, well then that was perfectly acceptable. I was in Africa, after all. As far as anyone knew I was flighty and aimless because I was far from home. Not in spite of it.

Marie searched my face; seemingly ready to rebuke any answer I gave. But answers did not form on my tongue or with my hands or with my feet on red dirt. They hadn't formed when I had bought the ticket or walked off the plane. My answers did not bubble up from my chest when I saw the girls for the first time, or woke up in a full sweat in a room that was not yet my own. So, I said nothing.

Marie spoke softly, a motherly warmth suddenly enveloping her direct nature, "Whatever you are here for, Isabel, we are grateful. But Africa is not a place to heal yourself. And Africa is not a place that needs healing. So, teach and learn, but don't expect anything more. Do you understand?"

Her words were not cold but they sent goose bumps down my chest. A small black ant with wings landed on my arm. I looked closely at the bug: thin red stripes streaked down its abdomen. I considered blowing the Nairobi fly off of my skin, as Nylie had suggested. "It's guts will burn you," she had warned. And then, I smashed the ant on my arm.

6

I dreamt my mother was air and I was fire. In my cold and watery sleep world, I saw her exhaling too quickly, sighing too loudly, and sending my flame to a point of near extinction. Then, in my dream, I saw myself at Ivy's funeral, the one I had never attended. I stood in all black with my hair twisted up into a scarf, and gently faded into the atmosphere. After all, no fire can exist without air. It was a startling dream, hot and sweaty, and I lie in the heat of my African room and allowed myself to remember Ivy for the first time since her death.

I only ever knew the facts of my mother. Her name was Ivy Supeet. Her mother was black and her father had been white but he was dead now. She was born and raised in New Orleans. Ivy's mother and grandmother and great grandmother had never wandered out of the South.

Occasionally, she would appear in Denver for a birthday, a basketball game, a stiff-armed hug. Like me, she was tall and had creamy skin and thick curls of hair, although you rarely saw her hair. She twisted it up in a cloth in an African way, knotted at the front and tucked under so no one could tell what was under there: braids or locks or a shaved head like my white daddy. She wasn't pretty. But she was striking. Her eyes emerged from her smooth face like black olives: shiny and waiting. Something about her movements seemed unnatural, as though she were visiting that tall, supple body. It was as if she were a child who had to maneuver those limbs, those breasts, those thin brown fingers. In my mind, she was a nurse, a healer, a muse to a famous artist. I wondered what she thought about. I could never tell.

The image of Ivy the African Goddess was a comfort to me. When life seemed unfair, I could tell myself my mother was a queen! And she kept a royal distance from me due to all of her queenly engagements. That

21

convenient distance kept alive the image, and allowed me to pretend anything that I wanted: I was a princess. I lived in a castle. I was loved.

The situation of my birth was so abnormal and not nice, and my father and his lovely wife were so normal and nice, that I never got the full story of the love between my father and Ivy. Here was what I learned from twenty-five years of questioning: Ivy had been a waitress in Denver, and my father a regular at the cafe. They were both originally from New Orleans and I suppose that's what got the conversation started.

Had my father ordered hot coffee late one night at the diner and had she added a little bit of peppermint vodka and sat down next to him? Maybe she didn't wear her hair tucked away back then; maybe its curly mass flew out in all directions, a reflection of her chaotic brain. Maybe at first, she was enticing *and* striking. Perhaps he couldn't take her artistic frenzy. Was she too exotic for a stockbroker with a title and reputation and spreadsheets? Maybe she was hard to hold onto: a girl with black eyes and coffee skin.

Or maybe it just wasn't love. Maybe it was an accident in the backseat of a '97 Silverado, tears on a positive pregnancy test. Maybe no one even cried. Maybe they all just handled it.

After one week or one year of my parents' brief love (I never could quite figure out the timing) my mother got pregnant and gave birth to me on a dry August day. A few months later, she went back to New Orleans because she wanted to live closer to her own mother, but she didn't want the strange child she had created to come along; to remind her of all the things she couldn't soothe.

Ivy had tied her hair up in a cloth, pressed the doorbell of my father's house with fingers that did not seem like her own, and handed off her daughter to the nice blonde lady with the nice smile. I never understood whether Theresa was a new or old girlfriend or had any idea of my existence prior to this encounter, or what she may have said when she walked to the door and saw a baby in the arms of a woman who had been held by my father, but not loved by him. I'm not sure what anyone says to that. But that was it. I lived with my father now. I was three months old.

Once, when I was about ten years old, I heard Theresa whispering on the phone in the living room. "Just calm down, Ivy, and take a deep breath. No one is going anywhere tonight. Isabel is safe and taken care of, I need you to do the same thing for you."

I had sat on my knees in the dark hall and listened hard. What was my mother saying on the other end? I felt defensive of Ivy, and bristled when I thought that Theresa or my father was talking down to her. I wanted to stand up and scream, "That is my mother! Why does she not call *me* when she needs help, why does she call *you*?" But I remained sitting on my knees throwing prayers up to the ceiling asking God to please look over my mother. Please give her someone to talk to and someone to love her. And please keep

Theresa from telling anyone that Ivy called and cried. And please Lord, don't let her die.

7

Maya, big-boned and nineteen-years old, was in the fifth grade. I was told she had repeated this grade for several years, and there was little hope of her getting promoted to sixth. She had big calves and big breasts and big eyes and big hands and she stuck out drastically from the other fifth grade nymphs with their flat chests and bony ankles and knees. I suspected she was purposefully failing the fifth grade so she could stick around the Manor. After grade seven, the girls had to find somewhere else to learn. If the Manor could keep girls in school during their formative years of primary education and prevent them from getting married, perhaps they would have the ability to find ways to attend secondary school. Perhaps there would be a way to attend a teaching college or professional university, if the stars aligned. But the reality seemed to be that instead of preventing marriage of a child who had no choice in the matter, Amani Manor pushed the problem back a few years. The girls were still being bound to men twice their age and against their will, but at sixteen-years-old instead of ten. The Manor didn't dissolve disaster. It delayed it.

Maya was logical and seemed to understand the game, and that's why I believed she was failing grade five each year on purpose. Not because she couldn't pass, and not because she was lazy, but simply because she did not know what else to do. To Maya, sitting in small plastic chairs discussing nouns, verbs, and adjectives for the third time in three years was more appealing than marriage. Maybe she just liked the fact that she had chosen this option. I would often peer out my window in the office, over my desk covered in dust and sticky notes with scribbled numbers, and see Maya sitting on a bench, knees apart, arms crossed over her broad chest. Eyebrows furrowed, she would sit and smile. Because she knew what she was doing. This wasn't her first choice, but it was a goddamn choice. Spite was so much

24

safer than softness.

I thought I understood Maya. I didn't love this new home. I didn't know Tanzania: I didn't have anything here. But I had chosen to come here. And right or wrong I stood by that.

I sat at my desk in the stuffy, windless office two weeks after my arrival and watched the shaved-headed girls lingering in the doorway. They seemed to be considering coming into my office to lay their words at my feet. I watched them weigh the pros and cons before giving an aggressive slam of the door and walking home. Maya was one of those girls; she slinked past my window and threw a glare in my direction after classes on a Friday afternoon. I recognized that type of stubbornness, walked outside and put my hands on my hips.

"Maya, are you doing alright?" I asked. The wind picked up and both of us instinctively covered our eyes from the dust. I leaned against the doorframe and saw Maya standing in the courtyard with her lips in full pout. She pulled small dead petals from a flower bush.

"I need something." Her face stayed hard but her voice was soft, soft, soft like a child.

"What do you need?"

"A blanket."

"Why do you need a blanket? It's not even cold." I searched for patience and spoke slowly.

Maya kicked up more dust with her plastic shoe and stared down at the brown swirls she had created with her feet.

"Maya if you don't answer me I can't help you."

She continued to create the dust storm with her shoes, forming a cloud around us, like a barrier from the world outside these dirt walls.

"Forget it." She turned and began to drag her feet down the driveway, slowly, begging me to ask her to stay.

I shuffled towards her and touched her thick wrists. "Maya," I whispered in a voice as soft as her own had been. "Why do you need a blanket?"

She looked down and rolled her neck in circles. Blinking back tears, she gazed past me, beyond me, as if peering into neighboring Kenya. Maybe her eyes had caught a glimpse of London, Tokyo, New York City, anywhere without this dust.

"My mother told me to sleep with my fiancée or sleep outside. So, I need a blanket so I can sleep outside."

My eyes closed and exhaled hot air through my nostrils and it cooled the sweat that had beaded on my upper lip. I pictured Maya with her knees tucked to her chest as she sat outside the mud hut, refusing with that fiery stubbornness to come inside. To lie with a man. To let anyone else decide her future.

"Just take a seat outside the office, I'll get you a blanket." I kept my voice low and Maya nodded.

"Put it in a plastic bag," she whispered. "I don't want others to see what I am carrying."

My eyebrows rose, acknowledging I heard her request and would oblige. Taking a blanket from the donation room, I wrapped it in a black plastic garbage bag and handed it to the waiting young woman with a gaze eight thousand miles away. She nodded her thanks. My head dipped in reply. No phone calls to the authorities, no storming into her parents' house, no lecture on her rights and the probability of pregnancy with every unsafe sexual encounter. Maya just needed a blanket, and that was all that I gave. I told myself I didn't do more because I was patient. Really, I was just scared.

The girls in the Manor were often shy, and staying in a windless office typing numbers into a keyboard was lonely. Daily, I felt more of an outsider as I sat behind those cement walls with sunburned cheeks that made the young girls giggle. There was too much division: between where I had been—what I knew and saw and experienced in life—and the lives and culture of the girls who roamed these classrooms every day.

Maya stopped speaking to me after the blanket exchange; vulnerability made her heavy and she turned her face every time I tried to smile or greet her in the morning. I was lonely, and it seemed, rightfully so. The world was harder and smaller than I had remembered, and each day felt increasingly pressurized: like I was living my life in a small, windowless oven.

A month after my arrival, the cook knocked on the office door carrying the tray of rice and beans that I came to loathe and crave. I thanked her graciously as I always did, and used a metal spoon to scoop a heaping lump of sticky rice and beans onto a plastic plate. I closed my computer, stepped outside and closed the wooden door behind me. I walked across the barren courtyard to the cafeteria where I could hear the familiar noises of my own childhood: shrieking girl laughter and whispered gossip.

The cafeteria was outdoors, painted tired yellow with a tin roof over plastic picnic benches. The voices echoed a little less loudly off of the tin roof when I stepped onto the smooth concrete and into their girl world of rice and beans and desert heat. Maya caught my eye, but shook her head, and quickly looked away. Then, I found a face I knew: the same face that held my gaze with milky eyes the first morning I arrived in Tanzania.

"Hey Loveness," I smiled and sat next to the girl, who scooted to the side to make room for me on the picnic bench. She wore a confused look on her face. "Do you mind if I sit next to you to eat my lunch today?"

"You are welcome, Madam," Loveness gave a nervous smile, as did the other girls at the table. And for the first time since my feet met African dust, I felt a little less alone.

8

Sunday evenings I called Theresa. It was the morning in Denver, before church, and I sat on the cement steps and leaned against the wall. From where I sat, I could see the courtyard on my right; quietly awaiting hundreds of loud laughing girls come Monday morning. On my left, I could see out into the village: immovable Acacia trees that stood fast no matter how hard the wind blew. This corridor where I sat was the threshold: the place between the truth of rural village life and the school walls that promised an ounce of hope.

Most of the time, during those Sunday evening conversations, I listened because my words didn't form. It was hard to explain everyday life. It felt like explaining to someone who'd been born blind why I chose a particular paint color for my bedroom. Would they understand brighter or lighter or contrast or hue? It wasn't Theresa's fault, not at all. But I squelched frustration by keeping it simple. I stuck to basics. What food I ate. Names that I had heard and liked. What kind of music was popular. The rest was unnecessary. It would have been explaining a deluge before she understood water.

Theresa told me about the world I used to live in: my father was doing well, just working more hours than usual. She was trying out a new gym next week, one that was closer to her home. I pressed the phone to my ear as two seven-year-old girls carried bundles of firewood on top of their heads to their home. Their dresses were humorously fancy: silk and shiny with large bows around the waist in startling green and pink. They contrasted with the world behind them: rolling waves of dust and the crackle and snap of twigs as their thin arms adjusted the bundles on their heads.

A younger child, perhaps three years old, came running up to the girls. The taller one set down her bundle of sticks, picked the toddler up and fastened the baby on her back with a cloth. She picked up her bundle of sticks once again. And the three went walking, slowly, confidently, into the dust.

Theresa could feel I was losing interest. She changed the subject, "I ran into one of your old friends the other day. Who was the boy with the African mother who used to play basketball at your high school?"

My heart sped up at her comment. I knew the man she was speaking about. I had seen him just a week before I had arrived in Tanzania, "His name is Penn. His mother was a friend of Ivy."

"Oh. Yes, I think his name was Penn, but Isa, don't call your mother by her first name, it's disrespectful."

I didn't say anything.

"Well, he is a good-looking young man, and must be successful too. He was dressed very nicely when I saw him at the gas station. Anyway, he said to tell you hi. It seemed like he knew you were in Africa…"

The three girls slowly vanished from view across the horizon. I wondered if their mothers missed them when they were far from home.

"Yeah, I ran into Penn about a week before I left for Tanzania. His mom is from out here, you know, so we talked about it a little bit."

I hadn't recognized Penn when I saw him two months ago at the Denver coffee shop. My mind was elsewhere, furiously researching visas, shots, residence permits and weather conditions of a place I had so suddenly decided to live.

"Bonjour," he said, tipped his camel hair hat at me and winked. I gave a closed mouth smile and continued researching vaccinations.

"Isa Carson, ignoring my good nature. The times don't change."

He pulled up a stool next to my metal table and took a seat next to me. I suddenly realized that I knew the tall, dark man so eager to talk with me. It had been seven years since I'd seen him in the gray halls at St. Luke's Catholic High School. My friends smoked pot with his friends underneath the bleachers after basketball games. He was arrogant on the basketball court and on the homecoming court where he'd pulled me aside after the parade, grabbed my ass and told me if I had gone as *his* date, then I could have been homecoming royalty, too. He was proud and immature and very handsome, even in high school. I had heard he came from somewhere in Africa. I had also heard he was homeschooled before high school, heard LeBron James taught him how to cross over, heard his father was a tribal chief. But that was the problem with Penn: you could hear a lot and still not know much truth.

"Penn Clemence. My god, how are you?" I stood and wrapped my arms around his neck. His back felt thicker, like a man's back. He smelled older, too, like pine needles, maybe cigarettes.

He laughed and took his sunglasses off, brushed a long-fingered hand through a black mane of coarse hair.

"I'm as good as can be! Got out of bed this morning, my legs worked and the sky was blue. Really can't complain."

I playfully punched his arm through a black jacket. His arm felt firm, and evoked a curiosity I could not quite identify.

"You are such a weirdo," I laughed. I had always liked Penn. His sweetness and flirtatiousness mixed with the confidence.

He stood and walked to the counter, "Want another coffee?" he stretched his arms over his head and I saw black hairs trail from his navel down towards his belt.

"Yeah," I said. "Americano. Black." Our eyes met. Black, like all of him and a piece of me. I wondered if he remembered Ivy. I wondered if he thought I saw him as black first, and a man second. I wondered if I did.

He came back from ordering and set a ceramic mug in front of me.

"Heard about your mom, Isabel," he said, pulling his chair closer to me so our knees touched. "Fucking sucks, I'm sorry."

I closed my eyes and inhaled the scent of fresh espresso. I preferred people to respond to my mother's death this way: upfront and honest. I didn't want to wonder if they knew or didn't know. I didn't want them to tell me everything happens for a reason. His precise reaction and black eyes sent a drip of adrenaline down my spine.

"It's life," I murmured, my voice raspy, low. I felt a catch in my throat and quickly changed the subject.

"I'm moving," I said. "To your old stomping grounds."

"Boston?" he asked, stirring sweetener into his cup, eyelashes long.

"Even more hometown than that. I'm moving to East Africa."

"Shut up. Belle girl, are you really? Ha, I always knew this day would come."

"You shut up, you didn't know I was moving to Africa one day. All you knew about me was I was fastest on the track team and was too cool for you."

Penn laughed and crossed his ankle over his knee. "I knew you were a fast girl, Isa, but more than that I knew you and I were connected by Africa. I knew you would make it there one day."

I shook my head and looked at his shoes. Leather, Cole Hann, he must be making money now, "You're ridiculous, Penn."

"No, I'm actually serious about this one. Your mom and I talked about it once. During one of your basketball games."

"What are you talking about?"

"She came to the regional tournament your senior year, remember?"

I stared into my coffee. I remembered. She came for three days and stayed in the Motel 8 close to school. She also smoked a joint with my gym teacher outside of the gym at halftime.

"Your mama looked like an African mama," Penn said to me. "My mama sat next to Ivy during that basketball tournament. I think they would just sit next to each other and bitch about people."

I continued to stare into my coffee. Penn's mother's name was Veronica. She wore her hair twisted up in colorful cloths like my mother used to do. Her accent was difficult to understand, and her voice was low; I liked hearing her speak. I liked that my mother didn't seem to have a hard time understanding her accent.

Penn continued, "But after that basketball tournament I came over to see both our mothers in the bleachers, all laughing with their elbows linked. She said to me, 'I love this woman. I wish I could see Africa. The way your mother describes it makes me lightheaded, I get so excited. But Isa, she will go to Africa one day. I can see it. I can feel it. That skinny pale ass has so much Africa in her blood it's practically dripping from her.'"

"My mom said that?" I stretched my legs out and hooked my boots on Penn's stool. Those words sounded like high Ivy words. I'd never thought of turning to Penn to find out more about the woman I longed for. It made me angry: how carelessly he gave up information that I generally worked so hard to find or to hide from.

Penn could sense my discomfort. He leaned forward and squeezed my shoulder.

I exhaled through my nose, "Where is Veronica, anyway?"

"I bought us a new place up in Avondale, actually. She lives with me. It's really nice; you should come check it out sometime. You know, before or after your trips to the Motherland." He smiled. His teeth were crooked. His eyes looked tired. But he also looked like he was about to burst into laughter at any moment. If the world swallowed him up, if he lost the job that paid for his pricey home in Avondale, if his mother smoked and cried and let the world take her life—it seemed he would simply laugh. His demeanor said nothing could hurt him; there is amusement in everything. I pictured myself at Ivy's funeral with a similar look on my face.

"Are you going to let me buy you a beer, Isabel Supeet?" He interrupted my thoughts with my mother's last name pinned to my first name. "Your coffee looks cold."

It was cold. And my computer was dead. My phone rang and I silenced it. It was Theresa. She was going to ask if I had gotten the typhoid shot. If there were any negative side effects. How much did it cost and did I price out the generic option? Did I buy tampons in case there weren't any available in Tanzania?

Numbers glowed on my phone and goose bumps rose on arms from Penn's touch on my shoulder.

"Yeah," I said, "Let's go."

Penn's mother was pregnant at nineteen. The Democratic Republic of the Congo was feeling the pressures of the recent Rwandan genocide. Clashes between the Hutus and Tutsis gradually trickled into the already troubled realm of the DRC. There were not many TVs, but people heard it on the radio: A Tutsi women's Bible study group huddled in a public restroom for eight days while they tried to outwait the rebel forces. Children slaughtered in their classroom for a slightly wider nose, a slightly more angular dialect than the tribe they had sat next to in the classroom just the day before. That seemed to be the premise of all wars and atrocities: the extreme fear of something different, no matter how trivial.

The real civil war in the Congo did not officially start until 1996; five years after Veronica brought her baby to America. She never saw the fighting but the stories scared her. They scared her enough to drug her newborn with drowsy cold medicine and strap him to her belly. She tied an orange and black sarong around her waist, draped another sarong over her shoulders, and drove herself to the airport with a friend's car. Her mother was Rwandan, which granted her dual citizenship in both Rwanda and the DRC, two places that Veronica had no desire to raise her smooth-skinned son. She applied for refugee status as a Rwandan citizen, and read the fine print that stated another application would be needed if her baby were to come along, too.

But she was only nineteen. She had a broken heart and a newborn baby and the unshakable fear that something awful would happen if she stayed in her home for even one moment longer. So, she skipped the second application for the child, which would have delayed her departure, gave the baby more sleeping medicine and boarded a plane filled with other refugees to start over again, in a new country, with a new address and a new place to refer to as home.

"Was she scared?" I interrupted Penn's story. My hands felt sweaty and my head was light. Two beers would do that to me.

"Fuck yeah, she was scared. But what else do you do? You got something you want, you do it."

I wrung my hands and thought about what my mother would have done in that situation. She would've gotten high, froze in her rubber sandals, and turned around and walked back to her apartment. She would've locked the apartment door and decided that was good enough, that I was safe enough. Maybe she would have tracked down my father and suggested that he take me to America.

"Finish the story," I commanded as I took the last sip of beer. Penn motioned to the bartender to bring another round.

"That's kind of the whole story," Penn announced, running his hand through a mass of coarse hair and finishing half his beer in one gulp. "Apparently, they flew into London, and didn't even de-board the plane. From there they made it to LaGuardia."

"No one stopped your mother and questioned her about the baby?"

"I guess not. Airports were different back then, not quite the same security. She said it was so hectic, she showed the man her paperwork with

31

her refugee status and walked out."

"She just walked into New York and started a life there? All by herself? That is right out of one type of jungle and into another."

"She took a cab to Boston. There are a lot of Africans there. She got an apartment. My dad was supposed to come and meet us. He came about ten years later. You know, African time," Penn flashed a smile; I sensed no bitterness in his playful words. Maybe he actually didn't care that his father failed to show up. Maybe other people let things go when they realize all of the questioning in the world won't give you answers or relieve the pit in your stomach. Maybe some people went about life smarter than me.

"What about you?" I asked softly. I touched the raised veins on Penn's arms. "Were you considered a refugee like your mother?"

Penn shook his head slowly, "No. I am a free man in the strangest sense of the word. I have no driver's license and I have no social security number. If you search my name, it will link you to my mother's refugee status. I can't get a job that requires a social security number and I can't attend any university that requires a permit or a green card." He studied the palms of his hands, "I am a ghost. I float from one muddled identity to another. We live in a world that requires us to know who we are, Isabel, and how to document it. There is no paperwork to tell me who I am, so I don't know. And neither does America."

Penn's story made me lightheaded. I excused myself to the bathroom and stood with my hands on the sink, caught my breath and steadied my head. I looked into green eyes and thick eyebrows. I pulled at my curls the way I always did: a hybrid between attempting to smooth and encouraging their outlandish behavior. My mother knew I wanted to go to Africa. Before I did.

My mind flashed to a four-year-old Isabel using coffee-colored crayons to draw the faces of my "best friends" and the faces of my "family." I used the peach crayon to color in my arms and my legs and my cheeks. Other than my mother, I was the darkest of the people I held close to me as a child, but every one of my paper crayon drawings showed a peach girl with a soccer ball standing in the Crayola sun surrounded by coffee brown best friends, brother and sisters. Not that it was really that strange. Schools are filled with sticky faced girls and boys drawing self-portraits with blue hair and purple eyes. Dogs were the same height as humans and houses. That's how children draw. But Ivy didn't see it that way.

"Your blood is African, Isa," she told me once when I was around twelve years old. "And I'm not talking about my mixed blood. I'm talking about your blood. You came straight from Africa in a past life. I can feel it. I smell it in your hair. I taste it on your skin."

I rolled my eyes at my reincarnation preaching birth mother and thought of Theresa, my father's wife, explaining the dangers of believing in multiple lives and how it harmed the Christian faith and rocked the very foundation that our church and livelihood was built on. In my mind, I heard Ivy clicking her tongue in passive disapproval and irritation.

Theresa was constantly pursuing eternal life. Ivy was constantly pursuing survival. Theresa found joy in attending church each Sunday, Bible Study each Wednesday, and the on-call prayer group whenever necessary. She loved sitting on the phone with her Midwestern family and discussing how a pie could be a representation of Jesus's love. How a Christmas light display could make others feel welcome, and thus potentially lead them into the kingdom of heaven. She was always completely earnest in these endeavors; she never quoted a Bible verse or looked intently into my eyes for show. Faith is what kept her going day after day.

Ivy, on the other hand, felt most alive on that narrow edge between life and death, and she held her daughter in her arms while she walked this ledge. My mother smoked too much and drove too fast and ate too little and didn't cry enough. I pictured myself calling Ivy on her cell phone that was never charged and telling her that I was moving to Tanzania with no plan and no reason. The carelessness would've excited her. She would have whisked me to the airport and made a joke about handling life more gracefully than she did.

But perhaps there was a small, glittering chance that Ivy was correct, maybe there was Africa in my blood. Maybe something was calling me to Africa that had nothing to do with Ivy or a fearful flee from home. Perhaps the desire was innate. Perhaps it was born in me before I was born to America.

9

Loveness was long and very lean, with graceful arms and milky brown skin. Her cheekbones were high and her lips full. When her head was freshly shaved you could see the curve of her magnificent skull. She was a swan in a past life, I was sure of it. That first month of school, I watched as she held her school books in one hand, and tied the baby on her back with the other. I watched while the two of them bounced down to the dried-up river, and Loveness pulled a mango out of her skirt pocket. She bit the skin and spit it into the river bed before sucking juice from the fruit into her mouth then pressing her lips to her child's mouth.

Her father had died when she was a baby. She lived with her mother on the far edge of the village and walked ninety minutes one way to arrive at Amani Manor. She was softer than Maya, and much quieter. An implied blush seeped up to the surface of her dark cheeks when she became flustered.

As I began my daily lunches with Loveness and other girls in the cafeteria, I watched as she pushed her rice in circles around her plastic plate, and offered the remnants to other girls she sat with.

"You should eat more," I said, motioning with my eyes to her full plate of cabbage and rice. The girl stretched her lovely swan arms over her head, so thin you could see the bones in her elbows protruding. She crossed thin arms over a flat chest and pursed her thick lips when she said "no." Another young woman. Another means of control. I understood.

One morning, before the school day started, I sat in the back office, boiling water for the weak coffee I made from leftover grounds I found in the cupboards.

Loveness tapped on the door, and it creaked as she pressed it open, "Madam, can you help? I forgot my notebook but I don't want to carry Samwel all the way back home."

34

I smiled, a faint feeling of pride that she had felt comfortable enough to elicit my help. Loveness unbound the baby from her back and tucked the wrapper around him even tighter. I held out my arms to the pleasant weight of a warm body.

"Of course, my dear, I can watch him until you return."

Loveness's shoes slapped the ground as she ran out the door. I pressed Samwel to my lap and took a sip of coffee. Warmth seeped into my thighs and down my legs as Samwel wet through the cloth he was wrapped in. There were no diapers here.

I laughed to myself and found another wrapper to clothe the baby. I held him up, a chocolate wriggling ball wrapped in a headscarf someone had left behind in the office. I stared into his milky brown eyes and spoke to him in the English words that his small curly ears rarely heard, "Be kind to your mother, even when you are older. She went through a lot to have you here today."

I had asked the teachers about Loveness and her baby. Their story was similar to Nylie's description of the girl: Loveness was not engaged to the boy who had gotten her pregnant, as if a child from a forced engagement was significantly different than a child from rape. The teachers claimed the baby was a burden to the teenager. Loveness, they said, watched with frustration as her mother was able to calm the screaming child with more patience than the teenager could muster.

The young mother cried frequently. She would tell me her tears were for her dead father, alone in his grave. She said she would picture what his skin looked like underground.

"I think about what he is doing down there and it's a bad thought to have in my head," she told me one evening, tears streaming down her perfectly crafted cheekbones. "I miss him."

I had seen some of how children, especially daughters, interacted with their fathers in the tribal community. Fathers who raised their eyebrows in acknowledgement of their child, but never truly spoke with them, or held their hand or asked them about school. They seemed distant, like an estranged uncle or a checkout clerk. Like a grandfather that lived several states away and mailed a check now and then. Yet Loveness' tears were constant for the man that I believed she never truly knew.

I shook my head to rid myself of the comparison of Ivy as the estranged uncle, the checkout clerk, the parent I never would truly know but longed for furiously. Love was a strange and nonsensical thing.

Some days, Nylie sat in the office after school to explain the world that I had stepped into. In her wild and staccato English, she told me the tribal community loved their livestock and believed in curses. She explained to me why some of the men in her tribe married so many women. She said, in the old tribal warring days, warriors died at an alarming rate. The old grandfathers in that village would tell stories about lions killing the warriors, and maybe that was true. But maybe they were killing warriors of different tribes, or neighboring villages, or of different sects or with different languages. Maybe warriors are warriors and if you give yourself that title you will kill or be killed.

The various stories reached the same conclusion: that polygamy stemmed from the concept of dead warriors. With so few men around, the ones that remained needed to do their part to maintain the population. They took on two wives or three wives. Some in this tribe had eight wives and one claimed sixteen. They were doing their civic duty. They were maintaining the population within the tribe.

Logically, it is difficult to understand how the tradition of multiple wives could be maintained when the warring days were over. Did anyone fight lions anymore? One guard that stood every night at the school gate had hiked up the cloth he wore around his waist to show me a scar that ran from the top of his inner thigh down to his knee. He got it fighting a lion, he explained, clicking his tongue at the memory.

When I told others in the village that story, they said no one had seen a lion in these parts for years. And the only wars in the past decade were after-school fistfights, mostly between girls, who resorted to teeth gnashing and open palm slaps, as there was no hair on anyone's head to grab. So, if the men were no longer being killed at an alarming rate, I could not understand how there were enough women for multiple wives. That is, unless they start marrying them younger. Girls with wide white eyes became wives before their breasts sprouted, while they still played hand-clapping games in the dust outside their mud homes.

Of course, not all of the men from the village had multiple wives. Some had conformed to more modern ideals, or simply didn't want the hassle of appeasing multiple women. But many others were pressured into marriage with their back against the wall. Perhaps you were content with one wife, but when your father asks you why, questions your manhood and your ability to provide not only to a family but to the village because you have settled down with one woman…well that is the type of pressure that can make you break. It's culture, after all. You have to stand by your culture. People will say things are permissible when they are done in the name of your roots. People will say a lot of things until they feel them with their own hands.

In this village, cows and girls seemed to be the only economic structure that held fast. Every morning, as the grapefruit sun lifted into the sky, the boys and men rustled their women and their girls awake to make chai. The young girls fetched water from the tap the government had installed a few years before, marching with their knees high to step over the sinking dust. The buckets were gracefully balanced on their unwavering heads. Carrying water on your head was a real reason to keep your chin up.

Daily life in the village fascinated me. Early mornings before classes, I slid on sandals and a scarf to shield my hair from the dust and picked my way around the village on exploratory walks. Sometimes, the students would smile and wave and beckon me over to sit with them and observe the early morning chores. I watched as the girls fetched water, and mothers squeezed the teats of the white and crying goats: milk for the chai. The mothers then lit a fire with a Bic lighter and burned the wood her daughter had gathered the day before. She boiled the water, milk and sugar in a large metal bucket until the bubbles came. Then, this mother, who was often no more than fifteen, reached into the cloth tied around her waist to pull out a handful of spices. Cloves, cinnamon, cardamom and anise floated on top of the boiling milky water like small sailboats in a storm. The spices gently seeped the mixture into a light tan color. Now, the air outside the mud hut smelled like burning wood and sugar and clove leaves.

It was only then that the boys and men would flutter their curly eyelashes and stretch their bony elbows and knees and rub sleepy brown eyes. Only then would they slip on their rubber shoes made of old car tires and glue, and reach for their shepherd staff kept next to the bed in case of emergencies. The men and the boys filed out of mud huts and crouched on overturned bucks or old plastic chairs or stools with tin cups in their hand as the women directed the young daughters to carry the chai, "Slowly and carefully to your *baba*. Slowly and carefully to your *kaka*. To your *babu*."

When the chai had been drunk and the sun climbed one rung higher on the ladder of the day, the men released the cows and goats and sheep from fences created with intertwined thorn bushes. They took the animals somewhere far away to graze, somewhere with more grass and less dust, a place where the wind didn't make your eyes tear.

The lucky boys pulled on blue shorts and baby blue button up shirts. They pulled out white socks freshly washed by their sister the night before. They rubbed excess dust from their black shoes; grabbed notebooks covered in brown paper, and began to walk to school.

Some lucky girls did this, too, but there were significantly fewer females on this trek. They shimmied into navy skirts that fell to mid shin, and tucked in the same baby blue button up over breasts with no bra. They pulled on white socks up towards their knees, socks they had washed the night before, along with their brothers' socks. They slid on plastic shoes and grabbed their notebooks covered with brown paper, and made their own way to school.

While the lucky ones were at school, learning reading and writing and the wonders of biology, the complexity of the English language, proper Swahili grammar and dividing fractions, the unlucky boys threw rocks at the sheep to keep them away from the road. The unlucky girls stayed home to tend to the naked babies and gather firewood and fetch water and walk kilometer after kilometer down that old dirt path to the market.

And then, there were the girls at Amani Manor. The Manor helped to clothe these girls in the same uniform the public schoolgirls wore so they did not stand out. These were girls with bride prices paid or babies on the way or a mother at home with a heavy hand and no room for extras like school fees. Any passerby walking down the road would assume they were school girls with physics on their mind: not a child dodging dowries, and clinging to education for as long as possible.

The uniform was also a way to get the girls' minds prepared for classes. White socks and black shoes symbolized preparedness to learn and the skirts represented sameness of every girl at the Manor, regardless of her age or tribe or situation. The powder blue shirts were donations from Holy Trinity Church and School in upstate Illinois. Mink Kelly had made it clear at the beginning: gifts like the uniforms were to be treated with the sincerest respect. The girls nodded solemnly as they accepted the shirt with two hands and wide eyes.

The stories and explanations Nylie told me in the windless office kept me up at night. I would lie awake and listened to the sound of crickets and stillness that can be so deafening to someone who has yet to learn peace. I felt the familiar anxiety of insomnia sink into my feet and drip up my body until my hips and shoulders and head were panicked. What was I doing in this strange world where I obviously didn't belong? Where had this artificial confidence come from? My fingers felt for the cell phone stuffed under my pillow, wet with sweat. I thought about Ivy and her slow hands. I thought about Penn and his laughing eyes. I thought about how I would accept either of their arms around my shoulders tonight.

10

It wasn't a sugar shortage so much as it was an increase of sugar laws that created such havoc. A new president was elected just weeks after I landed in Tanzania. The power went out for several days pending this announcement, just as Nylie had predicted. Apparently, the power company had preferred the losing candidate and cut power for the president elect's speeches. Despite the power company's obvious opinion, the new man in power seemed like a positive change. A new president meant a chance to improve the country through reducing corruption and bribery.

My second month in Africa, the president declared that the police were required to give receipts every time they pulled someone over for speeding. This seemed like a good and logical rule to prevent police from pocketing the money. The president also decided the school year was to be the same for all schools so no child skipping school and selling bananas on the street or beads by the highway could use the excuse "school is not in session for me right now, Madam!"

The attempt to cut out corruption was noble; the goals were good. But as is the case with most change: people resisted, and then found a way around it.

Countries on the east side of Africa were trying to do their part to eliminate corruption and bribery. But an entire nation could not instantly insist that all imports were brought in fairly and ethically. The government needed a test run. Sugar was widely imported into the country, and many of the tactics used to produce the sugar were unethical. Richard, the driver of Amani Manor explained to me that in years past, sugar was shady business. There was sugar harvested by child workers, sugar plants maintained by illegal immigrants, sugar grown by cheating and stealing, and he really didn't care. It all tasted the same to him.

The government saw the sugar trade as way to stick their toe in the fight against corruption. The Department of Agriculture imposed a sugar tax and a sugar restriction and sugar advisories so stringent that only twenty percent of sugar exporters could afford to follow the laws and stay in business. The only companies able to get their product into Tanzania had good connections and money to pay for permits and bribes.

At first, our tea was sweetened and the sugared *mandazi* tasted fresh and fluffy each morning. The initial weeks after the cut, I had to persuade stubborn girls to eat their porridge that lie bland and gray and sugarless in plastic bowls, while our tea stay sweetened. A good six weeks into the sugar cut, we felt the full force.

Nylie and I had given ourselves a list of things to accomplish for the week and written it on a hot pink sticky note and stuck it to my desk. It read: 1. Tax exemption (Water treatment plant for new wells in village) 2. Open bank accounts for employees (get list of employees with no bank account) 3. BUY SUGAR- Check the bigger towns.

And this is how it began. In the dusty sleepy village, two months after my feet touched the African soil, I felt the urge to stretch my miles and my legs. I decided that my daily duties now included long drives to questionable suburbs in search of a few kilos of the sugar that everyone seemed so desperate for. I rationalized it well enough: I was here to make business decisions for the school, and if that involved roaming to different neighborhoods so the girls would eat their breakfast in the morning, so be it.

The government didn't touch the tribal land we lived on. This was agreed upon decades ago, to keep the peace. Their officials would not come knocking on the door demanding taxes and the people in village were not subject to the rules of the rest of Tanzania. At least not officially. The tribe could exist the way they had since the beginning of time. They could live in their mud huts, marry multiple wives, sell their children as brides, all in the name of the culture—and the government would pay no mind. In turn, the tribal land was not provided with roads or electricity or law enforcement. It was a strange sort of quid pro quo; one that said, "I won't ask anything of you if you don't ask anything of me." Thirty miles separated Amani Manor, the center of this tribal land, to Casa, the closest Tanzanian town.

"Surely," Nylie said, "We can find sugar there."

Richard and I tumbled down the village's rocky roads in the safari jeep. Since my first faux pas with the air conditioning two months ago, I didn't touch the knobs. Instead, I rolled down the window and waved to the women in thick purple fabrics who carried yellow jugs of water on their heads. A few girls waved back. They either attended Amani Manor, or dropped off a young sister or daughter who did. The road curled and sighed in the red dust until eventually it released on black, tired asphalt: the indication that we had left the tribal land and were in government protected territory.

Richard and I made our way over the rolling hills of Casa to begin our journey. I loved driving on these hills. I loved the way my stomach hung weightless in the air for a moment before the car descended down the other side of the slope.

Richard drove us west, reggae music cooing from the speakers in the jeep that occasionally choked out dirt along with the music. He drove smoothly and silently to Casa from our village, which was gently nestled in the dust of majestic pink mountains. Richard always wore his tribal clothes, even on holidays. His shoes were shiny and the cloths he wrapped around his body were clean. We walked into situations as a team: he the man who knew the culture. Me, the woman who used the strange privilege of skin tone to push our team to the front of the line.

The houses were no longer mud, but cement and tin and corrugated iron. The sides of the narrow road swarmed with women in long colorful skirts or tightly tucked wrappers and men in jeans and t-shirts; not the thick course fabrics that were worn in the tribal land. Each curve in the road produced a new fruit stand or hair salon, where big women with thick wrists twisted strands of hot pink or lime green into the braids of teenage girls. People from the tribe were seen in Casa as well, picking up fruits from the food stands, or bribing a small child with a barbecued corn on the cob.

Richard laughed the first time he drove me to Casa for errands, "You look like the children when they leave the village the first time, staring with your mouth open like that. There is more to this world than the village, you know."

My monthly trips to Casa had previously consisted of stopping at government offices to pay taxes, stopping at the bank to pick up cash to pay salaries for employees of Amani Manor, and renewing the precious internet contract that kept me from disappearing into the dust completely. Then, I spent an hour in the iridescent lights of the biggest grocery store in the country, Snacky's; luxuriating in the freezer aisle and the foods that reminded me of home. Today, we added finding sugar to that list.

I first met Annie outside of Snacky's, underneath the neon lights and the multiple brands of lotion and cereal in the nostalgic shiny boxes. She had stood behind me and watched me fumble in the checkout line during my first month in Tanzania, clutching a precious chocolate bar, just short of the amount of change needed for the purchase. She laughed pleasantly and slid a few coins to the check-out clerk so I could take home my candy. She rattled something in rapid Swahili to the clerk, they both exchanged a laugh, and she gave me a smile.

We talked. Annie was from New York, a Peace Corp volunteer, and had already been in Tanzania a year. She worked in a village East of Casa and rented an apartment in town. Annie was a calmer, smoother, silkier version of myself with sure steady movements in her words and in her steps and in long, waist length blonde hair. I envied her confidence. I tried to match her strides as we left the store.

"Wow, so you stay out there in the tribal lands? You sleep at the school?" she asked as we stepped into the unrelenting sun. She gracefully moved sunglasses from her smooth hair onto her face.

"Yeah, I do," I said, suddenly proud to have impressed the woman with the sure and steady movements. We walked towards the parking lot towards the car where Richard waited.

"Max, this girl lives in the tribal lands!" Annie had called to a tall man with a thick chest and laughing eyes. The man walked towards us in the parking lot and wiped his hands on a greasy rag as he came closer. He was a mechanic, it appeared by his clothes, and he wrapped Annie in a hug that she playfully denied.

"Welcome to civilization!" he joked and shook my hand with a gentle grip. He winked at me and showed a perfect row of teeth. I was shocked at the precision of his English, the way he pronounced every syllable as if he were molding his words like clay.

"Isabel, This is Max," Annie had said that day while sweat beaded on my upper lip, "If you ever need help with anything in this whole city, Max is your guy. And from the way I've seen you try and pay for groceries, you are going to need help."

As we approached Casa, I clutched a paper cup of hot coffee in the sweltering heat and looked for the man I had met the month prior in grungy, grease stained overalls.

On this particular day, the old red jeep rumbled to a stop at the front of the grocery store, where the handful of white tourists and Peace Corp members huddled in the same place that I had met Annie. They were looking for a chance to speak English or find a food that reminded them of home, a piece of familiarity in the midst of newness.

Max sat out front, exactly where I had seen him before, smoking a cigarette and winking at another white woman who clung to a bag of chips. He laughed when saw me.

"Isabel!" Max cried, "Are you surviving those tribal lands?"

I laughed as he kissed my hand, and Richard looked away, obviously embarrassed.

"I am. The tribal lands are doing well."

"And those mud huts?" he teased, taking a long drag of his cigarette.

"The mud huts are… functional," I laughed at his intense curiosity of the village where I lived. Many people would live their whole lives without venturing there. He stamped his cigarette out with the heel of his boot.

"Max, I need your help today. We need sugar," I said and pulled my sweaty hair up off of my neck.

Max made kissing noises into the air.

I rolled my eyes and laughed, "Not that type of sugar."

He opened the back seat of the jeep and sat down. I closed my eyes and tried not to imagine the grease he was smearing on the back seat, "I need sugar. And not a little bit. I need a lot. I can pay for it, too."

"Eh, you got a businesswoman on your hands I see," Max said in English, though his words were directed towards Richard. He clicked his tongue indicating my forward attitude.

"Sorry," I pulled the sunglasses up on top of my head and took hold of Max's hand. "But Annie told me that you own this town. And that if I ever need anything, then I should ask you."

The man laughed, revealing dimples pressed into both chocolate cheeks. His smile trumped his grease stains.

"Isabel, I am so glad you asked. And yes, I believe I can get you sugar. You want that cheap sugar, don't you? You want that sugar that doesn't follow the president's new rules, eh?" From the back seat he grasped my hand, holding onto it longer than seemed necessary. I slid the glasses onto my nose to avoid Max seeing me blush.

"Yes, that's the sugar I want," I said with an artificial confidence. "Let's go find it."

Richard in his tribal clothes, Max in his grease stained slacks, and a tan American woman drove over the railroad tracks. We passed the women in their green and orange and yellow flowered fabrics tied snugly around their waists and wrapped around their heads and tossed over their shoulders. On their backs they carried babies swaddled in the same colorful fabric, and balanced bags of rice or firewood or avocados on top of their heads. The long-legged children walked quickly to keep up with their mothers, or to roll a bike tire down the side of the street, or to carry a load similar to their mama's on top of their head. Sad eyed donkeys pulled carts full of bricks or melons or cement on the side of a crumbling road. Strong shirtless men pulled the carts if they didn't have a donkey to spare, their dark skin gleaming in the sun and muscles twitching with each step. Every step seemed like a prayer. How those men kept moving mesmerized me. Why they kept moving fascinated me even more. I envied their motivation: waking up each morning knowing their entire day would be spent with their jaw set tight and shoulders tense.

At Max's direction, Richard eventually pulled down an alley, wet with yesterday's rain. A naked baby ran with mismatched shoes down the corridor when he saw the car coming. We parked between two narrow buildings and Max and the driver both got out.

"Stay here," Max directed, "Fifty kilos you said?"

"Yeah, fifty kilos." I looked down at my hands, too shy to meet Max's smile.

"*Sawa,* alright, we will see you soon." I cracked the window open and subtly locked the doors. I kept my sunglasses on to hide any nervousness. Sugar wasn't a necessity at the school: not like the water and rice that filled our days. But a part of my soul wanted the adventure that came with finding it. I wanted to meet strange men with dimples and ride around with them in my car. I wanted to speak in terms of excess: kilos of sugar, gallons of milk, thousands and thousands of miles. I wanted to feel the rush of newness that whisked me off of that plane the moment I arrived in Africa.

Spreading my hands, I gazed at my chipped purple fingernail polish. School rules required that all girls kept their fingernails clean and free of polish. They also prohibited bracelets (other than a watch), necklaces (other than a cross) or earrings. Heads must be shaved at least once a month, purely as a matter of cleanliness, and if your religion prevented you from shaving your head, then you were to plait your hair, and have the plaits redone once every month. I smiled to myself, considering my chipped purple fingernails, countless rings on my fingers, as well as the wild mane of dirty blonde curls that I refused to cut, let alone shave or plait. I questioned how suitable of a role model I was for these young girls for the thousandth time.

Even upon observing my behavior and appearance, the girls didn't question the rules. They were fascinated by the colors on my fingernails and the rings on my fingers and the French braids in my hair. The young ones, especially, would lightly touch the blonde strands, or attempt to rub the color off a fingernail or a toenail and see if it left a stain on their own finger. They seemed to think, "This is not the thing that I do, but I like that fact that you do it."

Or perhaps they did not consider this at all. I never thought to shave my head or wrap myself in similar fabrics, so why would they assume they should paint their nails or cover their hands in rings?

Max's wide grin appeared at the passenger side window, interrupting my thoughts, "We have your sugar, my dear."

Two men in wife beaters and long jean shorts carried kilos of sugar in thick cloth bags and knocked on the back-door window, signaling for an unlock. I obliged and watched their ropes of muscle tense and relax under the weight of the sugar. One smiled a perfect-toothed grin. The other followed suit, revealing a gap in both the top and the bottom teeth, perhaps from chewing sugar cane, perhaps from bad genes. I gave them an appreciative nod, but stayed in the car, seat belt buckled, touching the money inside my purse.

As I leafed through the bills, I mentally counted the shillings. I preferred to pull out the exact amount when it was requested, a trick I learned from Annie. If you have more, they charge more. I kept a silent count in my head as I rubbed through the soft and ragged bills.

Nylie said she had checked sugar prices at the well this morning; where she filled up large plastic buckets and tied them to her donkeys while she listened to the men speak money. Sugar was at 2.3 times the normal price. I had mentally multiplied 2.3 times the average price we paid for a kilo of sugar, and then multiplied that by the fifty kilos that were purchased. After counting the money, I had rolled the bills up into a big pink wad and shoved it into my bra as I sat in the passenger seat. The pleasantries of the sugar exchange were finished before the driver lightly rapped on my window and held out his palm. I fished out the sweaty pre-counted bills and paid the sinewy man who had loaded the sugar. He rubbed his baldhead and flakes of sugar that he had carried with his strong neck sparkled down onto the steering wheel. This was illegal sugar. This was the sugar that the president had prohibited, the sugar without the papers.

"Let's get out of here, sister," Max murmured. I could see his heart beating in his chest behind a sweaty T-shirt. I threw a fabric over the coarse, cloth bags in the back, just in case.

A surge of adrenaline pulsed through my veins as we turned the jeep around and made our way heavily back to the school, the sugar weighing down the back two tires. We had done it. We had the resources and had bought illicit, contraband sugar from someone who had supplies. The excitement and success of our plan felt like we were moving more than sugar, more than something to sweeten the tea and bake fried dough in the morning. It felt reckless and energizing. I instantly wanted more.

11

The first time I realized we had a problem was when Dasha stopped coming into Amani Manor. She was young and sweet, perhaps ten years old but no one could find her birth certificate so it was hard to be certain. Her mother had died giving birth to her. Dasha's father was a tall and handsome man, and his daughter had long legs to match his. She was top of her second-grade class and came to Amani Manor because her father was concerned about her education. He was an educated man himself, and he spoke soft words in soft English, which contrasted with his enormous size.

"Boys cause mistakes to happen in the education process. I want to keep Dasha here all the way through grade seven so only girls surround her. Her eyes won't wander and boys' eyes won't wander. She's safer here."

Dasha's father worked in Kenya while she lived with her grandmother and older siblings close to the Manor. Dasha excelled in preschool, skipped grade one and tapped her plastic black shoes into grade two every morning. She sang songs at the top of her little lungs and held hands with the girls on the way to lunch (although she stood a head taller than the rest of them.)

In January, three months into the school year, Dasha came into the office because she had wet her pants. I wrapped a red and white flowered *konga* around her waist and slipped her navy pleated skirt down around her ankles and put it in a plastic bag. I gave her a wink and told her to get to the toilet faster next time.

The next day she came in again with another wet skirt. Once again, I stripped her navy skirt down and tied the *konga* around her waist and sent her home with a plastic bag. They were doing an art project. She was probably too preoccupied to leave her work.

Two days later, her skirt was wet again.

My mind flashed to fifth grade, age twelve, wet jeans with a fleece pullover tied around my waist. I couldn't hold it. I waited until the last of the kids left the classroom, mopped up my chair and walked to the nurse's office. I told her I had the flu. She let me lie down and then called Theresa who picked me up and instantly knew I wasn't sick. Theresa didn't chastise. She drove me home; made me change clothes then help her vacuum the house. Everything was okay.

Then the next day it happened again. I was too embarrassed to go to the nurse this time, so I tied the freshly laundered fleece pullover around my waist and waited for school to finish. I washed my skirt and my pullover myself. I hung them to dry in the basement where no one would see them. I swore to my twelve-year-old journal this would never happen again. I promised in gel pen this was the last time I would ever have to hide this secret. That journal held a lot of secrets for a twelve-year-old. Two days later, my skirt was wet again. I had known pain like Dasha's pain. I had held secrets that I thought would choke me.

Dasha's father came into the office before I was forced to call him. His voice was soft and his hands were shaking as he knocked on the open office door. I knew what he was going to say even before he decided to speak.

"You are welcome!" I greeted as cheerfully as I could muster as I encouraged the man to enter the office. I crossed my legs and placed my skirt between my thighs to relieve the sweat.

He didn't say anything at first. His hands shook and he stood over my desk. His height did not project a menacing presence. Instead, he seemed feeble, like a thin, dried tree branch. Like a breeze would knock him down, crumble him.

He took an envelope out of his pocket, threw it on my desk and dissolved into the chair next to me. He placed his face in his hands.

I opened the envelope slowly; concerned any harsh noise would destroy the man next to me. Rape Kit Review. Victim's age. Nine. Victim's sex. Female. I skimmed more quickly through details I did not want engrained in my mind. *Injuries. Remedies. Evidence. Consistent urinating in pants. Conclusion. Victim's brother (20) participated in sexual intercourse with victim on multiple occasions over multiple months. Victim was encouraged not to speak of abuse for fear of murder (threats) and promise of biscuits (rewards).*

I folded the paper and tucked it into the envelope as quietly as I had opened it. My hands felt cool despite the scorching temperature. The room held still. Dasha's father had stopped shaking. Goosebumps rose on his arms.

"I'm very sorry," I whispered.

He gave one head nod. Jutted his jaw forward and looked straight ahead. A tan line encircled his left finger where a wedding ring had recently been removed. He saw me looking, "She knew about it, my wife did," he explained.

I gave the single head nod this time, "Did you call the police?"

"Yeah. I called them."

His face grew hard, the muscles in his forearms twitched. "That's why I am here. Dasha won't be attending Amani Manor any longer."

I held still and let the blood pulse through my palms. I tried to imagine it being pushed from my heart and down my arms, into my calves. I listened for its consistency; I sought familiarity in the beat.

"The police suggested she move to Kenya, to stay with her grandmother. I believe their direct words were, 'remove the temptation from your son.'"

I had braced myself for this answer and allowed the thud, thud, thud of my heartbeat to keep all emotions in check.

"They won't charge him?" I asked, my heart a metronome for my words.

"No. The police have concluded this is a family affair. Something that should be dealt with within the tribe and the family and the community. Their only suggestion was to get her out of here and into safety. Dasha is in Kenya now. Her grandmother came by bus to take her this morning."

"I understand what the police are saying, but if you want to press charges against your son…"

"Stepson," he interrupted. "He's not mine."

"If you want to press charges against him, you can. I don't want him thinking this was okay, or tolerable. He needs to be…"

"Madame, please stop." My words were a breeze that could snap him to pieces. "That is not how it is here. That is not how things work. The police tell you something you don't want to hear because they want payment to do it differently. And we do not have payment, Madame. I have spent every last piece of my savings bringing my mother from Kenya to pick up Dasha and drive her to Kenya again. That's it. That's all I have. That is five years of savings as a taxi driver. If I want to save up more? Maybe thirty years can go by and I will have enough money to pay the police the money they want to prosecute the man who raped my daughter. I don't have thirty years right now. All I have, right now, Madame, is a broken heart and a daughter on a bus to Kenya where maybe she will be safe now. Maybe. The only other thing I have is the dignity to come in and formally withdraw her from school. That is why I am here. Not for your guidance on the matter or your suggestion with the police or your sympathy or sleepless nights thinking of Dasha. I came to tell you she's no longer coming to Amani Manor. And I want you to know why. And I want you to know the system that we are up against. Power and money trump morals every time. Every time. Every single time. So, if you please, remove her from the class list, do not call her name for attendance, and say a prayer if it calms your heart. But that is all that I am asking of you."

I said no words. He made no eye contact. I counted my pulse in my temples, in my wrists, in the soles of my feet. He stood and we shook hands.

His eyes were already somewhere else. Perhaps at a confrontation of the boy he was not calling his son. Perhaps on a cramped bus slowly chugging its way to Kenya.

"I'll pray," I whispered as he released my hand, "I promise I will pray."

I did pray. And not because I believed God cared or could help, but because I thought that promise would mean something to Dasha and her father. A memory dripped from my head and spread like goose bumps down my arms and thighs despite the scorching heat. I had been like Dasha. I was twelve years old when my virginity blew away in the wind with the stars. I had been a child, too.

I was a Catholic girl at a Catholic school and a Catholic household where a woman's worth was measured by the strength in which she held on to her purity. I was staying in North Dakota with my cousins that summer. Sitting on bales of sun-scorched hay, we passed around vodka in an iced tea bottle. The sun began to set and I listened to the cows slowly begin to trek back to the barn. My cousin's friend who was ten years older than my thin twelve-year-old body, grabbed my hand and told me he had new Dalmatian puppies to show me, that his dog had given birth and they were in the kennel outside. With a foggy mind, I gripped his hand and followed him to the chain-linked kennel.

Once inside, he closed the door, and kicked the dog that had jumped up onto his knees. He didn't say a word, but held both of my hands up over my head with one strong grip, and unbuttoned my jeans with his free hand. My cousin's friend spun me around so my back faced his pasty body and grabbed my hips and raped me right there: amidst the squealing puppies and a barking mother. I did not cry and I did not scream, despite the pain. Why would you fight when you are certain there is no escape? His plan was well thought out, because even if I had screamed, a passerby would have assumed it was a puppy or their crying mother.

"I have friends in the police station," he said as he released my wrists and zipped his own pants. I brushed dust from my knees and tried to still shaking hands and quivering lips.

"If you tell anyone, no one will believe you because that's where my friends work," he continued, and left me alone to clean up the mess of my body and heart and soul in that dog kennel.

He didn't have to threaten me. I wasn't going to tell anyone. I already knew what girls who had sex were called, how the boys licked their lips towards them in the hallways of the middle school.

The days following were numb and flighty. Time did not feel marked by hours or periods of light and dark. My body did not seem to need me anymore, nor the things I could provide it: food or sleep or comfort. I had betrayed my physical self, and in turn, my body no longer trusted my decisions. It disconnected from my mind and I woke up the next morning wondering how I used to communicate my legs to walk, my hands to grab, my eyes to open.

A few days later, I returned home to Denver and bled through every pair of panties I owned. Theresa became suspicious and the truth rolled out like a tidal wave. There were no tears then. Only facts. Solutions. Shoulder squeezes.

I heard Theresa on the phone with Ivy on the night I told the truth. It was late and her voice was low, but sleep was not coming easily so I picked up the other end of the phone and listened as they spoke about my "situation." Theresa had plans and tears in her words: what doctors she thought I should see, a therapist I could talk with, a lawyer who could help us decide whether or not we wanted to press charges. Theresa choked out the words to Ivy as if I were her own daughter, her own flesh that had been violated. Ivy remained silent on the other line.

Eventually the emotion got the best of Theresa and she said, too loudly, into the phone, "Ivy, this is your daughter we are talking about! Can you say something? Can you make a suggestion? Perhaps book a plane ticket and come out and see Isabel and make sure she is okay?"

But Ivy knew she was only capable of stoking my fire. She thought I would emblazon all in her path if she said those words: "Are you alright, Isabel? Do you know that you are still worthy?" Or, worse than a further blaze, she would simply extinguish my flame.

Ivy took a deep breath and said into the phone as I listened on the other line, "She will be okay, Isa is a tough girl. I think we just need to let this blow over."

My mother was air and I was fire. Everyone knows a flame dies without oxygen. That's why water puts a fire out: it suffocates the air around the flame. Yet, strangely enough, Ivy died and I grew hotter than ever.

I wish she had told Theresa that she would pray for me.

12

The day after Dasha's father stepped into my office, I fell into the dangerous pit of hopelessness that had chased me out of America. It was a Saturday and the heat ignited inside of me a sleepy stillness that made lifting my head from the dust stained pillow seem like unmanageable effort. I was thirsty and my throat burned. But moving would acknowledge I was still alive. Alive in a world where children were ripped of their innocence, mothers died, and daughters left their families to live in dust. I did not want to be alive in this world anymore.

Marie, the head teacher with the intimidating demeanor, had words that replayed in my head over and over again, "Africa is not a place to heal yourself, Africa is not a place that needs your healing." My mind ran through options of who I could be this lifetime: the phoenix of a woman who rose from the ashes of personal tragedy. Or the girl who turned to sand when life felt difficult. The child who blew away when her mother no longer wanted to live this life.

I reached for a cell phone and held it with sweaty fingers as I debated who on this Earth could hold my pieces together. Theresa would be there, whatever the hour with caring words and genuine concern but without the understanding. Perhaps I could text Nylie, ask her a work question, inquire what she did on Saturdays when life was too heavy.

When night came, I climbed out of bed and into the dark outside and pulled my knees up under my skirt. My mind flashed to Dasha on a bus, a grandmother folding the child in her wrapper like a blanket. I thought about Dasha's brain, her thoughts, whether she was relieved or scared or angry or happy to be moving out of a place where no one moved by any means other than their feet.

Without any particular motive in mind, my fingers dialed Penn.

It rang four, five, six times before his voice answered, low and chocolate: "Bonjour."

"Penn? It's Isabel Carson…"

"I know who this is, Isa. Your name is saved in my phone with a small heart next to it…"

"Shut up."

"It's true!"

Silence. The comfort of knowing someone else waited on the other line brimmed my eyes with tears. I let them fall silently and prayed he could not hear the hopelessness in my voice.

"Living here is kind of hard."

Another silence. More room to speak. I wondered what he was doing. I thought about his long arms reaching overhead to stretch or thick fingers gripping the steering wheel of his car. I thought about his black eyes and black lips and how much I wanted to know the comfort of human contact.

"I just didn't think I would be so submerged in it all. I thought that maybe I would see the occasional challenging situation and I would be astounded and bring that memory back home. But it's more than that. It's astounding every fucking day and I don't know how to process any of it. I don't know how to deal with the inconsistency of knowing the pain we feel with the way we smile back home."

"Want me to come out there and sing you a lullaby?" Penn asked.

"You don't even have a passport."

"I'm a man, Isabel, I'm making false promises I can't fulfill, okay?"

I laughed out loud, "Then yes, come out here and comfort me."

I could hear him get in his car and shut the door. I heard him start the engine and mumble something about traffic in the mornings.

"Penn," I said slowly, wondering at the honesty that would ensue with my question. "How do you make money? When you have to float in that in-between place where no social security numbers and no true identities exist?"

The silence was more weighted this time. It was thick and velvet like the night sky and I let it lay on my shoulders like a blanket. Perhaps Penn counted his heartbeats too, because his words were consistent and on beat, "Some things you don't ask people, Sweetheart."

I said nothing on the other end. I heard a screech and cry from the outside village; a celebration was starting. The drumbeats pulsed in my head.

He was right and I respected his request. After all, Penn had never asked me how Ivy had died.

13

I was ten. Ivy and I were at the grocery store. A girl, no more than sixteen, with blue eye shadow and a stomach the size of a basketball, strolled lazily down the aisle. She leaned back beneath the weight of her pregnant belly and pouted her lips the way teenagers do. I stared at the girl, so confident in such a vulnerable state. Ivy used that moment to give me what would be closest to "the sex talk" I would ever get from her. She told me that she had gotten pregnant by accident and had been decently careful; it could happen to anyone so I shouldn't mess around with stuff like that.

When I was fourteen, Theresa sat me down with my father, gave me a small pink box with a thin silver ring in it and told me that my husband was waiting for me, so I must wait for him, too. She told me God had handpicked someone to share my body with, so I mustn't give it away until the day my husband arrived.

"How will I know if he will be my husband?" I asked, fourteen-year-old lanky limbs hanging over her couch, dreading this conversation more than I dreaded getting my braces tightened.

"Because he will have waited for you, too," Theresa said with a smile. She wore a pink cardigan sweater that looked sickeningly similar to stomach medicine. She was always wearing cardigan sweaters.

"So, you knew Daddy was your husband because he waited for you?" Dad got up at that point, put more ice in his scotch.

Theresa didn't answer but took both of my hands. "What is important for you to know is that you need to wait to have sex until you are married." She realized the mistake in her words. The Dalmatian kennel was not to be discounted.

Theresa rephrased, "When you choose to give your body up, you need to choose to give it to your husband."

I pulled the hair tie from my pubescent curls. The tangles got stuck and I freed each hair individually, "So, I will know that he is my husband because I am the first one he has chosen to have sex with?"

"Well not everyone who chooses you as the first person to have sex with will be the person you are supposed to marry."

"Well they are going to have to be. If I have sex with them," I flicked my eyes towards my father. He stared down at the ground with a red face. Theresa stayed calm and poised, just like her living room: intentional. Put together. Casually elegant.

"That's not what I'm saying. I am saying that the first person you choose to have sex with should be your husband."

"And if it isn't?"

"Well then, that's a sin."

"Why is it a sin?"

"Because sex is special. So, you have to have it with special people. Like your husband."

"So, is my mom a sinner for having me when she didn't have a husband?"

"Isabel, you know I don't like to talk about Ivy. She's your mother. You can ask her any questions you may have."

"Am I a sinner because I had sex before I was married?"

"No, because rape is different than sex. Your heart and mind are still a virgin."

"So, it's only a sin if your heart and mind have sex?"

"Isabel…."

"I'm sorry, Theresa, but I don't understand," My father left the room Theresa buttoned one more button on her sweater, as if this would tighten her argument and keep her emotions in check.

"Yes, it is only a sin if your heart and mind do it."

"So, is thinking about sex before you're married a sin?"

"I'm not sure…"

"But you said…"

"Isabel, listen, sweetheart. There are going to be a lot of things that we don't know and we don't understand. The important thing is, we continue to do them because we have been told they are right. But you will drive yourself crazy questioning it, my dear. Just accept what I've taught. Wait for your husband. Be kind. Everything else will fall in place."

Theresa tucked a stray curl behind my ear. My face was flushed from the conversation; I puckered my lips and crossed my long tan legs underneath me. Her gestures were kind but I could feel her convictions like a swift wind through my hair. Theresa and I were different. I couldn't accept what I couldn't understand.

Late in March, after school, Loveness knocked on the office door. Even though the school day was over, I continued working: entering another month of budget sheets into the computer. A girl called Miriam sat with me in the office, slowly turning the pages of a storybook. On my right was a locking safe that held the Manor's funds. I counted out weathered, pink bills, so worn they felt soft, like cotton. Meticulously, carefully, I counted so I didn't lose track. I was sweating. We all were always sweating.

Loveness's hair lay in light wisps on her head. It wasn't coarse and curly and dark like most of the other girls. It was fine; like baby hair. And when the wind blew the fine pieces fluttered. Her eyes were almonds and she smiled with her mouth closed, perhaps because of the light brown marks the fluoride had left on so many of the villager's teeth.

She had stripped off her school uniform and returned to her traditional clothes: a thick purple fabric that started at her torso and made its way down towards her ankles. Several colorful squares of cloth were tied intricately and thrown around her shoulders and neck, shoulders and back, and around her neck like a cape. Her feet were dusty from the run back to the Manor. She sank down low in the chair next to me and slid her feet out in front of her: silver chains around both ankles.

She swung a small bundle off her back and into her lap: baby Samwel, eleven months old with the same wispy hair, dark skin, cloudy black eyes. I held out my arms to scoop the tiny bundle into my own lap. He wore a shirt, no pants or diaper, and remained wrapped in the orange and yellow cloth that had held him to his mother's back.

"How are we doing today, Samwel?" I asked the baby. He wore a knit hat, embroidered with Christmas trees. Christmas flowers, Loveness had called them.

"You can keep Samwel, he is only causing me problems." Loveness crossed her arms over her chest, a thin smile teasing her lips.

"He would only cry if I tried to put him in my bed to sleep," I assured the sixteen-year-old mother.

"You don't have a baby. You can keep mine. He is nothing but a problem."

When I gazed into Samwel's cloudy eyes, he smiled a gummy smile.

"I don't want to have another problem like Samwel in my life." Loveness wrung her hands and kicked her flip-flops onto the ground. The silver chains clinked around her ankles.

"Why would you have another problem like Samwel?" I bounced the baby up and down on my knee. I recalled once again how Nylie had described Loveness to me that first month in Tanzania. "Angry," was the word she had used. Angry at the pregnancy. Angry at Samwel's father who had taken the more passive version of control: pulled her aside while she gathered firewood one night and reminded her that she wasn't strong enough, she was just a girl, and there is no way she would be able to tell him no. But Loveness sat with me nearly every afternoon in the office and I understood her better now. She wasn't angry. She simply knew who she could become.

"When I came home yesterday, there were thirty orange sodas on the table," she said. I understood what this meant and Loveness continued wringing her hands, jingling her ankle bracelets. Sodas were the most common form of dowry. Sodas and sugar. Maybe a cow or a goat. Maybe a few shillings. Courting with a future goal of marriage almost always started with sweets.

"Samwel is too much of a problem, Madam, it's difficult to manage him when I am at school, no?" Loveness said, her voice steady to the beat of her anklet's tinkling. "So, if I marry this time, I would like there to be no pregnancy until secondary school is over."

She didn't look up at me, but Samwel did. His hand's rested in mine. I wondered what he would tell his sixteen-year-old daughter with a child and dowry paid. I wondered if change in this community would reach his generation.

"How long do you think we have before you are actually married? You know, like sleeping in his bed?" I tried to imagine being sixteen and climbing into a strange man's bed. Would they kiss? Would they laugh and joke afterwards, or would she rollover and insist she needed to work on her homework, check on her baby, be a child?

"Maybe November," Loveness said, making eye contact for the first time. "Though, I may sleep in his bed before marriage. That's up to my father."

"I think we should talk with your father," I said. "What do you think?"

"I think," she said, crossing her ankles to a tinkle of bells, "You should explain to me how to prevent pregnancy when I am sleeping in his bed, Madame."

"I think we should think about not sleeping in his bed."

"I am going to sleep in his bed. When? One day. Maybe later, maybe soon."

"What's his name?"

"I can't remember," She spoke of her future husband like a bunkmate at summer camp. Someone she would have to deal with for a couple of weeks, but that's life. A college roommate. A stranger she would have to sit next to on a long plane ride.

We sat in silence for a while, considering the weight of our own thoughts. Maybe, like me, she was counting the pros and cons of carrying these thoughts further. Maybe she was determining if the weight of hope was worth the weight of disappointment.

"I wish you could leave and go somewhere new," I admitted to Loveness. I wrapped Samwel back in his *ngati*, the lightweight cloth villagers tied around their shoulders, and handed him to his mother. His lip started quivering, indicative of sobs that would soon follow.

Loveness slapped my arms. Red marks rose where her fingers had touched the skin.

"Don't say your wishes out loud!" she exclaimed, "or they will never come true."

14

"Where do you get sugar out there?" That was the text I had received from an unknown American number. I knew who had sent it even before I asked.

I formed my reply, "Depends on who is asking; who needs some sugar?"

"You are more creative than that, Isa, try again."

"This is Penn, isn't it?"

"Who else with an American number knows about sugar shortages in East Africa?"

"Good point."

"Seriously though, where are you getting your sugar these days? How much sugar do you need in a week?"

"You aren't very good at flirting."

"Isabel. Sugar."

"From Max. A mechanic in Casa. We get 50 kilos per week. At least we try to. New regulations make it tough. Why are you so curious?"

"You need to simmer down with all of the questions. How much are you paying?"

"I don't like bossy men. 4,000 shillings per kilo."

"I like bossy women. I can get you 2,500 shillings per kilo."

"I kind of like bossy men. How the hell do you know so much about East African sugar? Yes, I would like to get 2,500 per kilo."

"I'm a businessman, that automatically makes me a boss. I'll email you more info if you are interested. Would help us both out. You can still use Max if you trust him to transport."

"This is the sketchiest text I have received since being in Africa. And I have received some sketchy texts. Why am I feeling like I am doing something illegal?"

"You aren't doing anything illegal! When you have the chance to catch something elusive it feels wrong sometimes. But that's only because you feel guilty for being given a chance that others won't have."

"This feels strange to me."

"Liberating?"

"Kind of shitty."

"I think I'm in love. Your way with words is so fluid."

"Send me the email."

"Yes ma'am."

15

This was the plan: Penn knew some people at the shipping port who worked with the government. They pocketed 500 shillings for every kilo of sugar shipped in, and then ignored paperwork demanded by the President. The sugar would arrive by ship to a designated loading dock in the port. Max, if he agreed, would ensure that the correct boat came into the correct dock. Then, he would count out the kilos of sugar and the men at the docks would "accidentally" forget to ask for the paperwork. The extensive paperwork required information about where the sugar had come from, at what time it been harvested, who had maintained the plantation, and had it been harvested in a fair and equitable manner? Penn had heard that at first, the people at the dock were providing artificial papers, certifying that the sugar that came in ticked all the necessary boxes. But after a while, fewer and fewer dock workers collected the paper work or verified the stamp and the seal. If the authorities weren't enforcing the regulation, then neither would we.

"This sugar hustle is temporary," Penn had said, "It's too easy to circumvent the rules. Maybe some will attempt to follow the new sugar regulations for four more months, six tops, but after that, there is no way they will continue to follow these guidelines. It's too hard. Sugar at these prices is unreasonable. This is where economics finds us. Supply will meet demand, and the prices will fall. Our goal now is to get a little bit of money out of it while we still can."

The importers who were skirting the rules were making a killing. When importers who stayed within the guidelines were going out of business from attempting to follow the rules, only those who had or counterfeited the papers remained in the game. With more than 80% of competition cut, prices skyrocketed. The price of sugar had rested around 1000 shillings per kilo before the guidelines were put in place. Now, at 4,500 shillings for the average kilo of sugar, those who continued selling were raking in money.

A sugar "broker" transported uncertified sugar into the mainland, and a sugar "sales rep" would know not to ask for verification documents. This sugar sales rep had found a way to cover the kilos of sugar with banana beer and mangoes and rice seeds so that if the authorities did pull him over, he would show nothing but a truck full of crops.

It seemed as if everyone dealing with sugar was winning. The importer who previously had been put out of business due to complex procedures was now making more money than ever. Docks men were bringing home more for their family or their alcohol habit. Transporters had the hardest job: transporting sugar in semi-trucks without the proper paperwork on unlit, crooked roads riddled with crooked cops.

Max got our sugar from Casa and unloaded the supply into the back room of his repair shop, pocketing around 500 shillings per kilo. And there were a lot of kilos. We used sugar for *chai* and *mandazi* and the *chipati* pancakes that sizzled in oil on Fridays. No one seemed to be losing. Except those who hadn't learned how to play the game.

I agreed to Penn's plan, but only momentarily. I reminded myself there were more pressing issues than sugar prices. During the slower moments at school, Dasha's life with her grandmother drifted into my mind, then Loveness and her light-eyed child then Maya with headstrong refusals. The night I called Penn to agree to the sugar plan, it was admittedly for the need for a diversion. I needed something to distract my brain from the dust storm of fragility and inequality. I wanted to stick my head out of the sandstorm for a moment, and catch a breath of fresh air before submerging myself in the tribal world where I had voluntarily placed my feet. Sugar seemed to be just the way to do that.

There had always been hustle in my blood. When I was ten years old Theresa enrolled me in ballet school. I had the elongated neck and long limbs like a good ballerina, but my legs stretched me a head about the other students. Every Tuesday and Thursday, Theresa would smooth my curls back as tight as she could, and twist the length of my hair into a fat bun at the back of my skull. No matter how hard she pulled on my curls or how much gel she smoothed in, my hair never looked like the other girls. I cried whenever she wound a bun in my hair. Because she pulled so tight. Because I would never look like the smooth haired ballerinas I saw on the posters.

One evening, on a rare week that my birth mother stumbled into Denver, Ivy forgot to pick me up from ballet practice. I cried my ten-year-old eyes out because I was the abandoned ballerina with the curly, painful bun. I stood outside in snow boots and tights and pulled a jacket tighter over my shoulders. In ten-year-old time, Ivy was hours late. When she pulled up hurriedly in her old Silverado I slammed the door as hard as ballerina arms would allow.

"Theresa would have remembered me!" I shouted, tears escaping down my cheeks.

Ivy didn't say a word. She handed me three twenty-dollar bills to quench the crying. Sniffling, I sat in my black leotard with skinny pink-legged tights and snow boots, pulling bobby pins out of my hair.

"I've given you money so you need to be quiet now," she said.

Two weeks later Theresa got a call from the dance studio complaining that her stepdaughter was using the dance studio for her own business, and nothing commercial was to be sold on the studio's premises.

"Isabel is ten," Theresa had told them. "What are you talking about?"

At the grocery store across the street from the dance studio, I had bought sixty dollars' worth of butterfly clips, glitter ponytails, rubber bands and neon scrunchies. I had plastic headbands and hair ties with the colorful balls on either end. I had a few sparkle compact mirrors and a comb shaped like a seashell and laid out all of my products in a very attractive arrangement. After ballet class, my fellow ten-year-olds were no longer students, but customers.

My dad and Theresa sat me down on the couch and demanded an explanation that night. Where had I gotten so many hair supplies? my father asked.

I shrugged, "Ivy gave me money, so I started a store."

Theresa lightly slapped my knee for calling my mother by her first name. I sat on my hands, shoulders slumped. My father rarely yelled and never got angry. The thought of his disappointment ached my bones.

"Are you selling your products for more than you bought them for?" he asked, arms crossed over his chest.

"Of course, Dad. You don't make any money if you don't charge more money." I spoke quietly, respectfully, praying his anger would cool with the tone of my words.

He stifled a laugh. It escaped, billowing from his nose and his chest. His face turned red and a vein protruded from his forehead. I mentally debated if I should try and sell the seashell comb or keep it for myself. Theresa's lips gently curved upwards and she kept her eyes down.

When Dad's laughter had subsided, his eyes looked bright and glittery. I think he looked proud. "You can't sell things at ballet anymore, okay?"

I nodded my head, kicked the snow boots off my feet.

"But I think your stores are a good idea. You just need to tell me before you start anymore."

I nodded again, picked up my ballet bag and turned to go.

"Isabel," Dad stopped me. "How much money did you spend for your store?"

"Sixty dollars."

"And how much money did you make?"

"Eighty-four."

"That's my girl."

"Penn, I need you to lay out exactly what you need me to do for this sugar thing." A bolt of excitement surged through my body. The more I considered what was asked of me, the more it sounded like a game with rules and strategies. I was seduced by the thought of anything that could distract my mind.

"Isa, it's so easy I can't even stand it. Ask Max if he's interested in making a little extra cash. If he says yes, then give him the phone number I gave you. That will connect him to my friend at the dock and those two can figure it out. Then you get cheap sugar. If he says no, then no harm done, you step out of there. But believe me, this money is way too easy. Max is going to say yes."

"And how did you find out about all of this, again?"

"I dabble a little in African industries. Politics. It's fun for me; it's a challenge. I have friends in Kenya who needed hookups in Tanzania, and he gave me a few bucks to find those hook ups. Nothing seedy, darling, I promise."

I let there be silence on the phone for a moment.

"I like to associate with Africans here in Colorado. It makes me feel like I'm getting a little bit of the culture I missed out on."

"Do you wish you had stayed in Africa?" I asked, wondering at the appropriateness of the question.

"I could've died if I had hung around the DRC. So, I guess I am happy I am alive. Do I wish that being alive meant I could choose where I lived and how I made my money? Most definitely."

I let him breathe into the phone. It seemed romantic to me, this late-night conversation. I sat outside under the awning in the courtyard of the school and leaned my back against the cool cement wall and stared up at the sky. I knew for him it was the middle of the afternoon and he was most likely staring into traffic.

"I'm a piece of shit here, Isabel. I got to do something to change that. I can't get a real job. I can't get a formal education. I'm stuck acting like this is a life. I've got to do something. I've got to get out of here. I am driving myself insane. I'm not even driving myself insane, because I can't even get a fucking driver's license! I'm walking myself insane. I'm taking the bus until I go insane! That's so much worse."

"Hey, it's okay! Calm down," I mumbled to Penn. I struggled to find words to his rational frustrations and a surge of guilt rushed through my veins. I was free to travel, to wander. And not by any choice of my own, but my sheer circumstance of where I was born.

63

Penn inhaled sharply, "I need to get out of here. I can't do this anymore."

"Do what anymore? Wake up each morning? Go to work? Pay the bills? Because we have a whole life ahead of us that will require that."

Penn was quiet on the phone for a moment and I was concerned I had taken it too far, that my tough love strategy was not what he needed tonight.

"Remember how you asked me how I made my money?"

I nodded, as though he could see me in the dark through the phone.

"I sell cocaine, that's how I make my money, Isabel. I don't know what my other options are. And there is no future in that."

16

Theresa called me one evening as I roamed the school's garden. I was pulling plump tomatoes from the vine and filling my pockets until they weighed down my skirt.

"I just got the package you sent! My goodness, what a beautiful bracelet! Thank you for thinking of me, Isabel. I love it."

I smiled into the phone; the joy in Theresa's voice was not faked. I had wrapped up a beaded bracelet Nylie had made in brown construction paper and instructed Richard to take it to the post office, "My friend Nylie made that bracelet for me. I thought you might like it."

"She's one of the students at the school?"

"No, she works here."

"So, she's a teacher?"

"Her job is actually to fetch water for the school, but she speaks English perfectly, and Swahili perfectly, and the native tribal language perfectly, so she is a big help to me."

"Well that is just so sweet of her to make this bracelet. How old is she?"

"Like, twenty-three. And she's got a four-year-old."

"I see, shame what happens to the ladies out there, isn't it? She sounds like your friend though."

"She's a good woman, we get along well. She told me to send a gift from someone who loved me in Africa to someone who loved me in America."

"That's sweet," Theresa said. I envisioned her twisting the bracelet around her wrist. It was made from wire and beads that formed a small sun in the middle.

"Did she go to school?" Theresa asked.

"She did for a few years. But then she got married and had to drop out."

"What happens if girls run away from home? I know that sounds crazy for a girl to leave her family like that, but I wonder if anyone ever tries."

"Well I suppose they could run away. I just don't know where they would go. Or what they would do once they were there."

"Couldn't they just hop on a bus and get a job wherever they ended up?"

"The buses aren't close by, and there is no money to buy a bus ticket even if they were nearby. It's a good thirty-mile journey before you even find a paved road. Sneaking out would be some serious business. Maybe for a super athlete."

"So, they stay at Amani Manor until they have a better game plan? I was talking with some ladies at church who wanted to start a fundraiser. Maybe if we sent a little money over, then they could put off the marriage for a while…" Theresa wanted answers and solutions. She wanted a prayer to save these women, or a school to free them, or a lost American woman to heal them from the world's inequity. I knew that feeling, and I knew the reality was far from satisfying. Marie's words rang in my head; "We don't need your healing."

"Amani Manor is a place holder I suppose. Stay here, get fed, get educated, get knowledgeable about your rights before you decide your next move. Some of the girls stay long enough and get good marks in order to find an angel investor or a sponsor who will help them into secondary school and pay for their tuition. Some have families who have saved up for years in order to get them into secondary school as soon as they graduate from the Manor. Others are just delaying the wedding date. Some stay here to keep learning while their parents are out of town or travelling around so they don't have to keep switching schools."

"I guess I was hoping it was more of a miracle place that promised a future," Theresa sighed and I felt the breeze tangle my hair.

"I understand. I was hoping I would believe in miracles by the time I left this place."

I'd sat with Nylie on her bed when she had made the bracelet. She'd kicked off her flip-flops and sat cross-legged on a huge mattress inside the mud hut with smooth walls. A flood of dusty babies from the neighboring houses ran crying when I came into her room; they had never seen a *mzungu*, a white person, before. In the native language they asked Nylie, "Has this woman been burned by the fire to turn her skin this way, or is she a ghost?"

Nylie couldn't comfort her youngest, the ink black one-year-old, who screamed when he saw me. She told me to stay on the bed, and she carried the baby to a neighbor's house.

Her home had three rooms. The door entered into the center of the house. There was a small room here for storage. Buckets, sacks of rice and old bike tires collected dust just like the smooth foreheads of the black babies, the souls of those who were bound to call this place home.

The left side was Nylie's room. She had a huge mattress with a wooden bed frame, no blankets. She slept here with her screaming ink black baby and the seven-year-old daughter. Her husband slept there when he chose. On the far-right side of the house was the room of the other wife. She looked to me to be in her late twenties, maybe early thirties, with powder brown skin and a knit between her eyebrows. She watched me from the doorway of her own bedroom, arms crossed across her ample chest, and flicked her eyes as casual acknowledgement of my presence. She seemed to snarl when the shrill tribal words came out of her mouth. For sharing a husband, a house and the burden of another woman, Nylie knew very little about the other wife.

"I don't know how old she is, I don't know her first daughter's name, I don't know how old she was when she married my husband," Nylie told me one day.

Nylie was married at fourteen. She had never met the man before. The teenager had been away at secondary school, her first year up in the mountains of East Africa, where she had to put rugs on her bed just to keep warm at night.

"It was so wonderful and green," she had explained to me, "The grass sweats every morning, that's how green it is."

"Then, in December, I came home for Christmas break. I knew I was returning to school after the break, so I left most of my things there at school. I left my book bag, the bracelet my friends had made me, a few notebooks, my extra red school skirt." She shook her head side to side as she considered the things left behind.

"Our culture is not a bad culture. It is beautiful, and I am proud. But the things I was taught about being a woman? And the things I will have to teach my son about being a man? That is something that my heart will never understand." She was such an intense woman, seemingly peering into both my eyes and my heart with the mismatch eye color and unblinking concentration. The colorful cloths hung loosely on her long frame and gave no evidence of her body type other than this: tall. Thin wrists. Roses on the apples of her cheeks. Things that the purple fabric couldn't envelop.

"You never went back to school, did you?" On her bed, I analyzed the bottoms of my dirty feet, keeping my gaze down as to not upset a child that might make eye contact with this strange longhaired, light skinned woman.

"Nope." Nylie hopped off of the bed and stirred the fire in the corner. She called out to Happy, her four-year-old daughter. Nylie's instructions to Happy were in the native tongue, but I assumed it was direction to get a Thermos and two tin cups, because soon Happy held out a cup of chai filled to the brim without spilling a single drop. She handed the cup to me then, with cool, dry fingers, quietly traced the blue veins that ran likes vines up my hand.

"My mother woke me up early in the morning, on Christmas Day, while I was home for vacation," Nylie continued. "She shook me and told me they were having a party for me, and I had to get dressed right away. She plucked my eyebrows. She gave me lip shine. She put dye on my fingernails. I knew what she was doing even before she told me. It was my wedding day."

"Your mother made you do this?" I watched as Nylie counted out tiny white beads and let them roll lazily on a saucer on the dirt floor. She kept her eyes down and focused on her work.

"She doesn't have a choice. If my father is ready for me to get married, my mother must agree, even if she does not agree in her heart."

"So, you got dressed and they drove you to the wedding and then you were married?"

"Why do you want to know about my wedding, dear?" Nylie sipped her chai and kept her eyes focused on her work.

"I don't know. I just don't understand it. I wish I understood what my life had been like if I was born here." I drank my tea quickly, purposefully burning the roof of my mouth so I had something to feel other than the uncomfortable conversation.

"Understand that when Happy grows up, and my husband decides it's time for her to get married, I will have no say in the matter. That's all I know how to explain to you."

I swished the tea around. On the sun-drenched dirt floor, Happy was fashioning a doll from cornhusks and piece of red yarn.

"Will your mother have influence when you get married?" Nylie was intent on her beadwork. I was happy she didn't have a reason to make eye contact with me.

"My mother is dead," I said.

"Sorry."

"Thanks."

The silence that ensued felt milky, thick, like the end of the tea. In the corner, Happy was cradling a homemade doll in her arms.

"She wouldn't care who I married. She was kind of like your mother, maybe. She didn't believe she was allowed to make any decisions about her life or about mine. She let life happen to her. My mom just did whatever seemed easy at that time."

"Sometimes nothing is easy."

"That's true," I agreed.

"Did your mother love you?" Nylie finished the bracelet. It looked large and clunky on her slim wrists. The beads were shiny like sweat.

"I think she tried to. Do you think your mother loved you?" I caught Nylie's eyes for the first time since we began this conversation. They were a light, amber color. They reminded me of autumn and a surge of homesickness pulsed through my veins.

"Maybe she tried, too."

17

Loveness had fallen asleep after school one afternoon with a baby in her arms on large rolls of powder blue fabric. She had taken to coming into the seamstress's room after classes several days a week to watch the thin woman pump her foot on the humming sewing machine and learn how to make the tiny x stiches on the thin fabric. The seamstress, Harriet, was a quiet woman versed in the tribal language with minimal Swahili knowledge and she patiently checked Loveness's stiches each afternoon. Harriet had assigned Loveness the project of making sanitary napkins: intricately stitching plastic bags to strips of towels so that the girls could line their pants when the time of the month came.

Samwel drooled on his mother's chest and the seamstress hummed quietly: three generations locked in a moment of peace. I wanted to pause this moment and return to it on the nights my head spun with insomnia and doubts of the goodness of life and of humans. I wanted to be able to return to where Loveness' ear curled perfect and soft, and the hum of the sewing machine matched the exhales of a baby.

My moment of tranquility was interrupted by a buzz of my cellphone: an American number flashed on the screen. My mind quickly calculated the time difference: it was early in the morning in the States. Usually, no one called me from home for several more hours.

"Hello?" I kept my voice low as to not wake the sleeping mother or child.

"Isabel, how much longer are you in Tanzania?" The voice on the other end was low and frantic.

"Penn? What's going on? Why are you calling so early, is everything alright?"

"How much longer? Are you going to be there through the end of the year?" I heard a sniffle on the end of the line. I wondered if he was crying.

"Um, yes. I will be here until the end of the year, but what is going on? Are you in trouble?"

The other line was static for a moment. Deep breaths quickly turned into choked sobs.

I imagined Penn squeezing both of my hands with one of his. I imagined his palms warm from a mug of coffee, his fingers thick and dry.

"I found a way to get an American passport and social security number," he murmured, as if he was humming a song that only I could hear.

I exhaled sharply and wondered at his tears. "Well that's wonderful. That's going to open up a lot of doors for you isn't it?"

"I can go to college, Isa. I can get a job. They will let me get a driver's license and a gym membership. I can start making legitimate money to help my mom. I can learn something in a classroom instead of on fucking YouTube. Isabel this changes my whole world."

I paused for a moment, gazing at the tendons on the inside of my wrist. They were streaked with blue veins, the ones Nylie's daughter had traced with her tiny fingers the day before. "I'm happy for you, Penn."

I waited because I knew more was coming. I ran my thumb across the veins in my forearm in just the way Happy had done.

"The deal I have with this guy is that I need to help him move some products around the Eastern Region of Africa, and then he will be able to set me up with the passport."

I kept stroking the blue veins in my wrist. This conversation felt strangely personal. I glanced around the room and ensured that Loveness still slept, that the seamstress kept her head down as she sewed another navy skirt.

"So, I want to know if you would like to work with me to get products into Africa..." My fingers kept tracing. Memorizing. Mesmerizing. I wondered if my mother had taken the time to look at her body like this. I wondered if she had memorized her own veins and her own bones before she decided to die.

"Africa is a big continent, Penn. Why would you want products moved to specifically the place in rural dustbowl that I live? And what are products?"

I sensed a long exhale through pursed lips over the phone as he was given the chance to make his pitch. I pictured his shoulders easing away from his ears and Penn bringing the coffee mug up to his lips for the first time during our conversation.

"A guy I know wants to move the products into East Africa because of the sugar routes."

I imagined he blew on his coffee. I wanted to be the liquid inside of his cup. My cheeks instantly blushed at such an intimate thought and I glanced over my shoulder to ensure that Harriet had not read my mind and could not detect my desire through my cheeks.

"You mean the routes that Max takes to get cheap sugar..."

"Are tried and true routes for transporting…things. Illicit materials. Whether it is contraband sugar, fake Louis Vuitton Bags, bootlegged DVDs…"

"Or drugs," I finished the sentence for him. I spoke too loudly and Samwel's curly eyelashes fluttered.

I heard Penn sit up straighter, adjust the cap on his head, lick his lips as if he were preparing a speech. His voice got very low and he whispered, "This is going to change my life, Isabel."

Patience gnawed at my words and I closed my mouth and leaned into the silence that ensued. I tried to use all five senses as I waited for a logical answer: I listened to the hum of the sewing machine and small hiccups from Samwel's chest. I smelled the burning rubbish outside, and when the wind changed, cow dung. I felt the plastic shoes rub the place on the heel of my foot and sweat drip down the front of my chest.

Finally, Penn spoke, "If we can move a kilo of cocaine into East Africa, then I get my goddamn passport."

I sat, unmoving. I felt my chest rise and fall and snapped a hair tie across my wrist.

"That's a stupid move, Penn. A real stupid move."

Penn closed his eyes, or at least that's what I envisioned. I hated how easily he considered making this proposal. But I did not hang up the phone. He was what I knew of comfort and I was not ready to give that up. Penn had been my sounding board the last few months. He had been a voice of patient reason when 2 a.m. and loneliness became too much to handle. I was not ready for our first fight.

"Why would you think I would agree to something like this?" I bit my tongue so I wouldn't yell. I imagined myself as a pawn in Penn's game, that every genuine word he had spoken to me had floated away with a request for me to do something dangerous for him. My heart beat faster and I became more and more furious. My heart told me it was all a lie: every conversation about my mother, every sugar filled "sweet dreams;" all a means to his American citizen end.

"I just thought that maybe you needed some passports, too, Isa. I've heard what it's like out there; I know it's bad. And it doesn't even need to be an American passport. You know someone who needs to go to London, or Denmark, or South Africa or Kenya? We can get them there. That's a promise. You help me get my god-forsaken passport and I promise you I will help you get any and all of the passports you need."

"You're an idiot," I said. My wrist felt dirty where my fingers had traced. I moved out of earshot from Loveness and Harriet and the sleeping baby.

"And here is another thing. If I had agreed to this suicide plan, what on earth makes you so sure that your guy will follow through with what he promises? What keeps him from grabbing the cocaine and bailing?"

"Because I know his sugar routes. He screws me over and gets me a shitty passport? He screws you over and doesn't deliver all of what you requested? Then I have every DEA Agent from Manhattan to Nairobi on his contraband trail. You don't fuck with someone who has nothing to lose. I will tell them everything. The port they come in on, the road they use to the city, what the drivers are named. I know too much for them to fuck around. And quite frankly, you know enough so they shouldn't want to mess with you, either."

I pulled both hands inside of my jacket sleeves. I felt my heart pulse, pulse, pulse inside of my wrists.

I shook my head furiously; and watched Loveness through the dirty window of the seamstress' room. Her eye lashes fluttered open and I willed her back to sleep with my thoughts. I wanted her to know nothing more of the cruelty or complexity of this world.

"I can't do this."

"Isabel, this is a lot of information for one afternoon so I just ask that you take time to process this..." I felt my eyes fill with tears.

"Don't be angry. This is my future. This could be the future of the people that you live with. This is hope."

I shook my head again, frustrated at his logic in such an asinine setting. I listened to Penn rub his nose, and then rubbed his eyes. Was he crying? Were those tears he held on the brink of dark lashes and heavy, high eyelids?

I stayed standing and pressed my hand into my heart, felt the pulse of a confusion that knew the difference between right and wrong. I shook my head no to a man who could not see me. A man thousands of miles away.

"I'm going to drop this, Penn," I whispered, "and you need to drop it too."

"You don't fucking understand," I heard him slam both of his hands on the table. "You don't understand what it's like to not be free. So, no, I won't drop this. I won't drop this until I can get in the car and drive myself somewhere to eat. Until I can get a legitimate job to pay for my mom to go to the hospital. So, I can go to a damn school and get a fucking education. So, no, I'm not going to drop this, Isabel. Because without this, I am a chained man. Without freedom I am nothing."

18

On Monday morning, an envelope sat on my desk in an inch of dust that had accumulated over the weekend. It was surrounded by neon sticky notes; written reminders of teachers who needed salary advances, who needed loans, questions about budget in a hybrid English-Swahili shorthand. Etched in blue on the front of the envelope were these words: "Madame Isabel: These are the schools that I want to attend. Please help me. From your faithful Maya."

I was confused by the envelope. Surely this could not be the same Maya who failed fifth grade three times. This couldn't be same girl with thick ankles and a mean glare when asked to submit her homework. I opened up the letter and reviewed the schools where this mystery child had taken entrance exams. *St. Peter's School for Girls. Tulip Rose Preparatory School. Johnson's International School.* These were the top secondary schools in the area that accepted only ten percent of applicants.

Previously, my suspicious mind was convinced that they held prejudices against our tribal girls, refraining from giving them places on the campuses with the manicured lawns and water fountains.

"Madame, I assure you, that is not the case!" these headmasters exclaimed when I had called Tulip Rose and made my accusation. "It's not that we are discriminating against your students. It's simply that your students haven't met the requirements."

These were the Ivy League of secondary schools in East Africa. Getting in was an accomplishment. And yet Maya who couldn't pass fifth grade had formal invitations to attend each of these elite schools.

The next day, Maya walked past the office door, dragging her plastic shoes through the dust. Her white socks hung lazily on her calves.

"Maya," I stood in the doorway and waved to the girl. Her shirt was untucked and her hair unshaven.

Maya crossed her arms over her large breasts, poked a hip out to the side. Her gaze stayed fixed on me. She didn't move. She didn't blink. She waited.

"I had no idea you had applied to those secondary schools. That's wonderful! Those are incredibly hard schools to get into and you got into three of them…"

A fly landed on Maya's cheek and she moved just enough to encourage it to move on. No hint of a smile. No change in demeanor. Had I mistaken the envelope for a different Maya? Had I read the name incorrectly?

"What school are you going to choose?" I continued, my voice barely above a whisper, nervous that I had made an incredible mistake.

Maya puffed out her cheeks and let out a long, dramatic exhale, "I'm not going to any of those schools. My father won't let me. And my mother agrees."

My heart lifted back into my chest from the depths of my stomach. So, I hadn't made a mistake. This was the Maya who had gotten into the schools. She was the first girl to be accepted from Amani Manor.

"Why won't they allow you, dear? Are they still pushing the marriage?"

She shook her head and kicked up dust with her plastic shoes, "My father has no sons. I'm the last daughter. He wants me to watch the cattle."

I silently chastised myself for the assumptions I had made. She wasn't a lazy girl, or a girl without a plan; she was incredibly bright; bright enough to concoct a plan under my nose to further her education without arousing an ounce of suspicion. It hit me that every issue faced in this rural village was not a matter of unwanted marriages and child brides. Maya's father needed someone to work for him. She was the youngest, so she drew the short straw.

"I think you're incredibly smart, Maya, and I will do everything I can to help you go to one of those schools," I rubbed the dust from my hairline and picked dirt from beneath my fingernails.

Maya stood in place, hands crossed against her large chest, "You have dark skin for a white person."

"My mother had dark skin and my father had light skin."

"Do people like dark skin or light skin in America?"

"People don't like talking about skin in America," I answered. "That's why I'm in Africa."

Maya let out a half smile, the ones she released occasionally when they crawled out of her lips and onto a dimpled cheek.

"I thought you came to Africa because you loved me so much."

I laughed, "Go home, you crazy. We will think of a plan for secondary school tomorrow."

"Madame Isabel," Maya said, half-heartedly pulling the dirty socks up her calf, "I will do whatever it takes to go to school."

19

Dreams of Penn came. In one dream we lie naked in a bed under red sheets in a room with red carpet. My dream reminded me of details I forgot in my waking life. I saw again the scar on the right side of his forehead from a football cleat. I smelled his after-shave and watched him stretch his arms up over his head: first the right, then the left.

In my dream I ran my hands through his hair, and my fingers returned to me covered in white powder. Thinking it was a mistake, I ran my fingers through his hair again and again and found my hands more thoroughly coated. I panicked. As my heart sped up, I tried to brush off my palms, to clean my hands of Penn and the mess he had created. In my dream there was a knock at the door of the room with the red carpet.

Theresa stood at the door. Penn had disappeared but my hands were still covered in incriminating white dust. Theresa fell to her knees and started to cry but I just stood in the doorway, staring, unblinking the way Maya had done just the day before. One, two, three, four, five, six gunshots.

I sat up in bed in a sweaty wife beater with the hum of crickets and the pulse of a fan to remind me where I was, who I was. Instinctively, I wiped my sweaty hands on my shirt. Peeling off the wife beater, I threw it on the suitcase by my bed. A gunshot rang through the muggy air, silencing the crickets. The crack echoed in the dark night.

"That shot was real," I said aloud into the darkness that surrounded me. "That shot was not a dream."

20

Nylie was the one who told me, "Maya lost her mind last night."

I rubbed my eyes and slid a headband over my head in an attempt to smooth the frizz that tried to escape my tight braid. I hadn't slept well. My dreams became confused and muddied with reality. Had I spoken with Penn since the proposal of drugs and passports and the fight that ensued? Were the gunshots from the dream or had those actually occurred? I found myself continuously dreaming in America and waking up in Africa. The night before I had smelled bacon and woke up to the burning of trash outside my bedroom window.

"Nylie," I rubbed my eyes with the heel of my hand and tied a scarf around my shoulders despite the ninety-degree heat. "I don't know what you are talking about."

"Maya lost her mind," Nylie said matter of fact. She pulled some groundnuts from a bag and popped them into her mouth. Her flip-flop hung loosely over her crossed ankles. "She lost her mind. That means she went crazy."

"I know what lost her mind means. I don't know why you are saying it."

Nylie poured the remaining nuts into her hand and sat down on my desk. She was wearing plastic rosebud earrings I hadn't noticed before and it seemed that her hair was freshly shaven, "Why do you look so smart today?" I asked, and gently punched her shoulder.

"One of us has to look nice," Nylie grinned, the skins of the nuts stuck in her teeth. Clearly, she was referring to my tired eyes, my frizzy hair, the wrinkled skirt that I had difficulty washing by hand. All my clothes were slowly turning a muddled brown color as I washed them in the orange bucket outside the classrooms on Sunday evenings.

"Shut up," I said and Nylie laughed. I wondered briefly what this tall and graceful woman from one of the remotest tribes in the world would be like in America. Would she be concerned with fashion, boyfriends, cover bands? Would she be an activist, attend a university, study abroad? I shook my head to rid the thoughts from my brain. One of the most frightening things I could think of was the idea that something not too far-fetched, not too absurd, was completely impossible. It was wanting to be able to fly on cardboard wings for just ten seconds. It was grasping for virginity that had been there moments before. It was hoping my current best friend, who was strikingly similar to me, could have the same opportunities in life that I would surely have.

"Isabel. I am trying to tell you about how Maya went *crazy!*"

I sat erect in my chair, downed the last gulp of lukewarm coffee and prepared to listen to her story that I was certain was hyperbole.

The apples of Nylie's cheeks rose up towards her eyes as I gave her my attention. She began, "Well, you know how Maya is quite smart?"

So apparently everyone was aware that the nineteen-year-old fifth grader was a genius, except for me. I nodded my head.

"Well, she really wanted to attend secondary school, and she is smart enough to get into a good school. But her older sister got married recently and the husband paid a dowry of six huge strong, longhorn cows."

I continued nodding, signifying I was still following the train of thought through her heavily accented English.

"So," Nylie said, drawing out the "o" sound, "Because she is the youngest and refused to get married, and because there are no sons in the family, her father has demanded that she stay and watch after these cattle until one of her older sisters has a child that can look after these cows. Maya didn't like that plan. So, she handled the problem herself."

Nylie looked at my face and waited for a reaction.

"I don't get it. What did she do? Tell her father she wasn't going to look after the cattle?" I fumbled for an answer.

"Now no one will have to look after the cattle..." Nylie made her thumb and pointer finger into a gun and shot the imaginary cows in the office down one by one with a gentle squeeze of the perceived trigger.

My heart sped up as I patched the story together: the gunshots heard in the dark last night, Maya promising me she would do whatever was necessary in order to go to school, Nylie's pointer finger cocked like a loaded gun.

"She shot her father's cows," I said it as a statement, not as a question. My heart didn't race. It seemed to beat slower and slower until I was worried it would stop completely. "What did her father say?"

"He's out of town. Won't be back for a few months. They said he is grazing cattle in West Somalia. But I can tell you this, when he finds out what his youngest daughter has done to his livelihood, Maya will have wished she had saved a bullet for herself."

"Nylie, don't say that…"

"It's true!" Nylie protested, "If he doesn't beat her to death when he sees the dead animals, he will instantly marry her off and try to get some livestock back. That's why I am saying she lost her mind. If she had really wanted to go to school, this was not the way to do it."

My hands started shaking as a cook walked into the office carrying a steaming hot plate filled with fried dough. I took one and bit off a large piece and held it in my mouth. It was hot. Too hot. I let the dough burn me until I felt my heart return back to a normal speed.

"Where is Maya today?" I asked Nylie, who coddled her dough in her hands while the steam rose.

"At her uncle's house. He says she sure is lucky the father doesn't have a cell phone. But you know how this village is. Words travel so quickly. He's going to find out what Maya did soon."

I stood and adjusted the scarf over my shoulders. It wasn't cold, but goose bumps pulled and pricked at my skin until I rubbed my hands up and down my arms.

"Where are you going?" Nylie asked, concern rising in her big almond eyes.

I didn't answer. I couldn't, not yet. I pulled out my cell phone and stood outside the office door in the middle of the dust. I let the wind tangle my braid and blow the scarf off my shoulders, welcoming the grit between my teeth.

I held my cell phone up to my ear and my fingers dialed swiftly, without allowing my brain to consider or evaluate.

The phone rang five, six, seven times until a sleep filled voice answered on the other end, "Penn," I said. I weighed the next words on my tongue. I tried to bite them back. "Is it too late to count me in?"

21

When I was nine years old we watched a movie in my second-grade class about floods. I remember it very precisely: skinny legs in pastel print leggings and Theresa's attempt to smooth my curls with two tight French braids on either side of my head. I sat on a plastic chair next to Vikki with the light skin and the wispy bangs and the freckles she called angel kisses, and the teacher rolled a TV into the classroom and dimmed the lights. The cassette was swallowed into the VHS player. The movie explained the dangers of floods: how they can wipe away entire cities in a matter of days. The footage showed a boy clinging to a piece of plywood, desperately trying to stay afloat while paddling toward his dog in the distance.

That night it rained and my nine-year-old heart sank down to my knees at the foot of my pastel pink bed and I begged God to let the rain stop, please let it stop, please take the rain away and don't let it come anymore. I cried that night, my face buried in my pillow. I didn't want to see Theresa and my father clinging to plywood or a car tire as they floated down the cul-de-sac.

A few weeks later Colorado had the biggest forest fire I had ever experienced in my small life. Ash floated like sad snowflakes to the ground and covered the deck and the porch and carpet where the window was left open. The sunsets resounded in hot pink and orange tie-dye. The sky seemed to catch fire right along with the dried trees and grasses and unlucky country homes. I was too embarrassed to talk to God because this had been my doing. I had knelt on grass-stained knees and begged him just weeks before to not let rain come to this place again. And God was obliging: He withheld the rain. I had seen one problem and grappled at the only solution that I knew. It seemed to me that my nine-year-old solution had ultimately caused more damage than good in the long run. I wanted to save us all from a flood but in turn would I burn down our house, our neighborhood, our city?

The moment I hung up the phone with Penn, I felt like that nine-year-old. The problem directly in front of me seemed to be the life and success of a brilliant young woman with an anger problem. But would my solution ultimately burn down our home?

Penn gave me a call in my late evening, midday his time. I pictured him with a notebook in his hand, and a cigarette in his lips and every time he took a drag, his cheeks sunk in like smooth, chocolate caverns.

"This will work exactly the same way the sugar trade worked," he explained. I imagined him referencing points he had made on his notepad with a Zippo lighter. "The docks-men pick it up at the port, our port guys approve our documents without questioning what is in the shipment. Then, Max will drive the sugar to Casa and drop off the product at Amani Manor. You keep it in the garage for a few hours, two days, tops, and my guy will come pick it up."

My face flushed, I fanned my sweating forehead fruitlessly with my hand. I was tired. My eyes felt puffy from the night before and my stomach ached for something other than rice. I wanted ice cream, smooth and cold. Goose bumps rose up on my arms at the thought of the ice that formed on the top of an ice cream carton. My stomach growled and I grew increasingly irritable.

"I think you misunderstood me, Penn. I did not say I was in. I simply wanted to know if it would still be possible to be involved in your little scheme."

Penn exhaled out of his nose. I felt him trying to cool his temper before he responded, "Yes, Isabel, there is still time for you to get involved."

"And why do you get the first passport? How do I know that you won't just take the passport and bail on me?" I sounded like Ivy now: untrusting; accusing others of things they had not yet done.

"I will get my passport first so we know it's legit. I'm the guinea pig here, not your little friends you think you are going to save," his tone was caustic and it burned.

Penn was right: just because I got Maya a passport out of this village and out of this life did not mean that she was going to be saved. I was well aware of the white savior dilemma, and I struggled to understand if this had become me. What is the difference between thinking you are a savior and offering your resources to help someone? Just because she had the option to leave did not mean that she would accept it, or say thank you, or try to make the new life for herself any better than the one she was currently leading. But what was the alternative to trying, in any situation? Watching a life crumble in front of you? Standing stagnant until the world falls away and you are left hanging? That's what Ivy did. And I was not Ivy.

"I'm sorry, Isa, that was out of line…" Penn started to speak. I felt the sincerity on his lips but I did not want sincerity right now. I did not want right or wrong or true or fair. I wanted Maya to have the option to leave the village.

"How much blow are we talking about here?" I asked, chewing my lip, wringing my hands while my shoulder held the phone. Penn still seemed remorseful for his words, and his tone was too sweet. It made me feel sick.

"First of all, don't say blow. It's just a little dust. We are storing and distributing dust in a place that God doesn't care about, anyway. Just like we did with the sugar. But if you ask me, this dust is sweeter than sugar, the impact is greater. We will work with one kilo at a time. It's too suspicious having big delivery trucks on your rural roads. Max steps in, drops the kilo in your garage, and when my guy is ready for it, Max can pop in and pick up our dust the next day. Just put it right there in the trunk of his car."

"I don't understand why you need me for this," I began, "Why do you need Amani Manor at all?"

"Because they need a meeting spot. And what better place in the entire world than those tribal lands that you have been calling home? There is literally not a better place on the whole planet to make the exchange. The police don't give a shit what is going on out there; they won't get snoopy. And besides, you have a guard on duty twenty-four hours a day, don't you?"

"Yeah, we do…"

"It really is that easy, Isa. You don't even have to be involved. Just let them drop the product in the garage, and tell the gatekeeper that Max is allowed to come pick it up, and we are home free."

It was true; police didn't come onto the tribal lands. This lack of governmental involvement was a constant source of frustration. Rape cases were handled in the home of village elders. The gift of a goat to the family and the man was forgiven, while the girl carried a child the rest of her life. Goats seemed to be the standard apology. I wondered if the families with the most goats had gotten the most screwed over, had the most lies told to them, the most daughters pregnant with no promise of a marriage.

"So how much do we need to move until we get our passports?" My stomach turned with every question I asked. Light-headed, I sat down on the cement. A stray goat bit at the bushes nearby. This conversation took more energy than I could muster. I attempted to will my attitude to be all business. There was no room for fear and emotion and the complex contemplation of white and black and right and wrong. I tried to stick to facts; to game plans and to logic and not the terrible crime I was committing in a world that was not my own. As the conversation progressed, I grew increasingly uneasy. I dreaded every word that left Penn's mouth.

"One kilo per passport. That's it. One passport for one of your girls and one passport to get me home free in America. Two kilos of cocaine. Two different trips for Max. All you have to do is provide a place for this exchange to happen."

I wrung my hands again and again and again. The dust felt gritty underneath the silver ring on my thumb. I bit my lip. I slipped off my rubber sandals and placed my feet on the scalding cement. It burned the soles of my feet until the fire in my stomach settled enough to breathe normally, to think rationally.

"Isabel, I need an answer."

The bottoms of my feet screamed and my heart settled slightly deeper in my chest like a leaf floating down from a tired tree, waiting for the ground to rise up and meet her.

Theresa would love it if I brought back some of those fabrics I saw at the market: all red and blue and gold and green with intricate pattern and shapes swimming across the cloth. I should buy those soon.

I kept my burning feet planted on the ground.

"Isabel, you are fucking killing me right now…"

And I could get Dad an East African Football Corporation Jersey. I would get him a white one with the green stripes on the sleeves.

"Sweetheart, help me. Help us…"

I slid the rubber sandals back on my feet. The pain began as soon as I moved my feet from the scalding cement. It pulsed up my calves and into the backs of my knees. My heart slowed to accommodate the offending burn. My words were slow, marching to the speed of my heart: "Write this down, Penn. One Kenyan Passport. Address in Nairobi. Nineteen-year-old girl, I will send you a passport photo. I want it fucking legit."

Penn exhaled. I felt the tension release in his shoulders through the phone. "Thank you. Thank you, thank you, thank you. What do you want the name on the passport, Isabel?"

"Ivy. Make the name Ivy Supeet."

22

The first time I smoked pot was with my mother in New Orleans when I was thirteen. It was not long after the incident in the Dalmatian's kennel, and I was especially fidgety and nervous; my eyes darted rapidly toward whatever unexpected noise I encountered.

"You need to chill, Sis," my mother had told me, as she pulled out a gum wrapper full of crumbled greens from the glove compartment of her Chevy Silverado. I wondered, and not for the first time, if this had been where I was conceived; that if there had been a condom in that glove compartment instead of cheap weed, then maybe I would not have been here to smoke pot with my mother.

As her long brown fingers twisted the pot into a paper, I noticed how similar they looked to my hands, slim with the bone on the side of the wrist moving gently while she worked. I had been with my cousins when they smoked pot before, usually cramped around a bonfire we had made outside, or sitting on a fence, watching cows in that endless North Dakota field. I never smoked with my cousins. I would let them exhale near my face so I could breathe in the remainder of the smoke, but that didn't really count. It only counted if the paper touched your lips.

My mother adjusted the lime green wrap on her head and held the joint between her lips before she lit it. I wondered if my father liked big lips like Ivy's. Did Theresa's thin lips seem more manageable? I sucked both my lips and bit them hard.

"You doing this with me, Sis?" Ivy flicked the lighter until smoke snaked out of the paper. I nodded. I wasn't nervous or excited about the weed. I was simply grateful that my mother found me worthy to include. I held the paper in hands that looked like Ivy's and inhaled through big lips like hers. But when I caught her watching me with dark black almond eyes, I thought of what she saw looking back at her: light blue green eyes of her light blue green daughter who didn't really belong to the woman who spent nine months growing this child.

After we smoked and were heading down the road, I screamed for Ivy to stop. When she pulled over, I threw open the door and vomited on the weeds on the side of the Louisiana highway. Ivy had stepped out of the car and pulled my hair back into a ponytail when I finished. I was crying. Ivy offered me a Styrofoam cup of lukewarm coffee. The weight of being thirteen years old felt unbearable in that moment. I threw her coffee into the ditch by the side of the road.

"I hate you!" I screamed, wiping my mouth with the back of my hand. "I hate you for not being a real mother!"

Ivy did not speak but let me cry into her chest and into her neck. She placed her hands on the back of my head and pressed my face into her collarbones.

"I know," she whispered, over and over again. "I know."

African weed was brown and crumbled, like everything else in the region. I had bought a joint from a young man outside the pharmacy, who winked at me and made a smoking motion with his hand, keeping his pinky raised. I shrugged my shoulders, bought the joint and stuck it in my bra. I considered smoking it, crouched in the open field with nothing to hide me but open space, until I saw a white truck tumbling down the driveway. Max had come to the school.

The white pickup sat so low to the ground that instead of stepping down from the car, you would simply stand up, as if you had been sitting in a low, rumbling chair. My heart pounded when I heard the crunch of his tires on the driveway. The path to the school usually echoed with the sounds of students' plastic shoes and the hollow thud of donkey hooves carrying yellow buckets of water on either side of their wide ribs.

I was in the office, punching numbers into calculators before entering the same numbers into the spreadsheet. I practiced converting shillings to dollars in my head, and then back again. I could mentally consider exchange rates and bank fees. My mind thought in terms of the American African hybrid that I was. The owner of the school told me I was welcome to have any visitors from America come and see the Manor and visit me, and perhaps they could donate to the school. I remembered the first moment I placed my feet in this dust and woke up to the yellow paint and the drum beats and the shiny black faces. I mentally calculated the number of people who would willingly leave the comfort of their own luxuries and put themselves in this village. My list consisted of one person: myself. And that was a person who didn't have a great track record for decision-making.

Max knocked on the open office door, smiling ear to ear with a greasy paper bag in each hand. "Isabel, my dear, I have come with treats."

The guard stood behind Max, grinning broadly with fluoride stained teeth, a half-eaten hamburger in his hand. The wind picked up and blew the guard's red fabric off of his shoulder, revealing rolls of skin and a bald belly. "This is a good man!" he said in Swahili, pointing to Max.

The mechanic from Casa was handsome. He was thirty years old with thick dimples. His hair was cut short, and his thick-rimmed glasses made him seem collegiate, despite his grease stained overalls. Max was a big man, but he hunched his shoulders forward as if he were not comfortable being so large. His forearms bulged like thick ropes as he clutched the greasy bag of hamburgers in a tight fist.

Penn was the one who proposed our business plan to Max. I thought that if I had to tell Max about the plan, I would convince myself not to go through with it. I gave each man the other's phone number and told Max we had a chance to conduct a business deal. He had smiled his trademark smile, and said he was genuinely thankful I had thought of him.

"A gift for this sister," he slid a wad of wax paper over to me on my desk. "And a gift to this sister, too." Max pushed the other hamburger to Nylie who smiled with a closed mouth and looked up at Max through her eyelashes.

"Thanks," she whispered in Swahili, and crossed her legs, tapping her toe to the clink, clink, clink of her anklets.

We unwrapped this gift from a civilization two hours away, filled with exotic foods from outside the village. "Nylie, this is a friend of mine I met in Casa," I explained as casually as I knew how.

"I was just in the area," Max removed his glasses and wiped the film of sweat and dust off of his eyelids. "And I figured you guys could use a pick me up."

I ate the lies right up with the greasy food. Amani Manor wasn't in anybody's area. There was no nearby meeting place, no convenient road to see friends or family, no real reason one would live here, except, of course, circumstance.

"You just came to greet us?" I asked hesitantly, shaking my curls out from a tired hair tie. Panic rose in my chest. Was he dropping off the cocaine now? Surely it wasn't in a bag labeled "drugs" with skull and crossbones on the nylon wrapper. Nylie was here and she observed everything. She observed when I got a new color nail polish or a new piece of fabric to wrap around my hips. She noticed when I hadn't slept well the previous night. She observed when I had cried the day before.

"Yeah, I am just greeting you guys," Max sat on the arm of my chair and put his arm around me, squeezed my shoulder. I flinched at his touch. I had grown accustomed to a world where husband and wives touched to make children, not to comfort or console or caress.

Nylie continued tapping her foot. She rattled something to him in such rapid Swahili I could not catch her words. Perhaps the word girlfriend? The word *mzungu,* white woman?

Max laughed a little and shook his head. Nylie looked up at him through her eyelashes of her gold eye and her mocha eye, and answered again in the same rapid pace. I knew she was speaking quickly so I wouldn't understand. I watched with amusement as this tall, sleek woman made such a strong man bashful with her wit and her words.

Max laughed again and stretched his legs out in front of him. He looked at me and squeezed my shoulder, "She's a fiery one," he said, referring to Nylie, "Why don't you lovely women show me around your school a little bit?"

Nylie stood promptly, smoothed her hands across her shaved head and grabbed Max's hand to lead him out of the office door. I had never witnessed flirting like this, not within the village, where both parties seemed simultaneously interested in each other. I had witnessed men holding hands as they walked down the dusty roads. Occasionally women would put their arms around their friend's shoulder or waist as they made their way through sunflower fields, into the maze of dusty corn stalks or as they slapped donkeys with thin sticks on the way to the well. In this village, men and women greeted each with monosyllabic sighs. They kept their eyes down when they passed along the road.

The men ate in plastic chairs on one side of the house; the women squatted under a tree and carried on in their shrill rolling language. For such a small village, the connection between men and women seemed thin. I remember asking Nylie how old her husband was. She shook her head and shrugged. She had no idea. They hadn't talked about it. They didn't talk about those things, she explained to me. They talked about what foods he liked (meat and banana soup) and what he didn't like (cabbage) and where he would be taking the cows to graze (the border of Somalia) and when he would be home again (when he was finished grazing the cows.) There was no flirting or courting. There were no small gifts on her bed in the mornings, no "I love you," text messages, at least not as far as I could tell. But here Nylie was, holding Max's hand and blushing with her eyes.

I wondered if humans were biologically programmed to want only the physical intimacies of sex or something more. Did our genetic code ask for arms around shoulders, neck kisses, warmth of a hand on a stomach at night? Or were we culturally programmed to want lips close to our ear, fingers on our thigh?

Maybe a kiss on the mouth was like candy for a child, like the first line of cocaine. You didn't know it felt good, you didn't know you wanted it until you tried it. But after the first time, we are wired to crave it. To dream about it, replay it in the mind over and over and over until we can capture that feeling again. Maybe if you never try it, you never want it.

The three of us walked the perimeter of the school. Nylie pointed out important landmarks: there is the water tower. Over here is where grade seven studies. That's the garden. Max walked slowly, hunching his shoulders even more despite Nylie's confident gait. His eyes traced every building for security, for locks, for a place to rest his precious cargo without being too distinct or obvious. After we passed the garage, Nylie leaned up against the safari jeep, put one hand on her hip and stretched the other arm up the side of the vehicle, like a model from a game show where the participant just won the grand prize.

"And here is our car, Mr. Max," she said suggestively, laughing all the while.

Max stuck his head into the garage, pulled on the rope that slid the garage door down. He gave me a wink and whispered so Nylie could not hear, "Tell Penn we have a place to store his dust."

23

The man from the Dalmatian kennel got married. One morning before the school day at Amani Manor started, with my eyes still heavy with sleep and the sun turned light orange in the office, I learned this news. There he was; smiling on a social media site in a dark tuxedo. And her, white veil, creamy skin, dark hair—a Snow White smiling, too, and looking up at him in admiration. She married a man she would never know. She would have babies with him, grow old with him. No one completely understands the lives of others, even those with whom we are most intimate. Perhaps we would never know if our lover had been a bully in grade school, or had picked on kids in gym class in high school. Most would never even consider that their love was capable of hurting a child.

I prayed for forgiveness for the thought that came to me as I sat in that yellow orange office thinking blue black thoughts. What if he had a daughter and that daughter was hurt? Would flashbacks of our afternoon together haunt him? Did he think about that day? Did he pray about it? Did he even remember? Occasionally I fantasized about what I would say if I saw him at the grocery store or at a park. Or holding hands with his wife as they walked through the mall. But I never had words, even in my fantasy. In my heart I believed this man would never face what he had done— even staring in the mirror or into his own twelve-year-old daughter's eyes.

I wanted to call someone, to tell me my feelings were reasonable, that screaming and crying were reasonable, that thinking I could leave pain behind by moving to a foreign country was reasonable, too. But every response I imagined was like cake on a hungry stomach. I pictured their words satisfying me for a moment but just as quickly leaving me feeling sick and nauseous.

Work was finished for the day. The last of the girls began to trickle out of the gate and into their homes where they would fold up their uniforms until tomorrow. They would redress in the colorful clothes that their mothers had worn, and their mothers before them, and sing the same songs their ancestors sang while they carried water on their heads with long, strong necks, and slap donkeys with sticks as they trotted home with firewood for cooking dinner that night.

As the orange sun slowly made its way to the horizon, I called a motorcycle and asked to be taken to the town a half an hour east. I needed to get out, needed new scenery, new thoughts, new words, new voices in my ear other than the ones my twelve-year-old ears were reliving again and again and again. I hated myself for remembering so well, for still knowing the feeling of unwanted hands and an unwelcome tongue.

The motorcycle sputtered up to Amani Manor in a cloud of dust, and the driver turned his eyes away when I mounted the motorcycle in a skirt. He was in his mid-twenties with a perfectly cut jaw line, flawless teeth and a carefully lined up beard and mustache. He grabbed my thighs to secure me onto the motorcycle as we drove to town.

"Where are we going today, beautiful?" the man spoke loudly in Swahili over the hum of his motorcycle.

"Pharmacy," I responded slowly. "I'm having trouble sleeping at night."

"Sorry, Madam," he squeezed my thighs. I closed my eyes and let the hot wind rush past my face, into my hair. I wondered what Ivy would've said if I had called and told her about the ache I felt. I wondered if she would've comforted me or lit fire to my frustration.

The motorcycle dropped me at the pharmacy and gave me a wink as I got off his bike. I handed him a crumpled blue bill and told him thank you, I would be staying in town for a while and he didn't need to wait for me.

I knew exactly what to say when I got up to the pharmacy counter. I had heard the Peace Corp volunteers talking about this trick outside Snacky's.

"You just tell them you can't sleep at night, and they hand them over," they had laughed, in their baggie retro pants they had bought from a street vendor.

Annie had scoffed at the concept, "I came here to feel more, not feel less," she had said.

My hands shook as I went up to the pharmacy counter.

"I'm having trouble sleeping," I explained to the woman in the white coat who stood looking bored. She had long black braids with streaks of hot pink intricately twisted into her ponytail. Without a word, the woman handed to me a small clear bag with fifteen orange pills and zipped it closed. Muscle relaxers.

"One thousand shillings," she murmured. Forty-five American cents. I pulled out another crumpled bill, dropped the clear baggie in my purse, thanked the woman and walked out the door.

I knew my next stop, but first I swallowed an orange pill dry. My throat seemed consistently sticky with dust and it went down hard. I walked along the side of the road and wrapped my head in my scarf like a hijab. I was in no mood to deal with cat calls, taxi requests or souvenir selling that often came with walking these streets with a mane of gold hair.

I winded down a narrow passageway to a dimly lit restaurant and bar and sat in the back corner at a wooden table in a plastic lawn chair. I always sat there. The waitress was familiar. She wore her hair short and tight jeans, which was unusual for a woman in this area, but then again, so was working at a bar. She knew me by name and gave me a quick hug and squeezed my hand. The waitress was a sweet girl. I wondered if we would be friends if we lived closer.

I ordered a beer and an orange soda. The usual, though I didn't like orange soda. I really didn't like any type of soda at all but I did this to be able to drink my beer in peace.

The traditional tribal ruling was that alcohol was bad, a sin, and labeled anyone who drank, even casually, an alcoholic. There had been a few times on walks with the girls from the Manor that a drunken old man stumbled towards us and waved his shepherd's staff sloppily in our direction. He spouted out some phrase in his tribal language and intricately picked his drunken way through the rocks and thorns in sandals made from tire. Alcoholics did exist in the village. But surely Friday night beers didn't make this man this way.

The orange soda was my mask and my defense if a parent, or teacher, or benefactor from Amani Manor showed up. I would slide my hand around the glass orange soda bottle and act as if the beer belonged to someone else who was using the toilet, or perhaps by the person who sat at this table before me. Then, before leaving I would motion to a child inevitably crawling around on the dusty floor in the dimly lit restaurant and hand them the orange soda to finish. Wide eyed with excitement, I simultaneously was able to drink my taboo beer and become a wish granter to a dusty footed kid.

But this evening, I saw no parents from Amani Manor wishing to shake my hand and thank me for the work I was doing for their child. I encountered no teacher who pulled up another plastic chair and began talking with me about a salary advance or a raise. I saw no one, so I sipped my beer and watched my fingers dial Penn's number.

"Good evening," his voice sounded milky, smooth, enhanced by my pill and my beer. "How are you doing?"

"I had a hard day," I said softly, keeping my voice low in the quietly buzzing room despite the fact that no one in this restaurant was likely to speak English.

"Was this hard day related to our business plan?" Chills pricked my arms at the mere mention of the scheme we had concocted.

"It's personal," I sighed, took another sip of beer. Penn waited for me to continue. "I knew this really bad guy when I was younger and he hurt me. I just saw online the guy got married. It pisses me off." I spilled my secret the same way the child was spilling my soda: quickly, impulsively, leaving behind a sticky feeling residue.

Penn took a sharp inhale in a way that expressed shock and sympathy without any words, "I'm sorry, Isabel."

"Thanks," I said. "I want to talk to Ivy about it, but she's not around, so for some reason I am calling you."

"You can call me whenever; it doesn't bother me."

"Thanks."

"What are you thinking about right now?"

I wiggled one more orange pill out of the baggie and chased it down with the African beer.

"Do you think he told his wife about what he did?" I asked.

Penn exhaled into the phone. "I don't know. Do you think you will tell your husband about all of the things you have done?"

I thought for a moment, "No, I probably wouldn't tell him everything." The thought was interesting, that Penn would know more about my life than my future husband.

"Are you drinking?" Penn asked. I pictured him twisting the top of his hair with those long black fingers. I pictured tracing the lines in his palms with my fingertips.

"Yup. And taking pills." Words swam in my head and honesty flowed out more and more easily with every sip of beer.

"I need you to be careful," Penn said slowly.

"I don't belong anywhere," I responded, slipping my knees up under my skirt and onto the chair, just the way I had done when I was with Penn in Denver. "I don't belong in Africa or America or in black or in white or in Theresa's family or in Ivy's family. I don't belong anywhere."

We breathed together on the phone. My skin felt chilled and I swore I could feel his exhales.

"I know," Penn said softly. "I don't belong anywhere, too."

24

Dasha's father said he didn't know what happened. Dasha—the nine-year-old with long legs, clear eyes, and the stepbrother who'd taken her childhood and rang it out like a dish towel, —complained of a nauseous stomach one day. The next day she fainted. The grandmother took her to the hospital, a private clinic in Kenya. The doctors said it was low blood sugar. They gave her glucose tablets, hooked her up to an IV and said she should be fine. Her father said Dasha asked her grandmother for a haircut right before they left the hospital.

"Since we are already in town, and I need to look smart for school," the nine-year-old had explained.

As they took the IV needle out of her arm and helped the lanky brown girl into her shoes, Dasha fainted again. She never woke up.

Doctors in those parts call situations like this "bad luck." They couldn't explain what happened. No one looked into it for further detail. "The Lord called her home," "It was her time," and "Only the good die young," were the phrases used to explain away the death of a child.

I wondered what had actually happened, medically, biologically to her traumatized skin and bones. Had an infection developed from the rape that seized her body? Had she stopped eating due to the heartache and body ache? I read one time that a heart can actually stop beating in moments of stress and sadness. Had Dasha died in this way?

By text message, her father gave me the details of the funeral. The burial would be in her home country the day before my twenty-sixth birthday. The head teacher called the entire school together in order to make the announcement. The students sat at picnic benches in the dining hall: younger students at the front, increasing in age back through the benches. The announcement was made first in English. A hush came over the back of the

93

dining hall. The older students who knew English the best had understood the message. Then, the head teacher made the announcement in Swahili. The center of the room gasped. Perhaps they had started to understand the English version, but hearing it in the more native language solidified their assumptions. Finally, the words came in the native tribal language: the syllables bubbly and rolling. This was the announcement that upset the girls up front, the students who had yet to grasp English or Swahili and had only reacted to the silent tears and gasps of their older peers. The head teacher didn't leave time for further reactions or questions. She gave the date and time of the funeral in all three languages, and said everyone was welcome to attend, and that Amani Manor would drive students to the burial site before the funeral, if they wished.

Head teacher Marie asked that I send an email to the founder of the school and ask for prayers, "She is a religious lady. Tell her school will be closed for the rest of the week while students and family and faculty grieve. Tell her to send prayers."

I did what I was told and sent the email, but I anticipated the reaction of the American benefactor eight thousand miles away. She emailed back in a matter of minutes, my assumptions wildly correct, "Sorry for the loss of a student but the school will not be closed simply because one student has gone to be with the Lord."

I responded to the email the next morning and said I understood and would act accordingly. Then, I locked the office doors and began loading navy blue skirts with powder blue shirts into the van. The school would be closed for the rest of the week. We were going to a funeral.

For the short drive to the burial site, a small student sat on my lap in the front seat. We sang songs that every Tanzanian student was taught in their early years: "We are coming now, like a butterfly. We are coming now, like a butterfly. We are the members of Amani Manor and we are coming to you now like a butterfly…"

The drive was peaceful. Small girl voices and laughter rose and fell with the dusty hills on the drive to Dasha's father's home that would now serve as the place where Dasha would rest forever. The voices were silenced when the car stopped. Women covered their heads with their bright cloths and the students quickly followed suit: peeling their blue sweaters from their arms and draping them over their head and neck. A semi-circle had formed around a casket so small it seemed hardly large enough to fit a doll. Surely Dasha with her long legs and long arms could not squeeze inside that tiny box. The mud hut with the straw roof stood just to the east of the crescent circle. A teacher leaned over and whispered to me, "That is where the father lives."

So here was the offending house that has taken the life of a nine-year-old. It was those walls that kept the neighbors from seeing and it was those walls that had caused Dasha's heart to stop, I was sure of it. I instantly prayed for that house to crumble and fall to the ground, revealing any other secrets that the walls harbored.

The wailing didn't start until the casket was opened: slowly from the stomach at first, followed by high pitched and surprised screeches, like the African dogs that roamed the village at night. The students, both young and old, pulled their sweaters even more tightly over their heads. Some squatted down to the dust in their plastic black shoes. Sometimes, getting smaller made you feel better. One woman, who Nylie explained was Dasha's aunt, collapsed to the ground and convulsed violently. She continued convulsing and yip, yip, yipping like a kicked dog. Two men grabbed her by the thick arms and carted her away past the thorn bushes.

"She's grieving," Nylie had explained to me, when she saw the terrified look on my face.

What would my family have done if, at Ivy's funeral, I had fallen to the ground and convulsed violently in grief? What would my family have said if I'd pulled my sweater over my head and melted to the ground? That is exactly how I had felt like acting: explosive, fiery. I wanted permission to become ash at the grave of my dead mother. But I had stood in my father's kitchen, stick straight, too thin, hair curling at my chin and sticking to my cheeks, and refused to attend. I said it was too much for me to handle.

I said "My mother didn't really care about me anyway; she wouldn't mind if I didn't attend."

I said, "There should be no funeral for women who choose to die." If I had been honest, my reaction would have been the screaming convulsions I witnessed now.

When did it become true that those who release their feelings are considered unwell? I watched the wailing women with hair covered, throwing dust and screaming the dead child's name and I had never seen anything more reasonable. If you feel it then you release it. That was something I had never been taught by my black family or my white family.

Kind words were spoken in all three languages at the funeral. The woman who often sold mangos and eggplants to the school on the back of her aging donkey was there. She led the group in a high shrill song. This was the way that she knew how to comfort. A procession formed within the semicircle, collecting all mourners to walk by the open coffin, to look at the face that died too young and lived too short.

Dasha was the first dead body I had ever seen. There was an option to view Ivy before her cremation and the funeral. But I did not attend that, either. Instead, I said goodbye to my mother by buying too much weed in Denver, stuffing it all in an empty peanut butter jar, and flying where Ivy wanted her ashes spread: her hometown in New Orleans.

I sold the weed to my cousins and profited $300. Jordan was Ivy's niece, and five years older than me. Her father was Mexican and her mother was Ivy's sister. Jordan had warm caramel skin and the blackest hair of any girl I had ever met. When I was young, we used to pretend we were sisters and that our mother was a Native American queen and we were her princess daughters.

But on that day in New Orleans, there was no pretending we were sisters. My body had lengthened and leaned out and my hair grew lighter in the sun. Jordan was now several inches shorter than me, and had grown thick arms and thick thighs like her father. Her hair stayed black as a raven. We sat in that car and smoked the last bit of Colorado marijuana and defended ourselves, saying that we did it in honor of Ivy.

When Jordan lifted the ceramic vase of ashes, we took turns sprinkling them over the bayou. Small hairs escaped my ponytail, blew in the wind and stuck to my sweaty forehead. The thought that the wind could change direction and the dust of Ivy would stick to my skin caused me to sweat even more. I threw the ashes out quickly, hoping they would find rest in the swampy green water below. They floated in the breeze like the ash from the joint we had just smoked. That was all I had known of a dead body: sprinkling my mother with a foggy mind.

The African breeze picked up and I winced reactively as the dust swirled around my covered head. It became my turn to walk by the tiny coffin. I glanced, transfixed with seeing a human that no longer contained life. Dasha's eyes were closed and her lashes seemed longer than I remembered. Her lips were in a perfect pout and her skin flawless.

"She could've been a teacher," I heard myself saying out loud, "She was a smart girl. She could've been a doctor." One of the students grabbed my hand and led me out of the viewing area. I melted to the ground as the young girls before me had done.

"She just needed the chance to keep on living," I gurgled, comforted by the fact that my English rants would not be understood by most. I felt a hand wipe away coarse curls from the back of my neck and roll my hair up into a knot. "She could've done anything if she just had a chance. We should've given her a chance." My fingers gripped the ground. I was taken to a place of mental solidarity: me and Ivy's ashes and Dasha's lifeless body. I screamed, gripping harder.

Students knelt close to me and women covered their heads and screamed with me. They screamed because this daughter never had a chance. They screamed because their daughters would never have a chance. I screamed because I was twenty-six years old and my mother was dead and I was so far from home. I screamed because I missed something I had never had, never felt. I felt surrounded by women who knew pain, different than mine but with the same potency, the same directness. I huddled on the ground and felt a release that I had never known before, wrapped in brown arms and orange scarves and dusty tears.

It was hours before we arrived back at the Manor. I was shaking and dirty when I dialed the numbers on my phone. It rang eight times before the voice on the other end picked up; I heard a sleepy, weary hello on the other end.

"I need one more passport," I said into the receiver. "I'm not leaving without giving another life a chance."

25

Max and Loveness came into my office at the same time the next day. Loveness held baby Samwel on her back with an orange *ngati* and crossed her thin black arms over her braless chest. New plastic bracelets clicked on her forearms and rhinestone earrings sparkled in her ears. A hollow prayer escaped my lips that these were not wedding gifts.

A greasy black bag swung in Max's dark fingers. Out of the corner of my eye I saw the guard licking frosting from the top of a donut, his staff held between his elbow and his ribcage. He waved and gave a fragmented-toothed smile to Max. Max waved back and produced more donuts.

"Who is this man?" Loveness did not withhold the suspicion in her voice as she looked at me. She eyed the donut like it was a large bug.

"I'm a friend of Madame Isabel's," Max said. He seemed relaxed. He slouched onto the office chair and took a huge bite of his own donut.

"Are you her boyfriend?" Loveness took the smallest bite of her donut.

"No, sister, she has a boyfriend back in America," Max said with a full mouth.

Loveness shrieked with excitement, "Who is her boyfriend in America?!" She tucked her dusty feet up under her navy skirt.

"Yeah, Max, I am curious to know who this American boyfriend is as well." I studied his face while he spoke.

"Oh, he is big and very handsome. He is African, of course, Isabel loves Africans, but he lives in America keeping the house clean for her while she is here with you in Africa."

Loveness laughed loudly. She pushed Max's shoulder in jest and in turn, he pushed her thin shoulder back. I instinctively tensed up when he touched Loveness's arm. My molars clenched. What was that? Jealousy? Protective instinct? After Loveness's blunt statements about abstaining from pregnancy,

98

I bristled at the thought of any unwanted contact directed towards this girl. Perhaps this is what Theresa felt when she went through my bags and pockets after school. The woman tormented me, searching for love notes and cigarette butts, and even the wrappers of gum that we were not permitted to chew on school property. Perhaps Theresa wasn't crazy; maybe she hadn't lost her mind. The woman simply did not want me touched by anything that could harm me.

It felt strange that I found myself acting more in line with Theresa's actions instead of my mother's. DNA did not create loyalty. The blood running through my veins never reflected the ideas running through Ivy's mind and the intentions in her fingertips.

Loveness looked up at me. I held her hand, interlacing our fingers. I didn't care if she resisted, I wanted her to know sister love right now.

"Do you really have an American boyfriend?" she asked, rubbing my nail polish with her thumb.

"No. I don't," I rubbed her ink stained nails.

"Why? You are old! You should have more than a boyfriend right now, you should have four babies and a few goats," Loveness teased me.

"Because I had learning to do. And then I had to take care of you. Which was like taking care of four kids."

Loveness laughed and slouched down in the chair. Max was smiling as he watched the exchange.

"Isabel, I have to go now. I only came to greet you and because I had too many donuts. I think I will be by this evening as well. Is that okay with you?"

The uncertainty in Max's voice made my heart race. He would drop off the shipment this evening. An entire kilogram of cocaine would rest in the garage with the dusty safari jeep and the occasional lost sheep that wandered in; or perhaps the boy who kicked his soccer ball a little too far.

In the most authentic place I had ever been: in a place of dust and love and death and hurt and hunger would rest the most unnatural substance, an entire kilogram of white powder made from ingredients as synthetic as the plastic shoes on Loveness's feet. Cocaine belonged in the synthetic world of skyscrapers and bleached teeth and photo shopped models. It didn't belong here, in a place of honesty. Humanity was always so exhausted and hungry. These drugs wouldn't change that, even if they pretended to.

The irony of cocaine in this world mirrored the irony of the names of students I worked with every day. There was Goodluck, whose parents had both died in a bus accident when he was eleven. Happiness could not find it in her soul to smile. Lightness' skin was deep charcoal and her limbs thick. Then, of course, there was the man that took Loveness against her will, given her that ink black baby: Innocence.

I nodded to Max. "Sure, we like having you stop by. On your way out, tell the guard you are coming again tonight."

Max gave me a military salute and wandered out the door. Loveness crossed her legs and snapped some bubble gum while she watched Max leave.

"What does 'fucking 'mean?"

I coughed back the cold coffee I had just sipped.

"What?" I tried to stifle a laugh. "Where did you hear that?"

"I hear it everywhere. But I don't know how to use it. Are you fucking somebody or is somebody fucking good?"

I couldn't keep the coffee in my mouth this time; I coughed and spit it on the desk and the calendar in front of me.

Loveness enjoyed my reaction, "You can have a fucking house and a fucking cow and fucking car and a fucking wife. I don't understand when it is proper to use it."

"It's a curse word," I explained, dabbing at the spilled coffee with my scarf. "You say it when you are mad at something."

"So, if my goat knocks over my water I say, 'Fucking goat'?"

"Well, you shouldn't say that. But it is what people do say when they want to curse something."

Loveness nodded like she finally understood long division, a realization of an abstract concept that actually made quite a bit of sense.

I smiled and shook my head, then paused for a moment and watched her hands play with the beads of her bracelet, "I called you in here because I want to ask you a question."

The girl twisted plastic red beads around her wrist and didn't make eye contact with me, "What?"

"Does it still seem to you like you are going to be married soon? Are the sugar and the sodas still being given?"

Loveness crinkled her forehead and lifted the side of her face as if staring into the sun, "I am fucking married."

I wasn't as surprised as I would've been months ago. The dowry had been paid. They were already having sex, she was old enough and had a baby, so marriage was the only logical step.

I took a long deep breath and smelled the staleness of the office air.

"So, you are living at his house?"

"I am still living with my mother. Soon I will move to him. Sleep in his bed. Cook dinner. Have a baby."

"You are legal marrying age, aren't you? There is no legal way out of this?"

"Sixteen years old. I am allowed to marry any man who decides."

"When were you going to tell me that you were married?" The words were so much more confident in my voice than on my tongue. I was frustrated that she had not told me sooner; I felt betrayed. A marriage seemed like a significant life event that could have easily been mentioned during the countless hours the girl bride had sat in my office inspecting her eyebrows and humming hymns.

Loveness shrugged, popped her gum again, "There is nothing to be done."

We sat in silence and listened to the hum of flies, the wind. Songs from the church drifted over. A baby screamed. And then a girl, a playful shriek.

"Do you want to get out of this country?"

Loveness let out a long, tired exhale and pressed her forearm into her eyes.

"Yes, Madam. If that could ever be possible, I would like to be far, far away from this country, and far, far away from this life." Her tone wasn't dramatic or impulsive. It was factual. Calculated.

I hesitated to make a promise I did not know I could fulfill, "I can get you to Kenya if you want to go." I pulled at the blonde hair on my arms and envied Loveness's smooth, black skin. It was flawless, just like her cheekbones. After I had requested a Kenyan passport for Maya, I spent long and sleepless nights in the airless office researching safe houses or refugee centers in Kenya. The internet was slow and my search results were fruitless, sketchy, plastered with pictures of children with flies on their faces and mothers with their faces in their hands. I nearly called Penn on countless occasions, and begged him to get a passport to a different country, South Africa, Portugal, anywhere else so Maya could create a life. That is, until I met the poet.

Loveness snorted. "What would I do there?"

"Teach English. Make money. I am not sure I can make it happen, but I can try if you think it's something you may want."

Loveness interlaced her fingers on top of her head. She puffed out her cheeks and released a long, slow, exhale. "And if my husband finds me?"

"You think your husband is ever going to go to Kenya? Has he ever even left this village?"

"No."

"I don't want you to do something you don't want to do. I am just saying. As a secret. Between you and me. If you want to get to Kenya, we can try to get you there. To live and stay with a job."

A tear slid down her cheekbone and rounded down her chin. Her thick lips quivered. I wanted to enfold her. I wished into an existence a warm heavy blanket that could protect her from life and rain and sun and womanhood.

"I don't want to be pregnant again," she whispered.

I nodded, put a hand on her shoulder.

"I will help you in whatever way you want me to help you."

Loveness nodded, quickly rubbed tears off her cheeks and stuck her chin up in the air, "Fucking Africa."

I read too much in those days, that's how I met the poet. People say there is no such thing as reading "too much," but words are like water and it is possible to drown yourself. I read autobiographies and fiction and poetry book after poetry book. I liked to read African authors, to see if I understood them any better now that I lived in their world. I had a favorite poet who lived in Nairobi and after finishing his third book, I found him on Facebook and sent him a message.

"I live in East Africa, too," I wrote, "And it's very hard out here sometimes. Your poems keep me company at night." I sent it without a second thought, no anticipation of a response. I sent it because if he read it then maybe he would be encouraged and keep writing his poems. And maybe if he were encouraged he would become rich. And if he became rich he would love his daughter and send her to school and she would save the world.

But the poet from Nairobi did respond. He thanked me for my message and told me he had hard times sometimes too but his poems kept him going. He said messages from those who read his poems kept him writing. He asked me where I was from and told me my Swahili was bad.

"Writing in English is good practice for me," he wrote. "So please don't email me Swahili anymore."

We sent text messages for weeks. He told me about his father who was a drunk and his sister whom he saved from his father's alcoholic rage. He told me how his poems had inspired his younger brother to attend secondary school and how he lost his virginity to a maid who used to be a prostitute. He said he was always in love and had never been in love and all he knew how to do was love. He told me he knew pain and that was the reason he was able to write so well.

I tried to respond to his deluge of words. I told him I was a mixed woman and losing my virginity wasn't romantic either. I told him my mother had died and I never fit in and that was what I knew of pain.

"Americans don't know pain," he said. "Not like I have known, not like having a drunk father, not like being with a prostitute," and I am certain he firmly believed that these problems never occurred in a lighter continent.

He told me his pain had caused him to write and his writing had created books and his books sold very well and allowed him to create something more tangible than words: he allowed people into his home in the very middle of Nairobi, to stay and rest, free of cost. "Those with pain can find peace here," he wrote.

I stopped him here and gathered my judgements about this strange man. How dare he say Americans did not feel pain? How dare he claim that his intentions were more honorable, more intentional, because he was from this place? The root of my irritation stemmed from the idea that he was right: perhaps I would never suffer in the way the people who surrounded me would. Perhaps I could not create change in a place that was not my home.

"What do you mean people are allowed to go to your home?" I was glad we were texting so he could not hear the irritation in my voice, especially because I realized there was potential that this man could benefit me.

It is easy to keep a narcissist talking, and it's helpful to remember that sometimes, narcissists are good people who simply believe that sharing themselves is the best thing they can do for others. The poet explained more: he had met a Canadian man at a coffee shop in downtown Nairobi. The poet told me a story of how the Canadian man had requested almond milk in the place of cow's milk, which the barista found astoundingly funny.

"You can't milk a fruit!" the barista had exclaimed. "But there is a goat out back if you would prefer the goat milk to your cow milk."

As a photographer, the Canadian had come on safari and was inspired by the people, the generosity, the Kenyan way of life.

"Mostly, he was inspired by the words I spoke to him at the coffee shop that day," the poet texted. "I said my only goal and the sole reason I was put on this earth was to help people others could not reach. I told the Canadian I had been divinely called to lend a hand to the hurting and the vulnerable, and to be the voice and strength of the weak."

I urged him to text his story a little more quickly. I did not have time for purple prose.

The Canadian man agreed to pay the poet's rent on the large lime green apartment on the edge of town—if the poet would only keep his promise and take in the desolate. The Canadian was an old man, and when his son had told his father he was gay, the father had spat on the ground and told him never to return to his home again. Then that son died in a car accident. Paying the poet's rent to help the destitute was the Canadian photographer's attempt at reparations in his own life.

Now the poet and the man from Canada talked weekly. Or, more accurately, the Canadian man called and the poet talked. He wasn't required to have a strange, hopeless soul on the mattress in one of the bedrooms every night. But, more often than not, a tired body would find rest there.

If the poet encountered a woman in short shorts and high heels on the street corner looking for money, he let her stay and sleep and gave her thick black coffee in the morning, with grainy sugar that sunk to the bottom of the mug. He said if there was a teenage boy sleeping on cardboard he would gently shake him awake "like shaking dust from a star" and bring him home for a warm meal.

The poet spoke in abstractions and metaphor. He was flamboyant and strange and I imagined him in a cement house filled with strange art and animals.

"What happens, then, when they have overstayed their welcome in your house? Do they go back to the street?" I knew Amani Manor was not going to save anyone. I did not understand how this man's house was any different.

It was simply going to stave off the inevitable. Unless, of course, I chose to believe in miracles.

"Most don't want to stay for more than a few nights. Africans, we are proud! I give them rest, a warm drink, a few verses from the Bible, and they feel nourished to continue on their way."

I nodded through the glowing screen on my phone, shaming my heart for hoping for more.

"But there is this one organization through my church that I have been talking with. They need English tutors. They teach English over the Internet to students all over Africa and Asia. The man who runs this organization, he keeps saying to me, 'I will hire those Children of God who sleep on your floor! Just send them my way.' But the truth now, Isabel, is that prostitutes and street children do not speak English. He can only hire those who know the language well enough. English, on this continent, is worth more than a blood diamond to a white man."

Goosebumps rose on my arms. I pictured English words spilling out of Maya's mouth, laced with glitter and worth. Perhaps, in the faintest stroke of luck, this strange poet could become a partner in my goals. Was there a chance that Maya and Loveness, could escape to the basement of the poet? Were these women in the same situation as the prostitute on the street, the teenage boy sleeping on cardboard?

The poet was not fascinated with my personal life, but strange pictures of the village I sent intrigued him. A circumcision ceremony. Circle scars on the cheeks of children, indicating their sub tribe. He wrote poems about the pictures, told me he would include them in his next book. He said he wanted to know these people better, because he could identify with them through the pain in their eyes. He said he could see pain in their eyes that I couldn't understand because I was from America.

Hope was dangerous. I felt reckless as I allowed myself to picture Loveness and Maya in Kenya, speaking rolling Swahili with an Eastern Tanzanian accent. I imagined them with credit cards, bank accounts, smiling as they explained their job to those who asked how they became so successful. Mostly, I pictured them peacefully alone at night, drunk on the idea that no one could touch their peace.

I called the poet after my conversation with Loveness, with Maya in the back of my mind. I turned off all the lights in the office and sat in the dark room and spoke quiet, English words, because he did not want to speak in Swahili.

"Two girls from this tribe are in trouble," I explained slowly, deliberately, matching his slow poetic words with the cadence in my voice, "If I can get them to Nairobi, you can help them, right? You can give them a place to stay and help them find work until they get on their feet. Maybe eventually they can go to secondary school?"

He answered with a long, calculated sigh. "For you, my love, I will do this," he replied, intentional, dramatic. "There is one other girl staying here now. She came from the street. She's fifteen. I am getting her to a halfway house just outside of town in a month or so. Your girls will have to share a mattress with her, but they have a place to sleep. It's warm. We have so much food. At night I sing and we all read the Bible. They are welcome to stay here if you think it is a good fit. This isn't a place to live though. This is just a place to be safe until they figure out how to stand up in a new world."

A sort of pressure welled up inside of me, considering that I would be responsible for the future of someone other than myself. I imagined myself as Ivy Supeet: rolling up a joint for Loveness and praying to escape problems instead of looking straight at the challenger's face and baring my teeth.

After the talk with the poet, my emotions ebbed and flowed with such ferocity, my head felt light and untethered. One moment, gratitude for the strange man felt overwhelming. The next moment, I was certain he was a fraud, a creep, another man out to hurt the girls in ways that were becoming all too familiar. I would go for days at a time without responding to text messages, certain that the man was out for blood of the young and the headstrong. But then hope returned, laced with desperation. And I responded.

"What would they do in Nairobi? Would they be out of place there? You mentioned before that perhaps there were some English instruction jobs..." I felt like a mother reconsidering a child at the gate of the first day of school: perhaps she isn't ready; perhaps we should wait another year. What if the other girls aren't kind to her?

But we didn't have a year of praying that Loveness wouldn't end up pregnant. We didn't have a year of praying Maya's father would not come home to see the dead cows, encircled by flies, the meat stripped from their bones by the children wandering by. We probably didn't have a month.

"They speak English, right?"

"Yes, their English is very, very good. Loveness corrects the grammar in the newspaper at lunch sometimes."

She even uses the word fucking more appropriately than half of the native English speakers, I thought.

"Nairobi is overflowing with the need for English tutors. Not just in person but online tutors. If your girls speak English like you, then there should not be a problem getting them a job."

I pictured Loveness and Maya in a dimly lit computer room, poking keys with index fingers, explaining to an unknown face online how to create a past tense verb. I pictured them wearing Western clothes instead of the traditional tribal cloth. Maya walking, slowly, slowly, slowly to teach English classes after a full day of her own secondary school classes. Studying in her own room with a bowl of *ugali* at her side.

I imagined Loveness exchanging English lessons for daycare of the baby. I saw her rocking the child back and forth, back and forth as she instructed the other girl on the mattress how to conjugate verbs, and the meanings of the words hopeful, promise, suicide, enamored.

"You know there is a problem, though," the poet told me, "I don't know how long these girls need to stay in Kenya, but without a passport or visa, they aren't going to be able to get over the border, or stay for any length of time."

"They have passports," I interrupted him. I winced. I had spoken too quickly, too forcefully for the subject at hand. "Passports aren't a problem." I tried to lower my voice, make my forceful answer seem less harsh.

The poet was too concerned with his own tone of voice to consider mine. "Well great, then I suppose they are set. Get them on the bus. Nairobi Express. Or a flight, since I know you Americans have the money for it. Give them my contact number and I will come get them from the bus stop or send someone to fetch them at the airport. I will tell the other girl they are coming. She will love the company. And I cannot wait to tell this Canadian man that we have another two visitors. He will simply be thrilled. We have been singing every night and need a few more female voices. My voice is a little too strong and overpowering. Girls in the house will definitely light up our evenings…"

I'm certain he kept talking after that. Comparing his voice to the guttural growl of a lion, explaining his home was an umbrella in the rain. Not that these girls ever needed an umbrella in the rain. When the rainy season came, the clouds opened up and the people threw their faces to the sky, closed their eyes and exposed their teeth to the raindrops. You don't need an umbrella for the rain here. You need an umbrella for the dust. An umbrella for the stones thrown by the world.

"Isabel. Isabel? Isabel, are you still there?" My attention returned to the strange man sending messages with the power to save the lives. He was casual with matters that I observed with the delicacy of a dragonfly. "When will these girls be coming to Kenya?"

Headlights swept across the driveway. Fast Swahili chatter drifted into my ears as I sat in the dark office. Max was back to drop off a kilo of cocaine.

"As soon as possible," I whispered. "As soon as humanly possible."

26

I knew where to find Maya. Not because she told me but because I saw her thick hair in the back of the white pickup truck picking its way down those dusty streets one evening. She covered her head with fabric to shield her face from the sun, but I knew it was her. And I knew the pickup truck.

The truck belonged to a Somali man who lived ten kilometers from the Manor. He was an older man, probably in his late sixties. He had a definitive Somali look; I could've guessed where he was from by glancing at his eyes, his cheekbones, the texture of his hair. Legend had it he fled Somalia in the midst of the pirating days just a few years before. I heard that his brother was a pirate. I heard that he was a pirate. I heard that he was attempting to take over all of East Africa with his milky blue eyes and wispy white hair. I heard he came to this country to gather mistresses from all over the world, to have them do the pirating work for him, to loot and steal and bask in his eternal pirate glory. I think he mostly wanted peace. I think he came to live in the dust because it felt better than the Somali sand in his eyes.

I don't remember his name, but I do remember he had one hundred and ten camels. In a land where livestock determined one's wealth, he was a king who lived in a brick and mud house and drove a white pickup truck that sat low to the ground. It was no wonder people called him a pirate: camels were expensive, and one hundred and ten of anything made you a rich man.

The morning after I spoke with the Kenyan poet, I got up with the sun and drove the ten kilometers to the Somali's house. The sun rose pink and orange and full of juice that this land thirsted for.

I pulled in between the thorn bushes that formed a fence for the camels. The sun had begun to cast thick shadows of the animal's necks on the dust.

The man stood outside: his black skin thick and shiny, his eyes electric blue, his hair white. Long white fabric covered him to mid calves. He waved when I approached.

I slammed the car door and picked my way through the thorn bushes to his home. A fire was burning outside, a young boy tended it and boiled thick, yellow milk in a pot just above the flames.

"Welcome," he greeted me in English, "How can I help you this morning?"

The camels began to stir in their thorn bushes, gracefully gliding to a full standing position, making soft snorting noises with their enormous muzzles.

"I am looking for a friend of mine. I believe she may be staying with you."

"Sit down," he said, smiled warmly, and shuffled toward the entrance to his home. "Maaz will make you some chai. Let me see if I have any friends you may know here."

I sat on a wooden bench and the young boy poured the thick tea into a tin cup and set it in front of me. "It's from the camel's milk," he told me in shaky Swahili.

Maya stepped heavily outside, barefoot and sleepy. She pulled a faded purple fabric more tightly around her shoulders.

"Good morning, Madame," she said, dipped her head for me to touch with my palm in the traditional tribal greeting.

Maya and I sipped the thick tea in silence for a few moments before she spoke again.

"I suppose you heard what happened," she said, looking into her tea.

"I did hear what happened. It was difficult not to hear what happened."

"Does my father know yet?"

"Not that I am aware."

"Has anyone said when he is coming back?"

"I don't know, Maya."

Another long silence, another sip of tea that went down thick and sticky.

"He's going to kill me when he finds out. You know that, right? He will actually kill me."

"I know."

The camels seemed to sway with the wind.

"I can get you out of here. To Kenya. If that's what you want."

Maya kicked the dust with her bare feet and brought the purple cloth up over her head. I had never noticed before that her eyes were so light, a toffee color.

The Somali man sat on the wooden bench next to me and was given his own cup of thick camel tea. We stopped our conversation and finished our tea in silence. Soon he stood, grabbed his herding staff and woke those camels that had yet to rise and greet the day. He tapped the beasts gently on the hump and they rose: back legs first, then front legs. They made a soft, groaning noise in miniature protest.

"What will I do in Kenya?"

"You will get a job. You will attend school. We can get you a sponsor. Maybe not the schools we talked about. Maybe not the school that's first choice, but you'll be alive."

"And I won't have to watch cattle…" Maya muttered under her breath.

A hot feeling in my face suddenly rose. It wasn't from the sun, it was at my long coming reaction at Maya's careless and reckless actions.

"We need to talk about what you did…"

"Okay. Let's talk about it," Maya re-crossed her leg, folded her arms across her chest and smiled, challenging. "But I am happy I did it."

"That's the thing. I can help you, I can send you to Kenya and give you a push to make a future for yourself. But how do I know that you aren't going to do something wild and crazy there? How do I know that as soon as you cross that border you won't get upset again and get in a fight, or destroy someone's property and end up in jail?"

My mind raced to all of the things worse than cows that Maya could potentially shoot: a raucous neighbor, a family pet, heroin.

The Somali shuffled back toward us and squinted at the rising sun. The wrinkles at the side of his eyes formed cracks and dips that looked disturbingly similar to the ground we stood on.

"You aren't talking about taking my young daughter away from me now?" he laughed, a playful tone in his voice, "She's a good cook you know. And those eyes are pretty to look at." He was not rude or suggestive in his tone. He seemed to honestly enjoy having Maya around. I was wary with trust and did not want to give this man my complete faith, but he did give Maya a place to stay, and my heart did not feel nervous when he took a step towards me. The man with blue eyes and black skin did not say much, but I trusted him.

"I want to thank you, sir, for taking care of my young sister. I can't tell you how much you have helped giving her a place to stay given the situation…." I paused, assuming the old man knew the entire story. Of course, he did. News in this village travelled faster than the dust.

"She's a smart girl, Maya is. If you are able to help her, Miss Isabel, then do it. This girl will move mountains, *Inshallah*." The old man sighed. And then, just as smoothly as he came into our conversation, he floated back out, white vest flapping in the breeze like a lost seagull's wings.

I waited until he flew away before we spoke again, "Why does that man let you stay here?"

Maya puffed out her big cheeks and slowly exhaled, "He's an old man. Only sons. He came and found me after he heard what I had done to my father's cattle. He told me if I cooked and cleaned for him I could stay with him for a while. He also said he knew you would come find me."

"How did he know that?"

Maya stretched her feet out long under my legs. She smelled like Ivory soap and the earthy scent of camel milk tea, "Because you see his eyes? Blue eyes on black skin mean they see things. Future things. Blue eyes in Africa mean you are a witch."

"Is he a good witch or a bad witch?"

Ivy had believed in witches. She burned sage in the house to cleanse the energy in her home in New Orleans whenever something bad had happened, whether it was a skinned knee or a gas station robbery. When I was sick with a cold she would boil rosehips and brandy and force the still scalding liquid between my lips. "Brew" she called it. She never made the brew strong enough to save herself, though. She never did anything enough to save herself. I watched my hands move like her hands as I interlaced them behind my head and gently wrapped my hair up in my scarf just as she would have, as I sat outside with Maya.

"He is a good witch. But he can see things that we can't see. He knows the future. And he said that if I waited here long enough, and stirred the chai and waited, you would come for me. And I would get out of this place."

In the distance, the old man patted the nose of a young camel, his wispy white hair blew in the breeze. From meters away, his eyes glittered like sea glass.

"What else did he say, Maya?"

"He said that you weren't black and he said that you weren't white."

I crinkled my forehead, caught off guard by the comment, "What am I, then?"

"He didn't say that part."

The sun rose higher overhead and I squinted into the light, wondered if I was getting those wrinkles in between my eyebrows like Theresa had.

"Anything else he knows about me that I should be aware of?" I kicked Maya playfully but her face remained serious.

"He said the day you came the rain would come."

We both stood silent and looked over the flat land, the dust cloud over the camel's feet, the small squatty trees threatening with long white thorns. The children used those thorns as toothpicks when a goat or a cow was killed and the whole family feasted. They snapped the thorns off at the base and picked at their perfect teeth while they washed plastic plates in a tub of water, or gathered cow dung when the firewood was too far. We looked out past the pink hills in the distance, across from the yellow sun, a definitive circle. We looked out to the dark clouds that suddenly descended on the horizon. Deep gray wind swirled with the dust. The wind picked up the clouds and crawled closer, like a stray dog, hungry but wary, slowly, slowly making its way to our feet. And then, the rain started.

27

Max was soaked. Rain dribbled off his chin and soaked the green rubber rainboots he had pulled onto his feet. Even his teeth were wet as he smiled outside my bedroom door, just three doors down from the office where I sat at a desk and typed dusty keys. My heart began its usual anxious flutter in his presence, the visible representation of my crimes.

I tried to match his smile, and pulled the fabric tied around my waist loose and secured it over my hair, a shield from the rain. I walked outside barefoot and my feet were instantly muddy. The dust that usually clung to the yellow walls and crevices and ceiling and ground like paint formed a sticky paste.

"Where is it?" I asked, my tone betraying my fake smile. "Did you put it away?"

Max held back a laugh and rubbed rain drops from his glasses and water dripped off his chin, "Let's try this, Isabel. Hi. How are you? Why yes, I am cold and I would love a cup of tea."

I blushed, but my cheeks did not betray me in the darkness as I tiptoed my muddy way into the office and invited the tall man inside.

"Do you ever get lonely living here?" He looked around at the walls that held hundreds of girls during the day, teachers with golden hearts, cleaners and cooks and gardeners trying to earn enough to buy rice for the day, soda for the wedding, fabric for their daughter's first birthday.

"Sometimes. Usually not though. It's so busy during the day it's nice to have a little peace at night."

"Do you have peace at night?"

"I look for it. Sometimes I find it." I thought about my nights with my head in my hands, desperately looking for validation in any action or movement or crime I had created.

I tiptoed to the back of the office, filled the blue kettle with water and turned on the one-burner gas stove. The lights flickered and clicked and the room grew dark. Power always seemed to go out in the storms. Sparks fell from the power lines like raindrops and darkness sat gently on the village. Persistent, but peaceful, like the rain on the metal roof.

I warmed Max's tea in the kettle on the gas stove and added three scoops of sugar: sweet and liberal like I wanted him to perceive me. He took the mug in one hand and my wrist in the other hand and led me outside. He used the flashlight of his phone to light the way as we ducked under the enclaves of the classrooms, the toilets, the garden shed, the garage. There in the corner, sat a cardboard box filled with strange round tubs. The tubs were light pink, with pastel ducks dancing on the side.

"This is it," Max announced, let go of my wrist and warmed both of his hands on one mug of tea.

"This is… it?" I asked, surveying the strange tubs. I knelt down and read the label, "Infant Formula. Nutrition and wellness for your growing baby."

My head felt light and my feet numb. I pressed my wet hands to my ever-curling hair and smoothed it back. "I didn't know we would be disguising it as baby formula."

Max laughed nervously, afraid that perhaps I would change my mind and send him home with an entire kilo of cocaine disguised as baby formula in the back seat of his car. "You didn't think we would label it as 'cocaine' did you?"

My stomach felt sick. I envisioned one of the mothers who worked at the school hiding a tub of "formula" underneath her thick fabric and taking it home to her baby or grandchild. I pictured her mixing the powder with milk and pressing it into her child's mouth while the child choked and sputtered and spit out the offending liquid. What if the mother forced the bottle in the child's mouth once again, insisted they drink as the baby became more and more numb? I hated it. I hated the decisions I was making and I hated that Penn had asked me to make them. I hated the idea that no one had consulted me on the formula tubs, why no one thought it was relevant for me to be informed. My anger turned my tan cheeks red and I could not speak.

"You're not speaking. So that means you are okay?" Max slid his fingers into my hand inconspicuously. He stretched them out long and wide and allowed my hands stay bent around his. Silence as consent.

I nodded stoically, unsure what words could satiate my anger. Sending the tubs back would be suspicious. Denying the disguise without a better plan in mind seemed childish.

Max brought out the nervous laughter again, laid it at my feet. He was afraid; just like me. I could tell that now. If only he knew the fear that lurked in my stomach during every waking moment.

I exhaled long and loud and watched sweat drip down Max's temple.

"Let's get something a little stronger than that tea, shall we? I have gin in my room. At least I think it's gin. I couldn't quite tell from the label but it smells like trees."

We continued to link fingers as I led him back to the office and found the bottle in one of the kitchen cupboards. The label had been ripped off and small hearts drawn in permanent marker on the cap. I wondered if the American woman before me had been the one to start in on this bottle. I wondered if she had been lost, too.

We sat down under the awning of my bedroom door and I sat the bottle between us. I took a swig, swooshed the clear liquid around my mouth before swallowing and offered the bottle to Max, sitting with his knees up under his chin. He held the bottle up to his nose, then handed it back to me.

"You don't want any?" I took another mouthful of the clear liquid.

"I don't drink alcohol."

I swallowed again slowly, screwed the cap back on the bottle. A dark purple stain of embarrassment grew in my stomach. Perhaps from drinking, perhaps from assuming this man did. Maybe, more than anything, for realizing this man who transported cocaine into the primary school was not a bad man. He was not of questionable character; he had never been convicted of a crime or broken the law. I knew because I had asked. And I knew in my gut he was honest. Hell, this man didn't even drink, not even a taste. The reason he did what he did was solely because he needed the money. Maybe he had a kid at home. Maybe his mother was sick, perhaps he was building a house for his grandmother. I couldn't be sure. But I was certain he was better than me.

I was the one who drank, took pills too often, and had the idea pass through my mind that perhaps I should taste for myself some of that white powder held behind the infant formula tubs. I was the criminal.

I closed my eyes and leaned my head against the yellow paint of the wall, my hair sticking to my cheeks from the rain.

But I tried to comfort myself by saying there was a chance my motives were just as pure. Was sending a girl out of her village for a second chance at life as commendable as paying hospital bills for a sick relative, a coughing child? Maybe if these girls were my own children, my unethical acts would make sense. Maybe if they were my sisters, or nieces or related by blood. But they weren't. I was a distressed young woman who didn't belong, grasping for an ounce of meaning in life. Any life.

Max and I sat in silence, staring at the tiny stream forming at the base of the cement where water dripped off the awning and into the dust. How much water must drip before dust turns to mud? How much before a good person becomes bad?

28

The next time I walked past the garage with an armful of towels, the baby formula was gone. I had told the guard a friend was coming to pick up some things, and Max came and went without a problem. That was it. We were done. One passport completed.

Penn texted me before I had the opportunity to message him first: "My name is Penn Clemence. I am an American citizen."

I dropped the towels to the ground when I read the message. Dust rose. In just a few days, the mud had disappeared and once again our world was softened by the brown of the earth. A cleaner hired by the school clicked her tongue in my direction, knowing she would be the one to rewash the towels. I picked them up, shook them with the breeze. The towels were to be cut into rectangles, a plastic grocery bag sewn on one side for the girls to use as sanitary napkins.

I unloaded the towels in the room of Harriet the seamstress, who had started teaching Loveness how to sew. Harriet was increasingly quiet these days, with glittering eyes and a long elegant frame. Her clothes always reflected her latest invention or fashion: a skirt that rippled up and down, or socks with complex ruffles. I greeted her formally. She wasn't one for small talk, and as I began my work. Harriet stood with a bowl of rice in her hand and nodded her greeting.

I sat on the floor and began to cut small rectangles from the towels that were not covered in dust. Two girls in grade two sat down next to me and began to do the same. I wondered if they knew why we were cutting these towels so precisely. Did they know what would happen to their bodies, their minds when they got older? Would anyone ever tell them all of these secrets, or would they have to figure it out for themselves? I had, in a halfhearted manner, pitched the idea of a sex education class to the owner of the school. The conservative woman with staunch religious criteria did not even reply to the email. In a way, I was relieved. My bones and my heart and my body could not face the vulnerability of sex in a place where my soul felt so naked.

Taking a pause from cutting the towels, I crafted my text back to Penn, "Does this mean you received your passport?"

"I pick it up tomorrow. My guy got your delivery. He's happy. I'm happy. And I'm coming to see you."

"To Tanzania?"

The girls continued to cut their rectangles and stacked them gently one on top of the other. When Harriet pressed her foot down on her sewing machine, it hummed, creating the outline of a powder blue blouse.

"Born in the Congo. Citizen of America. Like mom made me legit all of those years ago."

"But why are you coming to Africa?" my heart sped up at the thought of Penn here, at Amani Manor. What would he think of this place in the dust? What would this place think of him? I instinctually smoothed my hair.

"My guy suggested I test out the passport. Looks more legit if you have traveled different places and return back to your country of citizenship. Looks the most legitimate when I travel to the DRC, or other countries where I may have family. So, I'm coming to Tanzania. I need stamps in this bad boy."

The girls cut the plastic bags and held them taut over the rectangle of the towel. Gently they danced a needle around the perimeter of the plastic.

My phone vibrated again, the screen flashing another message from Penn, "I have favors to repay. A lot of them in Africa. And a big one to you. I'm going to make sure I hold up my end of the bargain, get you what you need. I'm on your side, girl. Trust me."

I sat the phone down without replying. He seemed too comfortable, not cautious enough. Suspicion rose in my rice-filled stomach.

My phone vibrated again. "What do you want me to bring you from America, Sweetheart?"

Thoughts of red licorice in a crinkling bag came to mind. *Scented candles. Beef jerky. Tubs of mango scented lotion. Sour candies.* The wind picked up and slammed the door closed. *Face soap. Hair ties.*

The dust swirled around my ankles and caught in the fibers of the towels.

I replied, "I'll think about it and let you know soon."

Miriam, the thin willowy reed of a girl in fifth grade who borrowed library books, entered the room on her tiptoes and pursed her lips at me.

"Hey Miriam, come sit down," I said.

She obliged, squatted next to me, hovered her long thin arms over bony knees. Miriam's mother was a sweet woman who always sent her daughter with treats for me at the school. Usually the treats were papayas, or cow's milk. Once she had brought me batteries she had found on her way to town.

"Will you go back to America one day, Madame?" she asked.

"Yeah, one day I will."

She was always asking sad questions like this, "Will my sister die one day? Will my children?" Shiny tears begin to hover on her eyelid. She was searching, it seemed, for something to break her heart, to take her to her knees.

"Don't cry, dear, help me cut up these towels."

She continued to hover but cut the towels like I instructed. We sat in silence.

Just then, Miriam arched her back. She grabbed at her spine, her hands in fists. She yelled out, first in English, then Swahili, then the native tribal language. Then Miriam fell on the floor, a skinny heap, and laughed. She laughed and laughed and laughed and gurgled out rolling tribal phrases. She arched her back and shrieked.

I was so accustomed to strange noises and actions that I hardly flinched. When she stopped writhing, I touched her calf.

"Miriam. Are you okay?"

She lay in the dust on that floor and the two second graders peered at her behind long eyelashes, scissors still in their hands. Now Miriam cried. She cried and cried and cried and the wide-eyed girls looked at her as they squatted near the sobbing body. She gurgled out more tribal phrases.

"What is she saying?" I whispered to the one with the light brown eyes, the pursed lips.

"She is talking about shoes…." The young girl furrowed her brow and tried her best in English, and then switched to Swahili. "She is saying you can't wear shoes to bed…"

The young ones were obviously disturbed by the strange behavior. I placed my hand firmly on Miriam's shoulder, "Go get head teacher Marie, tell her to come here."

Both girls silently rose and ran out the door. Miriam arched her back again, shrieked. But my heart remained calm. I learned months ago that panic and fast movement did not lead to success in crises. Perhaps she was epileptic, maybe this was a seizure.

The head teacher, Marie, entered, her shoes clicked, clicked, clicked on the cement. She knelt down and took Miriam's shaking body close to her own.

"She's been cursed," Marie explained casually. She shouted instructions out the door to young girls peeking in. She told them to get a driver and a car and to hurry, that the driver needed to take them to a church.

Miriam's rigid body relaxed once again but she continued to gurgle her words in unidentifiable syllables.

Marie rubbed the plastic pearls that hung around her neck. "Don't worry. These curses happen all of the time. The pastor will pray for her and the curse will leave."

The young girl with light brown eyes explained in soft, birdlike Swahili that Miriam's backpack had been stolen the other day, so perhaps someone had found it and put the curse on the bag. The other small girl nodded, her small round head bobbing quickly.

After several minutes, Miriam stopped seizing. She opened her wet eyes and held her lower back with both hands. She gently rolled her neck in one direction and then the other. She seemed embarrassed. Miriam stood up quickly, covered her head with her sweater and ran out the door. Marie dusted her hands and stretched her arms over head. Gracefully, she made her way to standing and glided toward the door.

"Wait, you are leaving? Should I call her mother and see if she can take her to the hospital? I don't think Miriam is well…"

Marie shook her head, "No, not at this point. You know Miriam, she is always striving for attention. Maybe she is cursed and maybe not, but either way she's acting out on it. Don't embarrass her. Just comfort her when she is upset and let her be. Poor dear."

Marie left. The two young girls hovered on their haunches and looked at me for guidance on how to react, how to behave. Strangely enough, I was hoping to look in their direction for the appropriate reaction, the proper way to react when you see a fellow seizing on the ground. But they didn't cry. They didn't run. They simply watched my eyes.

"Don't worry!" I said in Swahili, pairing a shaky voice with cheerful words, "She will recover now. *Hakuna matata.* No problem."

The girls nodded. Picking up their scissors, they resumed meticulously cutting rectangles.

29

My nose found the celebration before my eyes. The burning of meat and spiced rice sifted up towards the relentless sun. The entire village made a circle around one mud hut. They joined hands and quietly stood, allowing stomachs to growl at the prospect of the food that awaited them. There was no singing and no chanting, not yet. The curtain that served as a door to the hut rustled and slowly, painfully, adolescent boys limped out. They were dressed in black, their brown faces painted white with intricate designs that highlighted their eyebrows, their cheekbones, their chins. The boys wore shrouds of black and kept their jaws clenched tight. They did not say a word as they filed out of the hut. They held their staffs tightly in black hands and their lips did not part. These boys were men now; their circumcision was complete.

The safari jeep rumbled awkwardly past the silent and solemn celebration. All heads turned and looked in my direction: the light skinned woman who insisted this tribe and this village was her home. The stranger in her loud car and her loud clothes and her loud life. I blushed at the attention and willed the safari jeep to travel faster down the rocky road. I wanted someone to laugh with me at the awkwardness of the situation, to feel the weight of unwanted stares. I wondered if Penn would be that companion. I wondered if he would like my taste in music or cook with me at night. Would he wince at the newness? Or, would he stand unfaltering with me as wind burned our eyes?

Penn had tried to bail me out of trouble once in high school. I had been caught with a stolen test in my locker. Penn had a stolen test in his locker, too. Everyone seemed to have access to the eleventh-grade physics exams in high school, but the random locker check fell in alphabetical order, and they checked the "C's" on this particular day. Carson and Clemence were just a few lockers apart. The science teacher, Ms. Worley was tall and thin and pursed her lips into a tiny line, pulled the test out of Penn's locker first and clicked her tongue.

"You think this school is a joke, Mr. Clemence? You think we tolerate cheaters in this school?" Worley jotted a note in her notebook and marched down the line to my locker, where I sweated in a plaid, pleated skirt and awaited the same fate that would inevitably befall me. Worley didn't even have to look for it, the stolen test floated to the floor at her feet in a dramatic expression of karma.

"You too, Ms. Carson?" Ms. Worley snatched the test off of the ground and looked me in the eye with her arms crossed over her flat chest.

I opened my mouth to speak, but Penn's voice came first. "That's my test, too!" He walked coolly over to my locker in his Catholic school khakis and loosened his tie a little at his neck.

"That's my test too," he said again, "That's not Isabel's. It just fell out of my locker and right to the base of hers." The teacher held Penn's gaze for a long moment. Penn had that laughing gaze, even back then, where no truths or words could keep the smile from his lips.

"You are trying to cover up for your girlfriend? Is that it?" Ms. Worley smirked as she led us to the office. Penn's smiling expression did not change. I reached out and grabbed Penn's hand as we marched to the principal's office. We both got detention for the next three weeks.

I worried our future days in Tanzania would feel like this: both of us with brilliant ideas and unrehearsed schemes that would ultimately backfire. Penn would continue his noble attempts to save me—and hold my hand while we awaited fate. Then we would both end up in a different kind of trouble, I was certain of it.

Penn arrived with Max in a safari jeep twelve days after he had received his passport. He had planned to stay in Tanzania for one month. Through an email, he explained that he would visit the school during the day, get to know the kids, and work out any logistics for our passport deliveries.

I booked him a room at the Rasta Hostel in Casa. The first week in the hostel you paid with money; after that, you could pay in weed or booze or food. Eagerness exuded from Penn's words as he planned his trip. I worried about his stamina to stay in such a dry and stagnant world. Things moved slowly here. Eagerness was often a curse in a place where the depth of your dedication did not have much impact.

On the evening Penn arrived, the sun was setting like the bobbin of a fishing pole as Max rumbled towards the Manor in his low truck. I hugged both of the tall muscular men, and welcomed them into the office. We made small talk. I asked Penn about his flight. I teased Max about arriving with a human being instead of a donut. I brushed the dust off the chairs and the desk the best I could before finding two warm beers and a bottle of Sprite for Max from the secret drawer in the bottom of my desk.

"Africa is just how I remembered it!" Penn teased, as if an infant remembered size of buildings and traffic of a continent he barely knew. I wanted to touch Penn, to verify his existence. So often I lay awake at night and asked myself over and over if the life I lived was as strange and mysterious as it seemed when I told stories to Theresa on the phone Sunday nights. Penn's presence validated me: yes, this was my life, and yes, it was unwaveringly complex and real. I reached out and held Penn's hand. He casually rubbed the bony part on top of my fingers and bit his lip when he looked at my face.

Max took his Sprite bottle and said he would drink outside. He was a confident drug runner, but he averted his gaze at any sign of intimacy. When Max left the office, Penn and I sat too close on the bench inside the muggy room.

"How is everything back home?" I asked trying to remain smooth and confident despite the nauseating heat. Penn pulled my legs up over his lap.

"Exactly how you left it. I know you probably feel a little anxious out here, but you really didn't leave anything behind. We all have too much and think we don't have enough."

Penn's eyes seemed tired and he would not meet my gaze. I wondered if he was nervous. He'd always exuded such confidence, an immovable certainty that intimidated me. I pictured Penn at the school dance, arms draped around one girl but winking in my direction. Or Penn in study hall, insisting, through a handwritten note, that I was the most beautiful girl he had ever known, and wouldn't such a beautiful girl let him copy my homework? But for the first time, I detected a hesitance in him, though he looked stronger and older than the last time I'd seen him. He was thicker, his shoulders were wider. His hair was longer, cut close on the sides with length curling towards the top of his head.

I nodded my agreement, suddenly shy at his touch, his fingers around my calves. For the first time in months, I worried that I hadn't shaved my legs.

"This is a hard place," Penn continued. "Harder than most everyone described it. I can't believe that you have stayed here and not really explained to anyone the conditions." Out the window, two dust devils trickled from the sky and blended into the horizon.

"How would you describe it?" I said quietly, suddenly insecure in the way I had explained this place, insecure in the fact that I had not been able to describe it all. "How do you explain where we are? What words would you use to describe all of this?" The blanket of night was speckled by bellowing sheep and goats, the crackling of a fire, the high pitch wail that accompanied tribal dances.

"Just impressed with you for sticking it out here," he murmured, pushing his hair back with his free hand. I sensed insecurity in his words, too.

I sat with a warm beer and a man I barely knew. They were both just numbing agents to alleviate the discomfort of everyday living. Life here did not allow the salve of friends or family or the movie theatre or Internet or the shopping mall. And that is all love is, isn't it? An ointment and a bandage? The same as any drug or religion: a temporary shield from the pain of the world.

I grew brave and counted all I could lose from kissing the mouth of this man whose truth was familiar but not his body. I came up with nothing. I sat up, looked at him straight in the eye and kissed him. Penn didn't retract. He didn't seem surprised. I thought he knew it wasn't love, I thought he knew it was coping. He leaned into the kiss as if he had been prepared for it. He tasted of American tobacco, a dark tang that made me homesick for late night dive bars. I led him to my bedroom, closing the thin wood door behind me and locking it with my skeleton key, not even pausing to consider Max sprawled out in the pickup truck nearby.

It was always too hot to spend any amount of time in my bedroom. When I needed to rest I laid a yoga mat outside under the awning between the school courtyard and the village and read or closed my eyes while the wind chilled my skin. Because of this, my room was simple. I had taped a couple pictures of Theresa and my father to the cement wall. My twin bed was covered with fleece blankets from American donors and an orange and yellow *ngati* that Nylie had given me. I did not escape the dust in my room. I did not escape the dust anywhere. But I wasn't embarrassed by the sparseness of the room, instead, it made me feel as if my life were big enough to feel full in spite of an empty bedroom. I pressed Penn's shoulders down until he sat on my bed.

Penn stayed calm. He was never one to overreact. He didn't question my moves and he didn't promote them. He let me take his shirt off, gently, carefully, and I placed it on my dresser. He followed suit. Gently peeling the sweaty fabric away from my chest. The fan rotated and hit my stomach, sending goose bumps from my navel all the way up to my neck.

I wiggled him out of khaki pants and allowed my skirt to drop to my ankles.

I observed him, took in every piece of his body. The same ten fingers of a man born in America. The same eyelashes of a man who led the free world. The same thoughts and English words of a man who had killed, or healed, or had never done anything at all. Every human body was exquisitely the same.

"What do you want, Isabel?" His voice stayed low, calm; the same vocal chords and words used by drug dealers and saviors. We stood naked in front of each other. My eyes didn't search him sexually, but instead, curiously, like a child trying to understand.

I couldn't answer and didn't know. I pulled him to my bed where he laid his sweating face on my heart, and we tried to remember what it was like to believe in love.

Afterward, we curled side by side in my child-sized bed, the heat preventing us from getting comfortable. Sweat stuck my curls to my face and dripped down the center of his chest. He kissed the bony place between my breasts.

"You're beautiful," he said and searched my face with his eyes.

But vulnerability was not my goal, not in this place, not in this lifetime. I sat up and pulled the blanket around my chest, "It's too hot. You should probably get to your hostel."

He wrapped a sheet around his waist, lay back down and guided my head to his firm stomach, running his fingers through my hair. I had forgotten how much a body craves physical contact until it returns after a long absence. I closed my eyes and pressed a cheek into his chest.

"A little sweat never killed nobody. Let's stay here for a moment."

My heart pounded more rapidly as I allowed emotion to leak into my bones. I did not know what to do with emotion. I didn't know in America, and I didn't know in Africa, and I did not know how to handle being naked in a world where I had covered up so much.

Fire burned my eyes and manifested as two single tears on the chest of a man I had once sat in the principal's office with for stealing tests and smoking weed and living a teenager's criminal life.

"Are you crying?" he asked, no accusation in his tone. He did not take his fingers from my hair.

"Just taking a breath," I said. He picked up his beer bottle and drank down the rest, then kissed the top of my head. A tightness coiled in my throat. My mind became restless. Tears poured.

"That's a lot of tears for someone who is taking a breath."

I squeezed my eyes tighter until colors appeared in the back of my eyelids.

He put his hand on my hip bone. "Your mother would be proud of you here in this place, I think."

I wiped my eyes with my fists. "That's not saying much."

"Did you two not get along?"

I matched my inhales to his, and slowed my breath down.

"It's not that we didn't get along…" The tenseness was building in me from truths I rarely admitted to myself, let alone to other people, "It's just that she didn't care what I did. It didn't matter to her if I became the president of the United States or if smoked weed outside the gas station all day. She didn't want a baby and that didn't change when her baby grew into a girl, and then into a woman."

Penn altered his position to pull a necklace from his pants pocket. The chain held a small tube at the end; he gently screwed it open to produce a white powder and a small spoon.

"So, what now?" he asked, "You become the mother to every African girl on the Eastern side of this continent to make up for the fact that you think your mother didn't care?"

He brought the small shovel to his nose and inhaled. His words didn't offend me like those of other people who analyzed my life, who attempted to understand my peculiar decisions, my unknown expectations.

Penn held the small shovel up to my nose. I considered inhaling quickly. I pictured that inhale alleviating the wrenching emotion, stuffing it back so far into my heart that it could never leak out. Instead, I bit my lip and shook my head no.

"Tell me about the girls then," Penn answered. He screwed the lid back on his small tube, to my relief. "Why do they need to get out of here? Other than the obvious."

"Well, the first one is Maya. She is incredibly smart but she has a hot temper. Her father told her she wouldn't be able to attend secondary school because he needed her to stay home and watch the cattle. So, she shot his cattle."

Penn's mouth opened wide as he threw his head back and laughed.

"And that right there," he said, "Is the person that you want to get a passport for. She is not going to take any shit from anyone. That chick means business."

I thought of Maya as a businesswoman, a lawyer perhaps, standing in a courtroom on her thick ankles, staring a defendant down and shaking her head slowly side to side.

"What did her dad do when he found out?"

"He hasn't found out yet. He's away. Lord, I don't know what's going to happen when returns. Maya thinks he's going to kill her. I wouldn't be surprised."

Penn shook his head and closed his eyes, "Who is the other one?"

"Her name is Loveness," Penn situated his hand more directly between my legs. "She's sixteen with a kid, and just married. The dude is like forty years old. She wants out more than I've ever seen anyone want out of anywhere. She said her mom could take care of her baby if we could get her somewhere else."

I tried to determine if Penn was becoming more distracted or if it was only me. "Anyone else, Isabel?" He breathed into my ear. His breath was hot and we sweated on top of the sheets.

"There are so many girls with potential..." My voice trailed away with his touch, the movement of his breath… "But I want to be done with this trade business. It is another burden entirely."

"We don't need saving," Marie's voice rung in my ears, "And we are not here to save you."

I fell into Penn the same way I fell into Africa: with reckless abandon, no thought of consequences, no thought of the future or the burden it could place on my shoulders, my heart. I fell into his words like rolling Swahili phrases. I fell into his skin like the dust coating my world.

30

Nylie was particularly giddy the next morning. "Good morning, my dear!" she sang as she swung into the office, colorful fabric sliding off her shoulder. She wore new shiny gold earrings, shiny silver anklets. Her teeth seemed shiny, too.

I watched her feet dance on the dusty cement and her wrists twist and twirl to the music that no one else heard, "Why are you so happy?" I asked, attempting to smooth my hair. I wondered if Penn would be coming by today.

Nylie hooked arms with me and danced me in a circle, "Because we are young beautiful women, Isabel. We are free and we can do anything!"

I had to admire this attitude of a woman with a thousand problems on her tall shoulders. There were no fences on this tribal land; they weren't necessary. There was nowhere to wander. In any direction the only thing visible was swirling dust, the occasional flutter of fabric from a lone shepherd. You could run as fast and as far as you wanted, but at the end of the day, whether you were a wife or a sheep, there is nothing but a dusty death if you tried to escape. That's another type of slavery: the kind that doesn't free you when the gates are opened and the chains are cut.

Nylie stopped her dance and knelt on the floor. She hooked thin silver chains nearly identical to her own (albeit, slightly less shiny) around my dusty anklebones, one on either foot. She clasped her hands and smiled when she was done, "My God, now we can be tribal girls together!"

She collapsed on the chair cushion next to my desk: an exhausted heap of exhilaration and energy. I jumped up and down a few times in my teal rubber flip-flops, delighted by the gentle tinkling.

"Do I get to keep these?" I asked.

"Yes, my dear, these are yours to keep. I got new chains for my ankles so I want to give you those."

I tried out the few native words I knew. My tongue never learned to roll its R's, which hindered my accent.

"Thank you, *ashe*," I said in Nylie's native tongue, "They are good, *sidai naleng.*"

Nylie clapped and laughed again. "Now your feet are tribal, and your words are tribal, too!"

I laughed with her, enjoying lightness in a place where heaviness could easily swallow a soft soul. I urged my mind to photograph this moment, I wanted to come back to this memory during the times late at night when the world felt too heavy to hold.

The urge to be swallowed occasionally had hit me; to allow the grief and weight of life crumble me and blow me away with the dust. It wasn't a passive feeling, not like the way Ivy suffered: the inability to open her eyes in the morning, to get out of bed, to finish her sandwich, to make it to work on time. My occasional depression was much more active: the failure to sleep at night, the inability to sit still. The constant moving of my hands, my feet, my neck. If I stopped or sat still, I worried I'd disappear like Ivy Supeet.

I wondered how Penn would react to my shaking hands and restless feet under the covers at night. I hoped he would hold them still and calm my breathing. I hoped if I ever kept him up at night with restless limbs he would take my hand and ask me to show him the African constellations.

Nylie was standing, waving her hand in front of my face, "Helllllo, Isabel? What are you thinking about? I said 'Could I have some of that baby milk?'" said Nylie.

I shook my head, twisted the new silver chains around my feet. "Baby milk? What?"

"In the garage. There is a whole box of the baby milk. Many, many cans. I think some donation car must have dropped it off, but there is so much milk, can I have one?"

"What? No! I mean sorry, Nylie, it's some special project the school board is doing. We have to give the milk to certain new mothers." My brain was not thinking fast enough. How was I not aware that Max had made another drop off?

"I know many new mothers who could use this milk. I can help you pass it out if you want, I know where they all live," Nylie countered.

"No, just no, Nylie, I need to read the email and figure out exactly what it is that the school board wants."

"Okay, well I can start telling the mothers of new babies..."

"No, Nylie. Just no! Okay, I've got to figure this out before we do anything. Okay? Let me just figure this out."

I rarely snapped. Never raised my voice unless I was telling a girl to use proper English when I heard a Swahili word from across the room. Nylie was taken aback.

"Fine. I'm going to go help in the kitchen today." She stomped her plastic shoes so they made a clicking sound on the cement as she left the office. I had destroyed the elation she had felt just minutes before, even if the idea of freedom had been only in her song and in her mind.

Sweat dripped down my temple and down the sides of my nose. Salt seeped into my eyes and burned. I sneezed. Dust flew from my nostrils like the dust that covered my shoes, my laundry, my dishes, my heart, my conscience, my pure intentions.

In the back room in the office, I turned the precious water on and let it sputter until a strong stream ran down the sink. As I washed my hands, I was astonished as always at how black water ran from my hands when all I did was sit at an office desk all day. When the water ran clear, I washed my face then cleaned above my upper lip, the salty sweat on the side of my temples and down my brown nose. Turning off the water, I let my hands drip onto the cement floor. I flicked my dripping fingers to the tired African violets outside of the open window that tried to press through the dry soil.

A herd of the dinosaur-like camels pressed their wide feet through the dirt. Their necks seemed to rise taller than the sandstorms and their pace was constant: they didn't speed up or slow down like sheep or the goats did when intrigued, startled or frightened. The cows and the goats were always scattering. They were constantly falling behind or jetting ahead. There was no sense of time or energy management in those animals, not like the camels. They moved slowly out the window, like boats through a sea of dust, riding the waves as smoothly as their soft feet would allow.

31

I needed a different taste in my mouth, a different smell on my skin. I wanted to have a different feeling under my feet or on top of my head. I called Penn at the hostel and told him to meet me. I flagged down a man with a *piki piki*, a motorcycle.

"I need to go to the junction," I said in Swahili, directing him to the space between towns that no one ever stayed at, that only existed to transition from one piece of Tanzania to another. Covering my hair with a blue and white flowered fabric, I climbed on the back of the man's bike and held onto the silver bars behind me. I was cautious of what my legs rested against. Too many times girls came into the office with white socks pulled up over their chocolate calves scarred pink by the exposed pipes of the *piki piki*.

If you press out of your mind that dust is the filth in your skirt or the itch in your nose, it truly is lovely. Perhaps it could be glitter, swirling its way down with the wind, up with clouds. Perhaps it could be sugar, drifting from a hand into a bowl. Dust is a screen and a filter that permits you to look the sun straight in its big yellow eye. It is a reminder: of where, exactly, the straps on your sandals were, how your braid hung across your neck, in what place, specifically, you left your notebook on the desk. It is a magic paintbrush that can cover an entire country with just one sigh of the wind.

My dust looked especially lovely today as the sun set in front of its sheen, causing each speck to glisten and glitter as the *piki piki* rolled forward. I held the cloth over my nose and mouth, inhaling the familiar scent of bar soap I had scrubbed the scarf with just days before. I felt exhilarated and light: two sensations I rarely experienced on this African plain. I was excited to see Penn. I was excited to be travelling so fast in a slow world where seconds barely ticked away.

Penn said he liked the hostel. Annie had told me about the Rasta Hostel one day, when we had run into each other in the middle of Casa. We had both covered our hair with an *ngati* and linked arms like old friends. She told me it was a good place to stay, on the occasion when I wanted to escape sandstorms and long skirts. You could buy warm beers at the hostel counter and the buildings surrounding the hostel served chips *mayai*, French fries fried with eggs, or *mishikaki*, spiced meat on wooden sticks.

The driver crossed from the dusty road onto cracked pavement, jostling me. My calves squeezed against the engine. I heard a faint hiss before I felt the shock of burning metal on my leg. I jerked my leg out and held my knees wide for the remainder of the journey.

Penn was at the junction before I arrived. It had been three days since I had seen him but it felt longer, like eternity had passed since I had seen his dark skin shadow my white sheets and felt the comfort of his voice in my language. He had been "catching up with colleagues," he'd said. I pushed down jealousy that I was not the only one he had time for.

In dark jeans with his long legs bent and splayed out to the side, he sat at a plastic table. He wore a black short sleeve button-up shirt and dark aviator sunglasses, a warm bottle of beer in his hand, a toothpick in his mouth. On top of his head was perched a straw hat and, on his wrist, a Rolex. Penn looked exactly like what he was: an East African drug dealer. I wondered what he was thinking. Did it excite him to be home, finally, to a place he had never known? Did it feel familiar? Were those nine months in the womb enough for him to recall the gurgling French roll of the tongue, the breezy Swahili, the scents of motorcycle exhaust and cooking meat? I desperately wanted him to feel comfortable here because I feared that, like me, he would never find a home.

I stepped gingerly off the bike and handed the man a crumbled sky-blue bill. He nodded his thanks. I removed the cloth from my head and wrapped it around my waist like I saw the African mothers do. Penn's face brightened.

"There she is," he said and stood to hug me and kiss the top of my head. "You smell like dust," he murmured.

I smiled and motioned for a waiter to bring a beer, a cold one, not a warm one like Penn seemed to have accidentally ordered. No sweat pooled at the base of Penn's beer like a cold beer promised to do.

"What do you think of this place?" I asked.

Penn rubbed sweat from his forehead. "Well, we are definitely in Africa. This is where you come and hang out a lot?"

Behind dark glasses, his eyes traced his surroundings: the bus stop unloading a vehicle filled magnificently over capacity with humans, chickens and baskets. Vendors selling gum, sodas, cigarettes from plastic containers atop their heads. A man in a blue jumpsuit welding, sparks flying, his eye protection merely child's sunglasses. The man who'd brought me a beer gently flipping over *chipatis* that sizzled in hot oil.

Penn stretched his hands up over his head. I could see the black hairs trailing down past his navel, "I have never seen someone look so African, Isabel. And I am African!" He gestured to my tie-dye dress and *konga* wrapped around my waist.

"The more you live out here the more you begin to understand why people do things the way they do," I said. "You wear the *konga to* shield you from dust. You braid your hair to keep it clean. You wear bright colors so you don't get lost in the sandstorms."

Penn took his glasses off and held my hand quietly under the table, "You really came into yourself out here, you know? You seem like you know what you're doing."

I blushed and looked away, "I don't know what I'm doing."

Penn nodded and played with my fingers with both of his hands. He seemed nervous, like he wanted to ask me something. He opened his mouth, then closed it again. He wiped beads of sweat off his upper lip.

I spoke before uncomfortable words could exit his mouth. "Nylie was asking if she could have some of the baby milk," I said, and pulled my hands away from his. "She seemed pretty adamant about it, and a little pissed that I wouldn't give her a single tub of it. I hope no one gets the wrong idea and tries to steal it."

Penn didn't say anything.

"Only here would baby formula be more valuable than cocaine," I continued, trying to coax a smile from his lips.

Penn nodded, pulled a cigarette out of his pocket and held it between his lips. In perfect Swahili he asked the man at the table next to him for a lighter. I was impressed. I wanted to be that cigarette.

Penn seemed distracted and uneasy. Was he concerned the mission was not going as planned? I had already seen Maya's passport: it had an embossed and glossy picture and reflected Tanzania's national symbol on the inverse page and was incredibly high quality. It seemed he should be happy with how quickly and efficiently things were progressing in this slow, plodding world.

Penn pulled the cigarette out of his mouth and gave a long, dramatic exhale. He tapped the ashes onto the red dirt ground.

"Why are you doing this, Isabel?" His eyes did not meet mine. He stared down at the ashes.

"Why am I in Africa? Ivy…"

"No," Penn interrupted, tapping more ashes from his cigarette onto the table, rubbing it between his fingers. "Why are you helping me?"

"I'm not helping you. I'm helping my girls…"

"Why? You are taking a big risk. Do you know what they do here to drug smugglers?"

I ran my fingers on the smooth braids that ran the length of my scalp and traced the condensation on my beer. My mind flashed to a million people and a million memories that would never leave my brain. I smelled gasoline from the bus stand. Hot corn on makeshift grills of charcoals and metal wiring. The faint scent of Penn's sweat, perhaps his deodorant, laundry detergent.

"Because I know what it's like to not have a choice in a situation. I don't want to see these two girls without a say in their life. Their life is worth more than my comfort, Penn."

Penn crushed his cigarette butt under his black boot. I don't know whether his discomfort, the topic at hand, or the cigarette smoke was making it difficult to breathe, but I felt relieved to see it crushed on the ground.

"You went to a good school," he said. "And you have a good family. You told me your dad paid for your car and your college. It seems to me you have always had a choice in a situation. And yet here you are. Restless. No peace to be found."

We sat in silence for a while. A child, no older than four, sold cigarettes to a priest, then put the money in his tiny shoe.

Penn squeezed my thigh through the thin fabric of my skirt and tried to smile.

I leaned in and whispered in his ear, "People at peace don't make change."

32

We were on schedule to make another cocaine drop off in the formula tubs that evening. This would be the third and final drop off; the last kilo of cocaine disguised as baby formula that would get Loveness a Kenyan passport and a ticket out of her forced eternity. My heart knew no peace while the cocaine rested at school, but I felt a sense of relief knowing that this would be the last shipment.

Max was a smooth talker and a businessman. I trusted his sober mind and values. Occasionally, he would whisper to Penn about his wife back at home, or his baby daughter and her first steps. But these pieces of information were too precious to speak to me, and he quit his soft stories as soon as I walked into the room. Perhaps Max was not a man at peace, either.

Despite his gentle nature and the continual donut bribes, the guards seemed suspicious. They stopped his low riding truck at the gate and stopped accepting his gifts of pastries and fruits so readily. Penn told me they questioned him nearly every time Max came to the school. He wasn't certain if it was because they thought they could get money from him, or if they were genuinely suspicious of his actions.

The stress of the drugs on the school compound entered into my skull and left through my skin in sweaty nervous ripples. I figured the best thing for me to do before the next pick up was to keep myself busy and distracted. I texted Nylie, who told me of a celebration that was to take place that afternoon. The orange sun hung heavily on the horizon before I told Penn I wanted him to come with me. He agreed and the two of us mounted one *piki piki* and paid ninety cents for the driver to take us to the home where the celebration was to be held.

The wind was strong and the dust was high. We heard the celebration long before we saw it. Women called and chanted in high shrill voices, singing call and response songs with intricate meanings that no one had been able to explain to me. Men grunted and uttered low guttural notes, and slammed their sandaled feet on the ground with such force the vibrations exited through their mouths. A fire was lit, and smoke rose. The sky turned yellow and then black, skipping its sickly-sweet pink stage all together.

Children tried to keep up with the sputtering motorcycle. Babies ran naked and toddlers were dressed in the best outfits their mothers could afford or barter. A child with big eyes and a runny nose wore a Dallas Cowboys dress, and another wore a large t-shirt belted with "Chicago Dulls" printed on the front. Misprints always found their way to this part of Africa.

Penn and I dismounted the overcapacity *piki piki* and I pulled the blue cloth from around my hair to my waist. The harsh scent of animal blood and meat cooked over open fire permeated the air. Smells of spiced rice spilled out from a nearby hut. My mouth watered. Penn's hand swept my skirt and my hand as we walked towards a few students I recognized. I blushed at the vulnerability of encountering the students while walking next to a man; of appearing even more naïve and lovestruck than I had the week I had arrived in Tanzania.

Loveness came up behind me, and interlaced her thin brown fingers into mine. She rubbed the chipped nail polish on my fingers and I squeezed her hand. She was wearing traditional clothes; as most tribal girls did at a village celebration. "Everyone is asking who this man is with you," Loveness whispered into my ear. "Everyone is asking if you are going to have a wedding soon here in Africa."

I took Loveness in: head to toe. A thick, deep purple cloth twisted around her waist, another fabric safety-pinned over one shoulder and expertly twisted to cover her torso and lower back. Smaller, thinner pieces of fabric were tied over her shoulder, around her waist, draped around her neck like a cape. These pieces of fabric all held the same pattern: orange and white stripes and zigzags, blue polka dots and crescent moons. Her ankles were adorned with several thin silver chains, six on each foot, and her chest bounced with plastic beads and small silver discs. She wore dozens of necklaces and looked so stunning I was shocked for a moment that anyone was speaking about Penn or me at all.

I laughed nervously, "No wedding soon, my dear. Penn is just my friend from America. I like having him visit because he reminds me of my home."

Loveness nodded, disappointed.

The wind swept away all self-control and my mind painted a picture of Penn and me in a yellow house in the country. Three dark skinned, green-eyed children ran and screamed in the yard. I tried to picture Penn with a briefcase, a suit and a day job. I pictured myself with cookbooks, and the desire to wake up every day and care for my family and not run wild and reckless and free. Settling down was not a thought that frequently crossed my mind. The thought of all I was expected to accomplish before I died exhausted me. I suddenly wanted to cry.

"When I get married, I promise I will invite you," I forced a smile for Loveness and pinched her arm gently. Life was heavy and long. In moments like this, I understood Ivy.

Loveness's mother bustled around, ushering Penn and me onto small wooden benches just outside her mud hut. Her mother wore no shoes, but was decorated even more intricately than Loveness. Her head and eyebrows were freshly shaven, and thick ropes of earrings hung from the large holes in her earlobes.

One time I had asked Loveness, "How long did it take your mother to stretch her earlobes out like that?"

Loveness laughed. She said, "The holes weren't stretched out, they cut the middle out with a spear." She mimicked cutting out the center of an ear lobe casually, as if explaining how you break spaghetti noodles before placing them in the pot.

Loveness's mother brought Penn and me lukewarm pineapple soda. Penn tried to refuse and I kicked his calf from my place on the wooden stool, a suggestion that he accept the gift. He graciously took the glass bottle and bowed his head in thanks. Loveness pulled up a stool next to me and watched as the boys who were recently inducted as warriors began to form a circle for a new round of call and response songs. They held their shepherd staffs high in the air, teenage muscles rippling with each bounce of the heels and sway of the feet. The smell of sweat and dust mingled in my nose. Young girls, embarrassed and enthralled, busied themselves by chasing after babies or stirring pots so they would not be caught with their gazes fixed on these boys.

"Where is Nylie tonight?" I leaned into Loveness and stretched my legs in front of me. "I was texting her earlier; she said she would be here."

Loveness glanced at the chains around her ankles. "I don't know. I haven't seen her," she mumbled.

The boys' chanting got louder and the girls' shrieks became shriller until almost every child and adult capable of walking joined in the circle. The women popped their chests, sending plastic beads bouncing on a sea of breasts. The men stomped rubber sandaled feet and created dust that formed a trancelike state for the entire crowd. I was not at peace and I was not happy. But at the sight of such unorganized unity, I felt my heart release.

Penn grabbed my hand, and I grabbed Loveness's wrist as the three of us stood and entered the growing circle. A young naked boy grabbed my shirt, pulled my head closer to the ground and graced my neck with plastic beads. My shoulders grew loose and my neck swayed to the beat that the voices created. Penn closed his eyes and turned his face up to the dust and the stars. We were alive.

Miriam, who had recovered from her seizure in the sewing room, shimmied her way into the center of the circle. Her neck jutted forward and her thin hips swayed with the clapping hands. She popped her flat chest and pursed her thick lips. Just yesterday, Miriam had sat on a couch cushion in the office at Amani Manor. She wanted a sticker; she saw that some visitors had given me a whole book of stickers with rainbow horses inside. Could she, perhaps, clean up some rubbish in the schoolyard for the exchange of a sticker? I laughed at her enthusiasm and her negotiation skills, and agreed to the exchange. When she brought the rubbish back to the office to show me, I placed a large pink horse on the back of her hand, and slapped it a little to ensure a stick. She beamed, and skipped out the door. How strange to see this young and innocent girl so educated in the art of ancient ritual. Her maturity far exceeded the powder blue school uniform. I said a silent prayer that Miriam would only want for child things for now: stickers and candy and recess. I prayed she wouldn't experience grown up burdens for many more years.

The scent of alcohol and ripe, sour bananas wafted overhead: banana beer, the local brew. A young warrior screeched and yelled, threw his staff over his head in victory. I felt a hand grab me around the waist and pull me in close with confidence. He asked me in Swahili if I cared to see his cows, and I laughed out loud when I considered the difference in flirting rituals.

I grabbed Penn's hand, pulled him closer to me, allowed him to breathe a sweaty breath down my back and hold my hips while I twisted and shook. I allowed my body to want him again, despite the vulnerability and chaos our nakedness created. Here, with this man, in an ankle length skirt in the middle of the dust that I had learned to call home, I decided to trust Penn. Hope was such an exhilarating, breathtaking game.

Penn pulled me close and whispered in my ear, "What is this celebration for, exactly?"

Nylie had told me this was a party for the warriors becoming elders. I wasn't naïve, I heard them talk. The celebration was not for warriors or elders, but those were good words to throw to a western woman. I had no concept of those two categories, or of the celebrations that may be performed for a "warrior" or "elder," so if there was ever an instance that needed to go unquestioned or swept under the rug, these phrases were attached. This cultural difference was such that I would accept their answers and not probe.

Miriam, the young girl dancing at the celebration, had told me what the event was really about. Her hips were so thin, I had to belt her skirt with ribbon every now and then just so it wouldn't sink to her ankles. I saw her carefully leave a hut, the one her family lived in, and lock the door behind her, calmly, slowly.

"Can I go in to greet your mother?" I had asked Miriam. I enjoyed the young girl's mother. She spoke minimal Swahili but she often acted out Miriam with a skirt coming down around her ankles and we both laughed.

"No, you can't go talk to my mother right now. She is helping the girls," Mariam said matter of fact, and began to load the donkeys' back with big plastic buckers as she prepared to make the trip to the well.

"Help what girls, my dear?" I had asked her, and helped sling the heavy yellow buckets over the wide ribs of the animal.

"Help the girls who have been, you know, cut…" Miriam made a slicing motion between her legs. I felt goose bumps rise on my shoulders. I nodded slowly, squeezed her hand and found my way back to Loveness's house. It was not judgement in my heart as I considered the female circumcision that Miriam was surely referring to. But instead, it was an overwhelming feeling that everything I had once considered was a direct reflection of where I was raised. And everything I had previously considered wrong? Well, did that just mean that I had never seen it in my own home before?

When the night got too sweaty and my feet too dirty, I sat down on the wooden stool, and with a gap-toothed smile, Loveness's mother served sweet chai. Loveness gently swayed in the back of the crowd. I wondered what she was thinking. I glanced at her mother and a wave of guilt washed over me. I would be taking away this woman's first child, her daughter, and sending her to an entirely new place. I did not blame this mother with deep chocolate skin and milky brown eyes for Loveness's plight. I did not see her as the one who had married off her young daughter, despite her age, despite her intelligence and candor and unwavering ability to be brave. I knew this mother was simply trying to protect her daughter from what the too strong and the too brave and the too outspoken have to suffer. Maybe that's how Ivy had attempted to protect me.

Soon, Loveness sat next to me. The sun sank behind the horizon and the rolling hills the girls at school called "the pink mountains" because of how the sunlight looked on the peaks. Loveness's thin mother stood, pressed her gold clinking bracelets up her forearm, past her elbow and onto her bicep. She leaned over a giant silver pot. Her strong arms used a large wooden spoon to simultaneously ladle brown-spiced rice and goat meat into cracked plastic bowls, then wave the spoon at screaming children. She promised with her tribal tongue to smack them if they didn't behave.

Penn stared intently at Loveness. She squeezed the rice with her right hand between her fingers and palm to make it stick, and then gently placed the rice ball on her tongue. She was ruthless with the meat. She ripped it with her teeth and sucked the bone. I smiled at Penn, then followed suit: leaving plastic plates empty except for small pieces of bone and grit.

A short, fat man with ink black skin and orange red cloths wrapped around his body wiped grease from his face with the back of his hand, and then called to Loveness for a formal greeting. I recognized him as Nylie's husband. He had come a handful of times to the school gate when the sandstorms became too strong or the rain fell too hard. He would honk the horn of his motorcycle and Nylie would come running out of the office, covering her smooth head with an *ngati* that she held with long, strong arms. That's all I had ever known of this man that married my friend as a child bride. He was stout and gruff and dark and the thought of him on top of Nylie's long body sent shivers down my spine. Loveness stood and bowed her head as he touched his palm to her scalp in a formal greeting. They spoke quickly and softly in tribal words I did not know. Loveness kept her face to the ground and kicked dust with her shoe. Her voice was higher than normal. He grunted something, grabbed his shepherding staff and walked briskly away, his rubber shoes smacking the dry earth.

"What was that about?" I asked Loveness as she squatted on her overturned bucket converted into a chair.

"He doesn't know where Nylie is. He was wondering if I had seen her."

"Do you know where Nylie is? I have been looking for her, too. She told me she would text me…"

Loveness flicked her eyes at me and I understood her body language. I closed my mouth.

Loveness's mother ducked out of the mud hut. She poured one cup of tea into another chipped tin cup and handed the steaming liquid to Penn, then me, then Loveness just as she had been taught: first the men, then the white women, then, finally, her own daughter. Penn held his chai cautiously and blew on it with careful lips. The mother rolled her eyes and grabbed the tea from his hands. She found another tin cup and poured the liquid between the two cups. We watched the steam escape and the tea cool. She didn't spill one drop and handed the cooled tea back to Penn.

We finished the chai in silence. The familiar feeling of concern dripped into my stomach as I wondered where Nylie was and what Loveness seemed to know that I did not. Penn and I stood to leave when I smelled dust rustle and heard the slap of plastic shoes against the dry and tired earth. Nylie sprinted into view.

Her forehead glistened with sweat and her clothes were in complete disarray. She was breathing heavily and dust covered her feet and her ankles and her thin calves. She melted down to the feet of Loveness, and Loveness instinctively began mopping sweat from her forehead with her own colorful fabric. She dusted her friend's feet and the back of her neck.

Loveness's mother poured another cup of tea. Nylie tilted her head down toward the mother and the elder woman palmed the thin woman's head as a greeting but they did not exchange a word. The breeze picked up and we all instinctively covered our eyes with scarves or cloths or the fabric on our body. As the sand storm subsided, I glanced at Nylie, still shielding her face with a neon blue fabric, decorated with intricate stitching of small African women: each dancing with a baby on her back or a pot on her head.

The fabric was beautiful. I had seen it before.

"Isn't that Richard's cloth?" I asked, as I watched Nylie pull the fabric around her shoulders. Richard: the driver from the school who picked me up the first day from the airport. Richard, who didn't speak much but giggled and smiled like a child when Nylie spoke to him.

Loveness's eyes flashed towards me again and Nylie pinched my arm, quick and hard. I was surprised by this reaction. "Well, isn't it? Why do you have Richard's fabric? And where have you been? I've been texting you and your husband came by…"

A crease formed between Nylie's eyebrows and her cheekbones grew tight.

"My husband came? What did he say?" She spoke quickly, softly. She seemed to forget that most people around her could not speak one word of English.

Loveness removed one piece of fabric from around her chest and tied it around her waist. In the distance, Miriam led a donkey with two large yellow buckets of water on either side of its tired ribs.

"He asked where you were," Loveness said. "And I told him Isabel had sent you to do some errands for the school. So, you better figure out what you are going to tell him when he asks what chores you were helping with."

Nylie nodded, her lower lip trembling. I knew she was attempting not to cry. For a smart woman, for a strong woman, and an independent woman, Nylie allowed emotion to flow freely from her eyes and her mouth. Perhaps that's what made her smart and strong and independent.

"Nylie, what's going on?" I looked over my shoulder and hissed into her ear, "Are you sleeping with Richard? Is Richard your boyfriend?" I kept my voice low. Penn had politely turned away and held hands with a naked baby. He rubbed snot from underneath the baby's nose.

Nylie stood quickly and placed her long fingers on my knees. "No! You have to believe me, Isabel, I am not that kind of woman! I would never do something like that. You must know I am not that kind of woman!" She was crying large tears now. For a moment, I worried about the water she was wasting in this desert by allowing the tears to fall from her eyes.

"Okay, okay, Nylie I believe you! You know I always believe you! Calm down and talk to me. Why were you with Richard then? What's going on, are you in trouble?"

We all sat silent for a moment. Soon, Loveness stood and helped Miriam unload the buckets from the back of the donkey. She poured one whole bucket into a clean silver bowl, and threw the plastic plates and tin cups into the water.

"Richard is not my boyfriend, Isabel," Nylie brushed away her tears hurriedly, like a child, "But he is…. helping me."

My heart sped up and I pictured Nylie's pouting face as I refused her baby milk. Was she stealing it? Was Richard helping? I should've covered the tubs better; I should have never allowed her to see what was inside. My mind raced. What would I do if I checked the garage and the tubs were gone? What would I say if a child had died because of the decisions I had made? I felt light headed and my vision blurred. I squatted close to the ground and drew circles in the dirt like I had watched the girls do when they were frustrated or angry.

Eventually, I gained control of my breath and of my blame. I spoke words softly to the woman with the wit and the emotional weight of someone much older.

"Helping you do what? Nylie, I always try and help you. And I can guarantee you it's a lot less weird for your husband if you are spending time in the evenings with me instead of Richard."

"He's helping me...." Nylie twisted plastic beads around her wrist, and around her ankles. I waited for her confession, forming a contingency plan in my mind, "Isabel, he is helping me get birth control shots."

Loveness scrubbed plastic plates with a brown bar of soap more fervently, desperately hoping the sloshing water noise would prevent her from hearing the conversation.

"Where are you doing that?" I whispered. A weight lifted off my chest. Birth control seemed so insignificant compared to the scenarios that swirled around in my brain: pregnancy, abortion, HIV, cocaine.

"There is a clinic in Casa that has a back room. Only a few of us know about it. They give you a shot there and it lasts for three months. That means that even when your husband has sex with you, you won't get pregnant."

"I see," I swallowed again and thought of this woman, now twenty-four years old, for the first time hearing about and understanding the concept of birth control.

The first time I'd attempted to get birth control, my palms were sweaty and my face was red. I went into the doctor's office and asked under my breath. I was twenty-two years old. Later, when Theresa found the plastic case of birth control pills, she cried.

"It's because of my periods," I lied through my teeth, "They are so irregular I have no other choice but to get on birth control." She stopped crying. She knew I was lying but she appreciated my answer.

"So, you don't want to get pregnant right now?" I asked. I could feel Nylie's guilt dripping out of her pores. I knew the feeling. "It's okay not to want to get pregnant. You aren't doing anything wrong, Nylie."

"I want to go to school again," Nylie said, a newfound confidence in her declaration. "I want to become a nursery teacher. There is a college for nursery teachers in Casa. I have been calculating and if I keep saving a part of my salary I can go to the college. But not if I'm pregnant..."

My arms were covered in goose bumps despite the balmy air, "I think that's really wonderful, Nylie, I think that you will be a really good nursery teacher."

She smiled and wrapped her arms around my neck. She seemed like such a child in that moment. Sometimes I forgot she was a married woman with a family and responsibilities that far outweighed the elegance of her body, the intensity in her strange eyes.

"What will your husband do if he finds out?" Loveness interrupted. Nylie jumped and searched the premise for anyone else who may have heard her English confession. Loveness's forearms were wet and black and shiny from washing the dishes. They glittered against the flickering fire.

"He will beat me. Or kill me. Or leave me out here alone. Then I would never be able to go to that college," Nylie said, matter-of-factly because she had already used all of her tears. "It's a woman's job to make children for her husband. Children are the joy. If I do something to prevent myself from doing my job, that is a disgrace."

I nodded. I didn't agree but I understood. I seemed to reach that point quite often lately. I understood the plight of the handsome man with a handsome wife and a handsome family who had a handsome father telling him that if he did not get more wives, then he was not man at all. I didn't agree but I understood.

I also had begun to understand the situation of a young and pregnant girl who was not forced on her back through sheer, brute force. But instead, reluctantly climbed into a man's bed and called him her boyfriend because there was no point in saying no.

I understood wanting your daughter to marry when she had the chance so she was not left alone in this dusty world.

I understood promoting more of the same, even when the same was wrong, simply to avoid conflict. I understood that sometimes you decide because you simply don't know what else to do. Perhaps I was coming to understand Ivy.

My mother had called me about a week before her death. She sounded stoned in that slowly frantic way of hers. "I haven't been a good mother," she told me. She coughed through the phone. I pictured her sitting with her knees tucked under her chin the way I did. I imagined her in a thin nightgown with sweat beading at her temples and dripping down her chin.

I did not argue with her. She had been a haphazard, mother, praying I would figure life out on my own, and numbing me every way she knew how when the pain in my eyes was too much for her to bear.

"I haven't been a good mother, and sometimes I wish you didn't know me at all. Sometimes I think you would have been better without my opinions in the back of your head or the knowledge of who you could grow up to be one day."

I remained silent on that phone and bit the inside of my cheek. I was frustrated. I needed to get gas in my car before going to work, and this was another sympathy rant by Ivy. She would be fine in a few hours, once she got some food in her stomach and sobered up. I smoothed my curls back with my free hand as I held the phone to my ear.

"Sometimes I think the best way I could have shown you I loved you was to let Theresa raise you from the beginning. Let that white lady pray over you and fuss over you and make you soft and spoiled. Because I was not a good mother. I'm still not a good mother. And I guess I just wanted to tell you that I'm sorry, Isabel. I'm sorry I'll never be who you need."

I bit my lip and exhaled slowly. Ivy needed assurance that how she had chosen to raise her daughter was okay. She wanted me to wave away her apology and insist that I had nothing but positive memories of my African goddess mother with tired eyes and slow hands. But I was too angry to give her that. I still felt the twelve-year-old inside that needed reassurance that I was precious and beautiful despite what had happened, but I never heard those words from my mother. I felt the fifteen-year-old who tried to explain away the woman who smoked pot outside the gymnasium. I felt the twenty-four-year-old who could not call her mother and cry because her mother was the one with the tears.

"Perhaps I should never have been part of your life," she said.

I breathed into the silence on the phone.

"Maybe you're right," I had said. "Maybe that would've been the best way to love me." I felt Ivy's sharp intake of breath. I was being cruel. But right then, I believed the world had been so cruel to me, I had every right to bite back.

"Alright, now, Isabel, I guess I just want you to know I love you. That's all I can say."

I sighed, and gave a haphazard attempt at taking back my words. "Mama, why don't I come down and visit you in a month or so? Or better yet, why don't you come visit me? I can buy your plane ticket and you can get out of that humidity for a few days."

But my words were like tears that fell from Nylie's copper and coffee eyes and into the never-ending dust. They flowed out with ease, but you could never, ever take them back.

33

Ivy told me that the way to see if someone was actually in love with you was to make him or her incredibly angry. Perhaps you run their car into a tree. Perhaps you lose their diamond earrings. Maybe you renounce their religion, their culture, their heritage, their parents. Maybe you forget to pick them up at the airport, or drop their cell phone into the ocean.

Maybe you die before anyone is ready.

Maybe you move to Africa.

And if they still love you, after all that heartache and pain and inconvenience you have caused. Well, then that's when you know that they really, truly love you.

34

My stomach felt sick the moment I awoke, the moment before my eyes had even opened. My mind floated to the idea that someone else had taken the tubs of formula, that they had surely been stolen while the guard dozed in the early hours. But a text message from Max confirmed what I refused to believe: he had picked up the drugs that morning. Everything was going according to plan.

The night before I had briefly glanced into the garage to see if Max had made the drop off the same way as before: same location, same mislabeled baby formula, same crate of random equipment in a cluttered garage. Our scheme was happening so quickly, so seamlessly, and my tired mind worried that it was progressing with too much ease.

Penn was cavalier about the exchange, and seemed to enjoy his vacation to developing Tanzania with a more carefree demeanor than I dared display. He hired a guide to take him and Max on a three-day safari.

"Giraffes are my favorite animal," he said. "They keep their heads above all of the bullshit."

My movements felt strange and aimless during his time away. Penn had been in Tanzania for only two weeks, and I forgot how I had gone about a day without expecting him to walk through my bedroom door at night, or a frantic call asking me how much he should pay for a liter of petrol. Did I love the man who stood before me in dusty jeans and yelled Swahili words to the students to make them laugh? Or did I love not being alone?

Penn returned from his safari one evening after I closed up the office and lay on the cement under the awning in the late-night heat. I liked this place underneath the awning, and I asked the cleaners to sweep it clean every day so I could read and write and stretch my limbs like the cats in the garage. As Penn approached I was laying with my eyes wide open on a yoga mat, listening to the stork-like birds clip their feet on the tin roof above.

He lay down next to me and placed his hand on my stomach. He kissed my forehead and held my dust-covered palm in his. "I got the passports today," he whispered and wiggled a dark blue book from his jean pocket. Inside was Loveness's face, mouth closed, eyelids heavy, wispy hair sticking out in all of the wrong directions. She held her right shoulder close to ear, as if she were shrugging or saying, "I just don't know." The photo made me smile despite her joyless pose. It was a Kenyan passport and felt good and thick between my hands. Her name was Agness Ontieno. Eighteen years old. From Nairobi. She was unmarried and unburdened by any previous culture of children and cows and young girls with husbands and more responsibility than choice. She was a free woman.

The second book contained Maya's face; smug and challenging. Ivy Supeet. Twenty-four. Kenyan. Free.

The tears started in my hips. A type of surrender lumped into my throat until it reached my temples where Penn kissed me and a flood poured from my eyes. The tears made tracks from my dusty face down my nose, off my chin and into a small pool where my clavicles almost met but never found each other. Penn continued to kiss my matted hair. He kissed the inside of my wrists and the tops of my shoulders. He kissed the back of my elbows and every place that no one knows they need love until they feel it there.

Penn followed me into my room. I continued to rain from my brain and my soul and my eyes. I wished that Penn's chest was the field outside because then my tears would be meaningful and nurture the dry land.

We did not make love that night but we made understanding. He allowed me to feel my release and my pain without judgment or condolence. I allowed him to be wrong and a criminal and legally unacceptable. He swore to me something more honest than anything I had been told under the sheets by a lover. He did not promise me love and he did not tell me I was the most beautiful woman he had ever seen. He did not tell me everything would be all right and he did not fill my ears with hollow sayings of pride and bravery.

Instead, he whispered, "We are so alive. We will never feel more alive than this."

35

I brought Maya and Loveness into the office the next day after school. I greeted them as Ivy and Agness, the names printed in fine black ink on their newfound cards of freedom. They exchanged looks of excitement and fear as I locked the thin office door behind me and turned the lights off. I brought up the Kenyan poet as a video chat on my computer screen, the man who promised to find refuge for these girls. The poet was a bald man with dark irises that stained the whites of his eyes. He had small teeth, and large, cracked lips. He introduced himself in perfect English with a slight British accent and spoke to them in parables and metaphors and when they grew restless at his formal speech, he quickly switched over to casual Swahili, but threw in an English word now and then.

"You girls will be staying at a safe home that I own," the poet explained to them in simple Swahili phrases so I could follow along.

"You will come here together and share a room with one other girl. Her name is Roxane. I think you will really like her."

Loveness and Maya stared intensely into the poet's eyes. They did not answer or move.

He continued, "You will stay at the safe house during the evenings and nights. You will be expected to complete duties such as cleaning and cooking, just as if you were at home. During the day, we have arranged for you to tutor adults in English. You will go the library together, complete your work, and then return home together, even if one of you is finished with your work before the other. Do you understand?"

Loveness spoke softly, "Is Isabel coming with us?"

I squeezed her shoulder, "I have to stay here, love. I need to take care of the school."

Maya crossed her arms over her broad chest and raised her eyebrows,

"Do we get paid for working?"

"Yes," the poet answered, "You will be paid at the end of each month."

"And we can keep that money?" Maya raised her eyebrows even further.

"Yes, you keep the money." I felt the waiver in the poet's voice. He was not a negotiator or a businessman, he was a poet. Conversations like this made him nervous. His lack of confidence sent chills down my arms. Was he changing his mind about allowing the girls to stay with him? Or was his voice in my ears a reflection of my own lack of confidence? My uncertainty creased the space between my eyebrows.

"What's in it for you, then, if we are keeping the money?" Loveness spoke up, her skin looked dark and thick in the computer's camera.

"Well, when you have made enough money, the two of you move out of my house, that's what's in it for me," the poet explained. "The goal here is not to have you live with me forever, but instead become self-sufficient enough to live on your own."

Both girls nodded in agreement. I felt the hair rise on the back of their necks and uncertainty rise to their lips. We hoped he was a soft man. There was no way to know for certain.

"This man works for an organization that people in Canada support," I tried to help the poet explain. "They give him money and check up on him to ensure that he is doing a good job taking care of girls like you. And one of the best ways they see he is doing a good job taking care is by making it so you girls can live on your own. You can get an apartment together. Perhaps go to school together. Maybe you find that you really love teaching English and that it is a good fit for you. But it's this man's job to make sure you are successful so that the Canadian man is satisfied."

Maya chewed her lip. She truly was a thoughtful girl despite her impulsive decisions. "Why do people in Canada want to help us?" She interlaced her fingers and set them on top of her head. Her hair was growing long these days. It was shiny and glossy and made her appear even bigger.

"The same reason that Isabel is here," said Loveness. "Because she cares about people and she isn't afraid of going somewhere new." Loveness's voice sounded more hopeful than confident. I imagined trying to call her Agness, her passport name.

"Isabel came to Africa because her mother died and she couldn't stand to be in America and think about it," Maya interrupted. She raised her eyebrows as she always did in immediate challenge. My face may have given way to the verbal knife she had drawn, because Maya's expression instantly fell. Her eyes grew large and her forehead became smooth; she looked up at me through thin eyebrows and big lips. She looked as young as the fifth graders that she sat with in class day after day. It was not a secret that my mother had died. I intentionally told head teacher Marie that part of my drastic move was to feel further away from a place I had known my own mother. But Maya's words were the voice of my subconscious; the piece inside me I hid under every smile and scarf and Swahili word.

The poet began speaking on the other end, rattling off something about everyone's plight in life and the winds of destiny blowing them to the destination in which the heavens had intended.

I pulled at the curls that hung sweaty on my shoulders and I wondered why I had never twisted my hair up in the way that Ivy always did. Why had I never sat her down and begged for more intimate stories of the one who had given birth to me? I wanted to sit back in that Silverado at age thirteen, throw the weed out the window and ask if she had gone to prom. The information seemed incredibly pressing now, to know whether or not my mother had ever gone to her prom. What did she wear? Who was her date? Did she let her hair free then, or was it tied on top of her head like a queen? Why hadn't I asked her these things?

Loveness tried to talk to me, but my mind was elsewhere. I saw a hand shove Maya in the chest, my protective young sister angry at the big-busted Maya and her big-busted words towards someone who only wanted to help.

"Maya, *fuck*, why are your decisions always full of so much fire?"

I heard Loveness defend my feet in African soil. I heard the poet say it was getting late and he was happy to meet those girls and we would talk soon. That they would love Kenya.

"*Lala fofofo*, sleep forever," he said: a kind fatherly way to tell the three of us to have sweet dreams.

Maya's words rang in my ears. I rose and found my rubber sandals on the cement floor. I told the girls it was time to grab their things and go and if they had any questions they could ask them tomorrow. Loveness, angry at Maya's outburst, slapped her plastic shoes on the ground and didn't wait for Maya to hold hands and walk home together.

Maya caught my hand and traced the pale lines with her thick fingers. "Isabel, I am sorry. You are helping me. I just meant to say you were like us. You have problems to escape," Maya's eyebrows creased, the closest to tears I had ever seen the brave girl.

"Maya," I inhaled sharply and counted my words. I breathed slowly. I wished for something to ease my heart. My brain came up with nothing. "I never once demanded you explain what was going on with your family or your fiancée or a nineteen-year-old in fifth grade. And I never, ever judged you. I expect you to do the same."

Maya gritted her jaw tight. She traced the lines on my palm a little harder. She sucked her lips and for the first time in ten months I saw fear on the face of a fearless woman. It frightened me.

"And what if we don't make it to Kenya?" she whispered.

I measured my words. I took a breath, "Then we keep going."

"And what if we make it to Kenya and we don't like it? What if they are

147

mean to us?"

"Then we keep going."

"But what if my father finds out? What if he hurts me? What if Loveness ends up getting pregnant, you know she's sleeping in her husband's bed, don't you? What if we make it to Kenya and we find out in Kenya she's pregnant?"

"Then, Maya, my dear, we will keep going."

Maya squinted her eyes and slid the sandals onto her feet. "What if you get too sad or too tired or miss your family too much and then you can't help us anymore?"

I held Maya's hands too tightly. I gritted my teeth like her. I dug my nails into her palm, "Then you and Loveness will just keep going."

36

Penn and Max came over for our own version of celebration. We sat outside of the office on smooth hot cement, still damp from where the cleaners dumped the mop water. We always sat on the damp space; it was cooler there.

Three strange, unlikely friends had successfully moved three kilos of cocaine without the slightest hint of suspicion and we had agreed to the fact we would count our wins and would not push our luck any further. I was relieved. I had been concerned that Penn would want to take the entire operation to a new level. I was afraid he would insist on one more kilo, one more passport, one more rush of adrenaline. I never suspected that the person to push our mission too far could be me.

"We did it!" Penn raised his beer bottle for a toast and my warm and dusty bottle followed his lead. Max grinned and held a green glass Sprite bottle towards the setting sun, "*Afia!*" he cried, "To our health!"

Afia was exactly what I had needed at that moment. The stress of the smuggling, the language barrier and harsh conditions had taken a toll on my body. My skin had darkened in the sun, and new blemishes appeared on my face daily. The heat streaked my cheeks pink and the thought of hot food on my throat hurt my stomach. My skirt fit too loosely and the girls commented.

"Boys like fat girls, Madam, and you are not fat right now." I laughed at the obvious contradiction with American culture. Boys did not like fat girls in America. Or perhaps they did. But girls did not like fat girls in American culture and the boys really didn't seem to argue. Theresa had commented recently how good I looked, how I must truly be taking the time to exercise out there under the hot African sun. I smiled and agreed. How strange of a culture, to glamorize the hungry and turn our noses down at happy minds, full stomachs, stress-less bodies.

Max had once again brought over hamburgers and donuts from Casa. I dug in greedily to the grease-soaked wax paper. Chickens clucked at my feet for a bite. I waved my shoe at them.

"So, what's next for you, Isa?" Penn asked. He stretched his arms overhead, his hipbones protruding ever so slightly. I was not the only one undergoing stress as we completed our project.

"Well. These girls are getting on the plane next week. The school is closed for a holiday so we can all go the airport together. They want new shoes before the journey, so I figured we could stop at the market sometime before the airport."

Max snorted into his hamburger, "Hell, I want new shoes before my journey, too."

Penn laughed, playfully punched Max's shoulder. Max didn't know Penn had cut a large check to his partner. I was certain Max would cry when he understood he was being given much more than shoes for his service. Max and I had created a deeper relationship, and I learned to anticipate his reactions. I knew he would fall to his knees, grab the dust and beg God to bless him despite his acts.

"God knows motives," he had told me once. "I'm certain he will forgive me for this."

"What are you going to say?" Max asked in his usual way, talking directly into the food he held in his hand. "What are you going to say when people ask why the girls are gone?"

Penn looked at me for the answer. It was strange to see someone so confident curious about my own answers and plans. I crumpled the hamburger wrapper and dropped a half-eaten burger onto the ground. "I guess I won't say anything. It's not that strange for girls to go missing around here. Maybe they attempted a run to another school. Maybe they ran off and got married to a miner from the tanzanite mines."

People still held on to the promise that tanzanite would allow them to strike it rich, or marry someone who dug hard and fast enough to come into money. This hope floated around in those dark caves like the particles the miners inhaled. Perhaps the girls were kidnapped; perhaps they simply did not want to live in the dust anymore.

I squinted my eyes tightly and remembered Loveness's mother. Loveness had told her mother the truth of her departure. She explained to me she could not leave without being certain that her baby was going to be taken care of. And she wanted her mother to know that Loveness did not hate her mother or how she had been raised. I shuddered at the thought of Loveness's mother breathing a word of the plan to anyone before it was accomplished; before I had climbed onto that airplane when my contract was over, and drunk my American coffee out of a paper cup every morning. What would the village elders do if they found out? Would they call the police?

Would they demand their children back? Would they find a way to punish me? Perhaps Loveness's mother would help us. Perhaps she would say the girls were going to Karanga, the small village four or five hours away where peanuts were grown. Maybe the girls got a job in the harvest.

I comforted myself with my answer to the men in front of me, "They won't question the absence of the girls right away. They may have gone somewhere with a friend over the Christmas holiday, probably being stubborn like teenagers can be. I suppose I will just continue the running of the school. I have two more months on my contract. I will love on some of these babies and fight a little bit more, and then, I guess, I will go home."

Max nodded sadly and peered into his Sprite bottle, looking for words there.

"Then what?" Penn asked. He allowed his sunglasses to slip off the bridge of his nose.

"Well. Then I start again. I find a new job. Hug my family. I will begin living the way I knew before I came here."

The silence was heavy, like the sun on bare shoulders. It stuck in my mouth like the rice with too much starch, like the dust in your teeth and your hair and your lungs.

"When do you leave, Penn?" I asked slowly.

"In ten days. And I guess I am starting off a new person. I can go anywhere or be anything. It's exhilarating. It's terrifying. This freedom."

"And where will you go?" Max asked. He spoke to the Sprite bottle.

Penn smiled with crooked teeth and glanced in my direction, "It depends on where Isabel goes."

I laughed nervously. Why did it matter where I went? I did not want this man when I was back in Denver. I didn't want any man for that matter. I wanted peace. I wanted absence of heat, of hunger, of being needed and wanted and pulled in every direction. I needed to sleep with my brain quiet. I wanted to feel chilled at night and the need to pull the blanket closer. I wanted a ham sandwich and a refrigerator. But in that moment, most of all, I wanted to make my way back to America and lay under white cotton sheets in an air-conditioned apartment without guilt on my chest that screamed, "deserter!" But perhaps I couldn't have all the things that I wanted.

We drank until my limbs felt soft and my head heavy. The sky was orange. We sat on the cement under the awning in silence, until Max said in a small voice, "*Mambo, dada.*" Hello sister.

I looked up to see a coffee baby toddling towards us. It was Salome, Loveness's youngest sister. Almost two years old, she wore a yellow and orange dress, neatly washed by hand in the nearby well. Her head was freshly shaved, her eyelashes long and curly.

"Come here, Salome," I greeted the young girl in Swahili, and she smiled with small white teeth and tottered toward me. "She's an adventurous little one. She lives right over there," I pointed to the brown field that lay endlessly before us. "But she is always wandering out to the school alone."

Salome came closer and whispered in my ear. "*Pipi*," she said softly. Candy. I scooped up the tiny bundle and wiped dust from her cheeks, kissed her forehead.

"Let's get some *pipi* and then take you home," I clucked, and Salome gleamed with the attention.

Perhaps it was the beer or the reflection of my impending journey home, but I took in my environment as an outsider for the entire walk to Salome's house. The pink flowers of the driveway leading up to the school bloomed and thrived despite the drought as the rain fell everywhere but here. It seemed that living in this village was the opposite of having a cloud over your head. There were promising clouds everywhere except directly above us. I took in the mud huts that sprung up like goose bumps on the skin of a woman named Tanzania. Perhaps a lover had touched her neck, causing the goose bumps to rise. Maybe she was cold. I hoped she was excited.

Salome hummed and skipped and danced the entire way to her home. In her sticky palm she clutched a Tootsie Roll I had fished out from a drawer in the office. She expressed no worry or concern about her future that would surely swallow her up. I wanted to freeze her like this, preserve her joy.

Salome and I walked hand in hand through thick dust that covered our feet to our ankles, past Acacia trees with branches that reached side to side, nearly parallel to the ground. We walked until her mother saw us in the distance, shook her head, tied the fabric around her waist like a belt and ran out to meet us. She slapped Salome's legs, scolding her in the tribal tongue.

"I'm so sorry, Isabel, I don't know where she gets this fearlessness," Loveness's mother clucked her tongue and muttered in rapid Swahili. My head felt heavy with the alcohol and I was suddenly immensely proud of the way I had understood her quick words. Pride in a place I would soon leave made my heart ache.

"It's really no problem," I said with a smile. "I needed to go for a walk anyway. Salome is just encouraging me to get my exercise."

Loveness's mother reached out and grabbed my hand, "We are really going to miss you when you leave, Isabel. You have helped us a lot here."

I laughed again, nervously, hoping my breath didn't give evidence that I had been drinking, "Well, I tried. I wish I had done something brighter or more fun. I wish I came here and built something shiny and new. Like a soccer field. Then you would have no choice but to remember me." I thought of two more notebooks full of expenses and budgets that needed to be entered into the computer before I completed the job I thought I had come to do.

She laughed along with me, and smoothed her hands on her freshly shaven head. I marveled once again at her earlobes that were not pierced but cut through the middle with a spear. I wondered what unspoken words lay between us in the middle of the language barrier. I was certain there would be things unsaid, even if we spoke the same language. There would be words we would never speak, words about Loveness and how she got a passport and how she would be leaving the village.

The village was like skin: it was what we were born into and it is where we would die. Although the topography may change, we were stuck in that skin. There was no reasonable or comfortable way to remove yourself. I wondered for the thousandth time if I was doing the right thing, helping to remove these girls from their skin and placing them in a new one. What if it didn't fit right? What if it itched or burned in the sun when the only thing these girls loved was turning their face up towards the rays? What if the skin was too big and didn't stick, sagging around their ankles, a new kind of weight?

Loveness's mother squeezed my hand and fingered the plastic beads I wore around my wrist. Gifts from another student: white plastic on a black string. "For good luck," she had said.

"I'm sure we will see things that allow us to remember you, my dear. Maybe we just don't know what they are yet."

37

I was nearly asleep in my room. The single lightbulb still glowed yellow and my half-opened eyes watched the plastic floor fan lazily tilt its head back and forth and back and forth, spitting warm air on my sticky body. I wore shorts and a large blue T-Shirt that used to belong to an old boyfriend, his fraternity letters scrolled across the front.

The knock on my door was frantic, hurried, and so light I nearly thought a bird had flown too close to the door; that its wings had batted the wood. But the knocks grew louder and more rapid. I twisted a pink and yellow tie-dye cloth around my waist. Penn wouldn't knock like that. The guard had not sputtered out his Swahili words, deep and gravelly, informing me I had a nighttime visitor. I crossed my arms against my braless chest and called to the hot air, "Who's here?"

The voice was as faint as the bird wings I had imagined. "It's Nylie, Isabel, open up the door. Quickly!"

I cracked open the door and Nylie scampered inside. After she had ensured I had closed the door securely behind me, Nylie peeled off the purple cloth she had tied over her head and under her chin. She was crying and short of breath. Her body shook and she wiped away tears.

I pressed her shoulders down until she lowered herself onto my bed as I squatted on the ground and looked up at her. My voice told the tall woman with her long, tree like limbs to breathe and calm down, to breathe and calm down.

Her breathing slowed. I unscrewed the cap of my plastic bottle, offered her a sip of water.

"What's going on, my dear?" I whispered, attempting to match her bird voice.

Nylie's chest shuddered and her eyes were glassy. She calmed her trembling lips to tell me, "My husband found out about the birth control shots."

The mere statement of this reality brought on a new deluge of tears. I wiped her nose and mouth with my pink tie-dye cloth like she was a child.

"How did he find out, Nylie?" I kept my voice slow and steady, slow and steady. I attempted to keep it in rhythm of the turning fan.

Nylie choked for a moment on tears. "Someone from the hospital told him. They swore they would never tell anyone and they called up my husband and they told him." She shuddered.

I reached up and grabbed her thin arm, attempted to console her shaking body. Nylie winced and pulled back.

I could feel the knot between my eyebrows pulse into a headache. "Did he hit you?" I asked.

She bit her lip and unwound the purple cloth that was covering her head and shoulders.

I held my breath. I did not gasp. Horror was the worst way a person could react in any situation.

Nylie's neck and shoulder and left arm had been burned. The scorched skin was beginning to rise up from her body, to bubble and puss and turn white like the moon. Her left arm was bleeding. She removed another cloth that she had haphazardly wrapped over the wound. I mentally measured the length of the laceration: perhaps ten inches long. It throbbed and pulsed with every beat of her heart.

"What did he do?" I whispered. I hated how normal it felt, to see blood and tears on a trembling woman. To watch her chest rise and fall with the knowledge that there was no way to escape the violence that would almost inevitably befall her.

"He got mad," Nylie started, suddenly more empowered. Her voice stopped shaking as soon as her body did. "Someone from the hospital called and told him. And he said he didn't believe it but then he drove to the hospital and saw my records and confirmed that it was me. I was the one taking birth control shots. Then he rode his *piki piki* home. He found a thick branch and he hit me."

The tears fell from her auburn eye and the coffee brown eye with the same desperation. "He hit me in front of my son. He hit me so hard and I fell down and I started to cry. My son kept pulling at him and told him to 'stop hitting mama, stop hitting mama.' And you know what my husband did? He turned to my son and told him that his mama was a bad woman and she deserved getting hit."

I placed my hand gently on Nylie's knee, cautious of injury that perhaps I could not see. Her hands stopped shaking and she began again. "Then he took me to the room. He locked the door and told me that if I were going to try and stop him from putting a baby in me, then he would try even harder.

He held me down by my hurting shoulder and pushed my head so hard I thought my neck would break. And then he had intercourse with me again and again and again and again. But my neck did not break."

My heart caught on my ribs. Breath became painful. This was the feeling that Ivy had run away from, the feeling she had tried to numb out of both of us. I felt like my mother, listening to a broken girl speak. I hated it, I wanted to scream at Nylie to stop, that my ears burned with every true word she spoke. I knew that pain. And the only thing worse than reliving it in my mind was knowing that Nylie was reliving it, too. But I was not Ivy. I told Nylie to continue. I swore I would help her carry her pain.

I felt the tremble from Nylie's own lips well up into my chest. I felt it burn the sides of my ribs and climb into my neck and temples. How dare he. How dare no one stop this.

Her confidence waxed and waned with the story. During the calmer recollections, her English was better, crisper. The hectic parts were cluttered with wails and the occasional Swahili or tribal word.

"When he was done he left me and opened the door. My son climbed into bed with me and fell asleep with his arms around me. And when we were both asleep, my husband's other wife came into the room. She yelled and she screamed, 'Njoo! Get out!' She screamed that I had not just disgraced myself but I had disgraced the entire family. And then...."

Nylie sucked her lips in and bit them. She tried to find the words in English so I could understand. I pictured her doing a mental calculation of her young life: child bride, poverty, young son, abusive husband. This moment is where I stopped believing in karma.

Nylie took a deep breath and began again, "Then, she took boiling water and poured it on the bed. She poured it not just on me but on my son. She did not stop pouring when I screamed and she did not stop pouring when my son screamed. She poured out the entire pot."

I watched Nylie in hysterics now. She curled up in a fetal position on my bed and her body shook with tears and pain and sorrow. "I have been a terrible mother," she cried in Swahili. "God forgive me, I have been the worst mother in this world. My son, he screamed when the water was poured but my body protected him from the burn."

I felt the strangest emotion as I watched Nylie on my bed. An unanticipated wave of envy overcame me. I was jealous of Nylie and the insurmountable love she held inside. Her son was too young, too fragile to protect her. And yet she cried her eyes into swollen prunes and cursed the day she was born because she believed she had committed a crime that had caused pain to her son. I would never be able to love anyone that much. I supposed no one had loved me in that way, either.

I told her to wait on my bed for a moment, that I would go get medical supplies from the school's clinic. Instinctively, I locked the door behind me in case Nylie's husband had followed her here.

My mind is often selfish, as many human minds are, and it wandered to Ivy. Had my mother ever cried for me? My thoughts could not rest on one instance that would have Ivy shedding tears for her daughter. It was this selfish thought that broke my heart and led me to my own tears. I allowed Nylie peace and quiet for a moment while I walked outside under a pale moon and stars that shimmered like tears on black cheeks.

"Your mother loves you," my father had told me, eight years old at my birthday party. We had tied donuts on strings and hung them underneath the deck outside, then had competitions as to who could eat the donut the fastest without using hands. I smiled during my party games, but waited until late into the night for my mother to call me and tell me happy birthday. She never did.

"She loves you but she shows love in different ways," my father continued, searching for words to a concept he didn't understand. "You know I love you because I tell you I love you every morning. You know Theresa loves you because she tucks you in at night and cooks you the food that you like. You just have to know your mother loves you in a different way. But she loves you just the same."

"You know Nylie loves you because she believes she is the bad mother when life is unfair," I said aloud to Nylie's son, although he was not there. I spoke into the thick darkness, and jiggled a key into the lock of the clinic room. I rummaged around for supplies to treat burn wounds, skin lacerations, broken hearts.

"You know your mother loves you because she wants to make a future for herself to help you," I continued. Addressing this boy who was not here was calming me down, helping me make sense of the situation.

"You know your mother loves you because she wants to give you all of her love and make herself the best she can be for you." The door behind me slammed with the hot wind and I jumped.

"I hope when you are old you will know your mother loved you," I whispered into Africa's night, "Even if she is not around to explain everything."

Nylie had calmed when I got back. We sat silent as I pressed anti burn cream onto her peeling skin, her thin biceps and bony shoulders. She winced as I cleaned her laceration, then quickly and tightly wrapped it in antiseptic and gauze.

"Where is your son?" I asked quietly when I had finished my medical duties.

"He is with my neighbor. She will take care of him as long as I need."

"And how long do you think you will need?" I sat down on my bed and pressed the heel of my hands into my eyes until I saw bright patterns and designs in the blackness of my closed eyelids.

We were quiet for a long time. The power cut and the fan clicked to a stop, the lights flickered off.

"I know that Loveness is leaving. I want to leave, too," Nylie said. Simply. Confidently. You know your mother loves you because she would leave her home to save you.

I pressed my palms harder into my eyes; the shapes became more obvious, more random and brighter. I felt as if I was in a different body. I was a girl, disturbed by her past and uncertain of her future. I was a child making decisions with uncertain hands. I could not oblige. I could not refuse.

"I don't know if that's possible, Nylie," I murmured. I mumbled this sentence in a mixture of English and Swahili words, hoping that perhaps the disconnect would loosen the blow.

"If you don't do it for me, do it for my son," Nylie said in perfect English: jaw set, fists clenched, gaze determined. "I know it's possible, Isabel. Let me save my life. Let me save my son's life."

38

As Nylie slept fitfully on my mattress, I dug into the back of my dresser for grainy brown African marijuana and a lighter. I sat in the dark under a cement awning and rolled a joint with Ivy's thin brown fingers. I pulled a mass of snarls and curls back into a ponytail and wrapped it in the tie-dye cloth just as Ivy would have done. But when I dialed Penn's number into my cell phone, my words were brave and my actions strong and I knew I was not my mother.

"I need you to come over," I murmured into the phone. I flicked the lighter and inhaled dusty weed.

"You're tempting me darling, but it's so late. I can come see you tomorrow…" Penn's voice was sleepy, potentially stoned like mine.

"I need you tonight, Penn. I need…." My voice caught and I took another hit off a joint rolled in the dark. "I need another passport."

Penn was silent on the other line. I knew how to weigh his silences. This one was heavy. Full of decision. Reactions. Anticipation.

"I don't think that's a very good idea, Isabel," he said finally. I heard a bed creak and I knew he was sitting up. Perhaps turning on the light. "I know you know how risky this is. And we did it with no issues. But if we try to throw one more passport into the mix I feel like we would be messing with karma. I really don't think it's a good idea to push our luck."

I took a deep inhale and felt lightheaded. "Penn, look at me, look at who I am. I am a light skinned woman with a loving family, a college education, a roof over my head and as much food and clothing that I could ever ask for. Look at where we are. This is a place with good people with good hearts who often never see their child's second birthday, or who rarely feel a full stomach, and do not have enough money to make sure their babies are clothed. And you know what else? I am not an ounce better than any of these people. My life is no more valuable than any other person in this whole country. Karma doesn't exist, we are all just subject to fucking circumstances!"

I saw the guard with his flashlight making his rounds around the school. I quickly stubbed out my joint on the cement and brushed away hot ashes with my hand, "Penn. I need another passport."

"Isabel, I heard what you said. And I am telling you right now that I think we are pushing it if we get one more passport out here."

"Do you remember what you told me on the phone that night when you wanted a passport. Do you remember what you said? You said that if I helped you then you would get me everything that I need. I held up my part of the deal. Now it's your turn. I got you freedom. Now follow through on your end." My words hissed out with the ash on the joint.

"Fuck," I heard Penn exhale on the other side of the phone. "Fuck, fuck, FUCK." I heard him pacing now, pushing his feet through his sandals on a similar cement floor. The seconds dragged slowly. He continued to pace.

"I'm not going to say I am a good man. But I am sure as hell not a man who lies. Fine, Isabel. Let's get you another fucking passport."

I felt regret rise up into my chest. If he had simply said no, then I wouldn't have had to go through with this. I wouldn't have been able. His "yes" solidified everything I feared: I was getting what I wanted. Nylie would get a passport.

I bit my lip to keep myself from speaking the words my tongue so desperately wanted to say, "Are you sure? We don't have to do this!"

The marijuana high seeped to the top of my skull. The breeze cooled my sweaty face.

"Good," I murmured, leaned my head to the back of the cement, "So what's the plan?"

I heard a lighter flick. I heard Penn tap his cigarettes against the top of the box. I heard him inhale deeply and exhale every word he would not say to me out loud.

"I'm coming over right now," he said.

Nylie was awake when I walked into my room again. She tucked her knees up to her chin as she lay on her side. Her eyes were wet. She was holding photos that I had left by my bedside. "Your family looks like you," she said gently, staring deeply into a photo of Theresa, my father and me in the Bahamas. My tan arms were wrapped around Theresa, and my father was making a funny face.

"You think so?" I asked, and instinctively sprayed body mist on my dusty clothes to hide the scent of African weed. "That's not actually my mother, she's just my father's wife."

"That doesn't mean it's not your mother," Nylie said, "If she loves you and takes care of you, then she is your mother."

I took a brush and started pawing at my hair. "I suppose you're right," I said.

"I'm your sister but our mother *and* our father are different," Nylie explained, and I felt my heart speed up. We were sisters, in vastly different circumstances. Unfairly different circumstances.

She pointed to a picture of me with a few other college friends lying in green grass at a concert. We all smiled and I wore a flower crown over a tangle of curls. "Wow, this is so beautiful!" she exclaimed. "Look at this grass! Look at the flowers in your hair. I wish I could go to America."

"Well, maybe one day," I started, and instantly regretted it. I had a continual debate in my mind on the concept of hollow promises: whether they gave hope to someone when continuing on felt impossible, or if they set up a delicate creature for disappoint. Despite my continual debate, I threw questionable promises around daily. *I promise I will come back to see you again after I return to America. I promise I will stay in contact with you if we ever grow apart. I promise I will search for your sister. I promise your father loves you. I promise it will be okay.*

I didn't know what to say in place of those hollow promises.

I took a deep breath and stared at myself in the mirror. My eyes were red and cloudy from the marijuana and my newly brushed hair was big and loud and untamed.

"We need to talk about this passport thing, Nylie," I said. My mouth grew sticky. I needed water.

"I know. And I already know the kinds of things you are going to ask," she sat up in bed and smoothed the cloths around her waist. She gently readjusted the bandage on her arm.

"Thank God," I thought. My foggy mind couldn't handle logic right now.

"I would like to go to Kenya with Loveness. She has already told me about the man we would live with and how we would need to go to work every day and help teach English. And then she told me about how maybe one day we can all get our own apartment, me and Maya and Loveness. And then I was even thinking that it would be better with three women sticking together instead of just two, so I am helping them by going to Kenya with them. Also, I am more mature than those girls and I know how to handle things better."

Nylie crossed her ankles and looked up at me expectantly. She furrowed her eyebrows as I laid out the medical supplies out on my bed. My hands shook.

"And your son, where will he go?"

"He will stay here," she interrupted me. "I have neighbors and cousins who will take care of him. It will break my heart to leave my baby, but it will break my heart even more to let myself fall apart without even an attempt to fight for my life."

"You are ready to leave your son?" I asked. Tears welled up in my eyes at the mere thought of a mother leaving her baby. Unlike Loveness, Nylie had fallen naturally into the role of mother. Perhaps it was the age difference or the fact that Loveness's mother seemed to be the primary care giver of Samwel. The separation would be harder for Nylie and her son. That baby was part of Nylie's soul.

"I am prepared to survive," Nylie countered firmly.

My hands were numb. I patted the bandage on Nylie's arm. "My mom killed herself. That's how she died. She wasn't prepared to survive like you are." The words came from a foreigner's mouth; they did not feel like my own. I did not recognize the strange American woman who stood in the poorly lit bedroom in the middle of Africa. I did not recognize her skin or her smile or the way she walked. I did not recognize the truth coming from her mouth or the strength or ferocity in her decisions. I wanted to be her.

Nylie kept her head down and her eyes closed, "You and me? We are both prepared to survive, Isabel."

I began braiding the coarsely brushed hair: one braid on either side of my head. I braided quickly with nimble fingers in the way my mother had never been able to do. I formulated plans in my mind and prepared to execute them in a way my mother never could.

"Nylie. what will happen if you don't go to Kenya? What happens if we can't get you a passport and you have to stay here?"

Nylie wrung her hands. She wrung them so hard that I worried that she would break the skin and I wondered what would happen if she lost even one more drop of blood.

"You know that if we do get you to Kenya, it won't be for almost an entire week. What are you going to do until then?" I saw headlights in the driveway. Penn must be here. My heart sped up as my mind slowed down. I regretted the joint and longed for a clear mind.

Nylie picked up on my panic. She rose with her tired, broken body and put her hands on my shoulders. She looked in my eyes and her hands shook. Goosebumps rose on my arms despite the heat.

"What else in the whole world can we do except try to keep going?"

39

I was a sophomore in high school when I told my basketball coach what happened on my knees in the dog kennel. I was moody and crying for no reason. She took me into her office after practice and told me to sit down. Her office smelled like rubber from the basketballs and shoes. There were no windows. I wondered if she liked being a basketball coach, smelling all of this rubber every day. But I didn't ask. Instead, I sat on my hands and tried to look bored.

My coach closed the door behind me. She asked what the hell was wrong with me? Why couldn't I hold it together during practice?

The truth was I found out my sixteen-year-old boyfriend was texting a girl the year below us, a girl with big breasts and pasty pink lips. The mere thought of him putting another girl's face in his mind broke my heart. I was young. I was convinced I was in love. But one thing I had learned was that you do not tell your basketball coach that you cry during practice because the girl with the glitter lipstick gave her phone number to your adolescent crush.

I stammered through excuses and nothing surfaced in my brain. Instead, a stranger truth came out, some subconscious excuse that would be more powerful than any teenage angst that I could contrive at this point.

"I was attacked when I was twelve years old in a dog kennel in my cousin's backyard. That has been on my mind. That's what has been bothering me." That truth felt white hot on my fingertips.

My basketball coach was a good woman, but I don't believe she understood what it felt like to break. She had married her high school sweetheart and took the first job offered to her out of college. She didn't know what it was to be a mixed girl in a white school, to be raped in a dog cage, to have her high school love text the girl with the lip-gloss. She said she was sorry and told me that someday perhaps I would realize this whole thing was happening so that I could inspire someone else who has gone through a similarly difficult situation. She told me it was all God's will. She told me the Lord knew I was strong enough to help someone who needed that guidance and that experience, so God chose me to complete that struggle, to walk through that fire.

Perhaps no child knows the intricacies of God like an adult. Perhaps that comes with experience. But my teenage self had experienced enough to know that God had not handpicked me to suffer. It was cruel and disturbing to claim that God wished pain on his own creation.

I had a sobering realization that moment as I sat in a basketball coach's office: God hopes you know he loves you, but won't go out of his way to ensure it. God hopes you don't get hurt, but he doesn't lose sleep at night when you do. God is just too tired to do all of that.

God is Ivy Supeet. And I was not God. I was so much braver.

Penn arrived with an entire pallet of the tubs of "baby formula." He set it in the corner of the garage as we had done three times before. When his muscles bulged in his forearms, a pulse of desire streaked through my veins.

"Hey," I said. I smoothed my hair back with sweaty hands.

Penn dusted his hands on his jeans, "Hey to you."

I reached around behind him and pressed my face into his shoulders. "Are we fighting?" I whispered. I felt his muscles relax beneath my words and touch, but he did not respond.

"How did you get this shipment so quickly?" I asked, relaxing my grip.

Penn pulled his elbow away harshly, "I drove to the docks myself. I picked up the shipment and I turned around and drove here. Max already knows we are doing one more shipment. He should be here tomorrow morning in order to pick it up."

I rung my hands together, scared to upset him, "And I suppose it was less risky for Max to pick up here than at the docks, right?" I asked shyly. His tone made me nervous. I could tell he was angry.

Penn turned and grabbed my hands, "Isabel, we aren't fighting. We want the same thing. Freedom. Mine was a little bit more selfish, but we want people to be able to roam and learn and not be restricted. Maybe we just have different priorities on how far is too far when reaching for freedom."

"I know," I felt hot tears escape my eyes, and I brushed them away hurriedly, the emotions of the day finally consuming me. "But I can't stand there and watch someone's life fall apart because I'm too scared. That's what Ivy would have done. Nothing. And I am standing here on this fucking African dirt for an entire year to prove to everyone that I am not Ivy!"

Penn held my hips, then held my shoulders, then held my head to his chest. "You are already more than Ivy, Isa."

I held his shoulders tighter.

"I love that you want more for your life and more for these girls' lives."

I nodded and continued breathing into this man's chest. I hated his ideas and loved his passion. I loathed his actions but craved his courage.

"I love you," Penn said, blandly, as a test of his words on my shoulders. And with those words, we awaited our downfall.

40

I sat in that dusty office early on a Sunday morning, three days before Maya, Loveness and Nylie planned to depart. I watched the power flicker on, start up the fan, blow all the papers off my table, then cut back out. It was nearly humorous how unproductive I was being, spending more time picking up receipts from a cement floor than inputting them into the computer. My mind was heavy and I had watched every DVD volunteers and missionaries and vacationers had left behind, so I felt inclined to busy my mind with computer work.

I heard a knock at the office door and instinctively pulled a sweater over my shoulders, despite the sweltering weather, to cover the spaghetti straps I had worn on a day off. Annie peeked her head in the door.

"Hodi?" she asked. It was one of my favorite Swahili greetings, the simple request for permission to come into a room.

I giggled with delight and threw the sweater off my shoulders and gave my friend a hug. I relaxed in familiar arms.

"Where have you been?" I squealed, and the fan started up again, scattering my freshly arranged receipts throughout the office. Annie had moved to a village further south in recent months. It was a greener part of Tanzania, and I saw her cheeks turn pink from the sun from her drive over to this village. I missed having a friend I could pass on the streets in Casa, who I could gossip with in American slang, talk politics and music and English books and men. She was back for the weekend, she had told me. She figured she would see how I was surviving out here.

Annie slouched into the dusty couch and we caught up like two American women might at a coffee shop. She told me about the village where she worked, the problem of young marriage and genital mutilation of children that she described with terrifying detail despite her calm cadence and voice.

Her hair was long and think and she braided it with sure hands like the girls at Amani Manor. She crossed her legs and silver chains clinked around her ankles, just like Nylie's. Annie had adapted better to her African life. I did not see the anxiety in her brown eyes like I saw when I looked in the mirror.

"What's strange is I can bet you all my Peace Corp salary that your kids are experiencing the same type of genital mutilation over here. The only difference is they don't know that fighting this torture is up for discussion."

I nodded and silently agreed with her. My mind flashed back to the night that Penn and I sat outside Loveness's mother's house and drank tea while the men and women continued their call and response dance, and I spoke with Miriam: the thin girl with the gyrating hips. I knew the practice that was happening in the name of culture.

Annie grabbed my hand in the stuffy office and sat me down on the dusty purple cushions near the door, "I have to get you out of here. Because no offense, *dada,* but you look terrible. Let's get fresh air. Let's go swim."

I couldn't disagree with her. The thought of clean clear water rushing through my hair, flowing between my toes, gave me chills. I welcomed a distraction and blew dust off the keyboard before closing the laptop.

The pool was an hour's drive from the Manor in the heart of a hotel and hostel that advertised stunning views of Kilimanjaro. I had never been inside but my eyes lingered longingly every time I drove by with the promise of a pool. Annie had invited me to the hostel before, but I had reluctantly declined with feeble excuses: "Too much work, too cold, too tired, too busy." The truth was I felt guilty escaping from the village for a cool swim and bare skin when those around me did not have the opportunity for even a sip of cold water.

We drove the dusty safari Jeep down rocky roads and picked our way in flip-flops through thorns and needles until we found the entrance of the hotel. Immediately, we took off our sandals, felt the cool stone beneath our feet and enjoyed the smoothness of walking barefoot for the first time in months. You could never take your shoes off at the school, or any other place that I spent my time; it was too rocky, full of too many thorns and ants and plants that could bite. Walking around barefoot seemed like the most extravagant of all luxuries.

The pool was up a flight of stone steps, and was advertised as being surrounded by "authentic" plants from the area. But I had never seen the trees or flowers or bushes that surrounded the pool in the native tribal land. True authenticity would mean scrapping all of this and covering the hotel with dust. And when the pool dried up and everyone got hot and thirsty the concierge would say, "I'm sorry my friends, but you may not leave." Now that would be an authentic experience. That was what I knew of Africa in those days. I shook my head of the negative thoughts and ran my fingers through the ferns surrounding the walkway.

Annie rattled on about recent laws put into place to save "our kids" from things like mutilation, early marriage, thirteen-year-olds with children. I nodded amicably, but my mind seemed unfocused and changed direction with the wind. Nylie's bruised eyes, the baby formula in the garage, the passports…floated non-sequentially through my head. My brain would be able to think better when those girls got off this God forsaken soil, I was certain of it.

We stripped off sweaty T-shirts and long skirts and let the sun bleach the hairs on the back of our necks. I shivered despite the sun. My thoughts twisted and turned. It was strange to be around English speakers. I felt strangely self-aware when I greeted them with, "Good morning," enunciating every syllable purposefully. There were moments I could not find the English word for what I wanted to describe, when the Swahili phrase sounded so much more fitting, so much more descriptive. Annie and I joked about needing to integrate a few Swahili words into the English language.

"There are words like *shagala-bagala,*" Annie said to me and laughed with her teeth showing, "that sound so much more accurate than our English words for 'disjointed' or 'uncoordinated.'"

We sat by the pool and laughed at puns and jokes that only we would understand, people who have chosen to live somewhere they don't belong. A European woman with pasty thighs and brittle gray hair commented on the dryness of the environment, the disorganization of the staff. I glanced and took personal offense to her words.

Annie clicked her tongue and chastised the lady in Swahili, which made me laugh; I was happy to be with another woman who saw the world in the way I did. I lay back on the chair. My pulse throbbed in my head as the sun hit my stomach and thighs and every other precious body part I had covered in fabric for so long. Goosebumps rose on my stomach and the back of my neck prickled. My stomach turned and nausea rose in my chest when I closed my eyes. My body felt strange and not my own. I blamed the stress and the sun, stood and dove into the blue water below me.

If your hands are freezing, you ease into the warmth slowly. You start by running them under cool water, then warm, until your fingers have thawed through enough to withstand the hot water. I suppose the same goes with heat. If your body has been a hot, sweating orb for long enough, it is best not to submerge it into ice water right away. Perhaps you start with warm water, and then cool.

This not how I eased my body into the swimming pool on that one-hundred-degree day. My brain became startled. My entire body felt like it had consumed a huge, spicy peppermint and washed it down with a bucket of ice water. It seemed to me that my body froze, and upon hitting the water shattered into twenty-five million shining, shimmering pieces. Like I was an ice cube dropped onto a linoleum floor. Pieces of me chipped off and broke, and fell into the most difficult, hard to reach places. For a moment, I thought I had died. It was a comforting thought: my heart had stopped and I had gone to heaven, where heaven was cool and wet and blue and muted. It was the most beautiful thing.

Later, I was told that the bartender had fished me out, and continued to splash the pool water in my face with a whiskey glass. I admit those few seconds of unconsciousness were mesmerizing. I felt an embarrassing sigh of frustration when I realized I was still on this earth, and, moreover, still in Africa. There were still hungry faces I made eye contact with daily: the most disturbing face the one I watched in the mirror. There were still humans with no choices. Students without the luxury of dreams. Another kilo of cocaine until we successfully received the last passport.

I closed my eyes again and let my brain drop into the cold unconscious I had found moments before.

My father called me at my apartment in Denver to tell me that Ivy had taken her own life. I had been walking to my car, headed to the gym, wearing shorts and a t-shirt on a cold November day. Snow covered the ground. When I heard my father's words I sat in the snow. Then, as he continued talking, I lied down, like the snow was some grassy hill waiting for my body to rest. My calves pressed into the ice and the back of my arms grew numb. My neck felt paralyzed by the cold. I wondered how long before my whole body went numb. I wondered how long until my brain unremembered the words I heard on the phone. My limbs were peaceful numb, and my brain followed. The sky turned peach. Maybe nothing bad ever happened. I don't remember hanging up the phone.

My father and Theresa found me there, in the snow, about the same time as the paramedics. Someone had called the fire department to report a strange girl, unmoving in the cold in gym clothes. I had wished no one showed up. I did not want to thaw my body or my brain or my heart. I wanted to die there in that snow. At that moment my mother and I were the same.

In back of the jeep in Tanzania, my body was on fire but my mind did not have to think. I wanted to rest there forever. My mind searched the jeep's ceiling. I had never seen the car from this angle before. I tried to remember the name of the hostel with the pool. It did not come to mind. I exhaled a happy sigh that perhaps all of my memories had been washed away with that pool water.

At the hospital in the Catholic convent just outside of Casa, the nuns took my temperature and my blood and squeezed the water from my hair.

Annie kissed my forehead before she headed back to her tribal village with its own problems and her own solutions.

"They say it looks like malaria," she whispered to me before she left. "You're lucky. I want to stay here with nice grandma nuns for a few nights." I smiled at Annie and squeezed her hand. The nuns had tucked me tightly under thick blankets with my arms underneath the covers, and left a pitcher of warm water on the small wooden desk just out of arm's reach. The Sisters came in later that night wrapped a fabric around my waist to cover my bare legs and slid me into a wooden chair where they insisted I eat thick sticky rice and green beans.

Sapphira, the prettiest nun, with her caramel skin and wavy gray hairs swept back into her habit, sat next to me. She held my thin fingers with her thick hand. "It's official, my dear," she said in perfect, unaccented English, "You have malaria. That cold water must have been a shock to your system, that's why you fainted. Nevertheless, you are here now. I am going to have to intervene and insist you rest here for a while, at least a week. Malaria is nothing to mess around with."

I felt cold, like the ice cube I imagined my body becoming just hours before. I prayed I could shatter again, to feel the illusion of completely disintegrating and falling apart. I felt exhilarated by the lack of control. I no longer wanted to make the conscious and heavy decisions that hung in my heart.

"Okay, Isabel? I can send someone to fetch clean clothes for you later on in the week if you need. Until then, you can wear some of Antonia's clothes." Sister Sapphira referenced the corner of the room where a teenage girl scrolled through my cell phone.

I stood up and snatched the phone from her hands, "That's not yours," I mumbled in Swahili, and was taken aback at how exhausted the trip to the corner of the room made me feel.

"Sister," I began, as I absentmindedly scrolled through missed calls and text messages accumulated in the past few hours. There was one from Loveness, asking if I had seen Nylie and what I was going to do about her. Three missed calls from Penn. A text from the head teacher, saying she wouldn't be able to be at school tomorrow because her child was sick. There was a message from an unknown number claiming they knew I could help fund their sister's education. I sighed and clicked the screen to black.

"Sister, there is no way I can stay here for a whole week. I have so much to do back at the school."

"Doctor's orders, sorry, they are irreversible. I am sure whatever you need to accomplish next week can wait a few more days until you are well again."

I closed my eyes and sighed, figured that most things could be handled without my presence, albeit less gracefully than I hoped. Then I paused briefly on the thought that entered into my mind. Our girls were heading to Kenya this week. On Wednesday evening, Loveness and Maya were boarding a plane with Penn, who was going to ensure they arrived in Nairobi safely before he made his journey back to the States. If all went as planned, Nylie would be joining them. There was so much to do before Wednesday. I opened my eyes and stirred the rice with my spoon. The rice seemed to continue to move even when the stirring stopped. My head throbbed.

Sapphira left me after she checked my tongue for swallowed pills and the majority of my green beans were gone. I called Penn as soon as she kissed my cheek good night, and told me she would check on me in the morning.

"Where the fuck have you been?" he exclaimed as soon as I answered the phone. He was high on dust. I could tell from the way he sniffled into the phone, the way his voice was higher pitched, more forceful.

"I have malaria," I said. "I fainted at the pool. They took me up north in the pink mountains to the nuns." My voice sounded confident and calm for how sick my mind had felt just moments before.

"Sorry you are sick. When are you coming back? They finished the pick up today and I should be getting Nylie's passport tomorrow. But there was a problem with the pickup. The guard stopped Max while he was leaving. Started asking him all of these questions about why he was always here and what he was keeping in the back of his truck. Max threw him a few shillings just to get out of the gate, which makes us look even more suspicious. The guard is on to us, Isabel, or at least onto Max. He's a damn idiot, why would he just pay him off right away instead of telling him it was donations for the school...?"

My body felt heavy and my eyes felt dry, "Penn, you are reacting too strongly. The key is to keep our cool for a few more days. Sit down. Have a drink. Say a prayer. And for God's sake keep that damn blow out from underneath your nose." I winced for a moment and said a quick prayer for forgiveness for using the Lord's name in vain in a convent.

I heard him breathe heavily, assumed he was biting his tongue to keep angry words from overflowing from his wide lips, his hot exhales, his perfect tongue...

The lack of focus in my brain was refreshing. The stress seemed too unclear to worry about, too abstract to rationally consider. So, I didn't. I drank the rest of the tea from my ceramic cup. My hair reeked of chlorine and my lungs hurt from coughing. I had forgotten I was still on the phone with Penn.

"Isabel. Isabel! I said can I see you tomorrow?" he was yelling now. I was unsure if his harshness was due to my lack of focus or the drugs he had taken. I put my lips up to the phone.

"I love you too, Penn. I know you said that the other day and I don't know if you still mean it today, but I love you too." I waited for him to respond. My mind seemed to whisper and move from one island in my brain to another, I let my consciousness flow, "But do you know what's strange?

Even if you have parents, even if you have a whole big crazy family who loves you, even if you have a committed wife or husband or fifteen children or a job where you are the boss or a club where everyone depends on you, you still do life on your own. You have to flow on your own. No matter how many people you choose to love or to not love, or surround yourself with or not surround yourself with, you still have to do the hard parts by yourself. You can sleep next to someone or have dinner with someone, and still, at the heart of it all, we are alone. The only thing we can depend on is ourselves. And how hard we are willing to work. We each have to decide what is important."

Penn's breath stopped for a minute and he found space to speak, "You are okay right now, Isabel? You are somewhere safe?"

"I'm at the convent. I'm a little bit sick."

"I know that you are doing all of this alone. I know you have to do life alone and death alone, and a part of me thinks you even experience things like sex and friendship on your own, but you got to stay up for a few more days. No matter how alone you feel, you need to stay with us until we load onto the plane. Because maybe you feel alone. But we don't. Not when we are with you."

41

I dreamt fitfully of water and ice and shattering. I woke up sweating and shivering and threw up in the pit toilet outside of my room early in the morning. Afterward, my head and hands felt steady. The concrete steps outside were grainy with sand but inviting. The convent was lined with smooth barked trees and bushes with purple and white flowers and brave pieces of grass that pushed through moist soil. It was a sliver of peace that was foreign to my understanding of Africa. I drank it in like a dream. My shaky hands urged a mango off the tree and I bit a small piece of green skin off with my teeth, then spit it into the bushes. I smashed the orange flesh with my fingers through the skin and sucked the sweet fruit through the hole in the skin. I ate without self-consciousness. I sucked and slurped and squirted juice on my skirt without considering how my face looked, the orange strings that would surely be stuck between my teeth. As the sun rose higher in the sky, a small child sat down next to me wearing a tattered t-shirt that proclaimed, "I love spring!" and adult size flip-flops. He clasped his hands and glanced bright, shiny eyes in my direction.

"You want some?" I asked in English, and eyed his dirty fingernails. "Go wash your hands," I instructed in Swahili and nodded towards a hose hanging over a bush. He clapped sticky, chubby hands and scrubbed his palms together before sitting back down inches away from me.

I pulled another mango from the tree. I bit a small piece of green skin and spit it away, and handed him the fruit. He took it in two hands and smiled victoriously.

"Thank you," he said in Swahili, then began humming an English song the younger grades often sang at Amani Manor, "Your mother may let you down, your father may let you down, your brother may let you down but Jesus never will…"

I liked this small boy's company. I'm sure his parents were nearby, perhaps working in the garden out back, or mopping tile floors with water gathered from the river that flowed a mile from here. I sucked my mango enthusiastically and he followed suit, pausing only to mention other people who may let you down when Jesus wouldn't.

My head felt significantly better. The chills were gone and my thoughts seemed more coherent. But when my mind ventured back to Nylie and the passport, my stomach turned into knots and anxiety sank into my blood. How was anyone well when they cared like this, when they had responsibilities that involved another's life? Loving was such a physical burden.

Between the sleep and the peace of the convent, my body was beginning to revive. My phone buzzed with a message from Annie, telling me she was sending good vibes my way. She also noted that promptly after pulling me out of the pool, the bartender asked for her number, and when she declined, he asked for my number. I laughed when I read her message and the mango eater next to me laughed, too.

I smiled for a moment, and then grew sad at the thought of what would happen to this long-lashed boy if he ever came down with malaria. He wouldn't be brought to a convent, given his own room, and told to rest for a week, free of cost. Maybe his mother would be able to bring him to a public clinic when it got bad. The church could take up a collection to pay for the malaria medicine. I had seen that done before. Maybe they would have taken him to the witch doctor, who would burn sage around his head and call out demons in the name of a higher power. Maybe they wouldn't have done anything. Maybe he would've just gotten sick and stayed sick. Maybe his mother would've kissed his hot forehead and said, "I am sorry, my baby, but there is just nothing I am able to do."

I walked inside my small room and found *mandazi* the nuns had left on my small wooden desk that morning. The dough had hardened from being left out too long, but occasionally I preferred the bread that way. It took longer to chew. It made your mind think that perhaps there was more sustenance there. I brought out the bowl and offered the bread to my friend. He took it happily and we sat, sticky and sweet, and we turned our faces towards the sun.

"I see I have been replaced." A familiar voice startled me from my half-asleep state of mind. Penn stood in front of the sun; it shone around him. His jeans hung loose on his hips but his shirt fit taut, revealing the curve of his shoulders and the fullness of his chest.

"I am not one to wait around," I smiled and patted the seat next to me. The way my heart sped up at his presence startled me. I had not anticipated the joy his presence brought.

The small boy held a *mandazi* in each hand and spoke to Penn with his mouth full, rapid fire in Swahili.

I took another bite of the dough.

"Just because I'm black doesn't mean I speak the language, man," Penn said, and feigned hurt feelings. The boy looked at him quizzically, then turned back to snack, his face towards the sun.

"So, malaria, huh?" Penn said. He sniffled and rubbed his nose with the back of his hand. He looked stressed. His eyebrows furrowed unnaturally and his hands would not stay still, digging into the cracks between the concrete with a rock like a child.

"I already feel better than I did last night."

"Good," Penn said and stared at his shoes. He seemed to want to bring something up but could not find the words to do so. "Is there anything I can get you or anything...?"

I reached out and grabbed his hand. He squeezed mine hard. It felt cold despite the sunny morning.

"What's going on? I feel like something is up," I traced the lines on his pale palms and he watched my fingers move.

"Yeah, well, there is a little something up." Penn reached into his bag and pulled out a small blue booklet. He dropped it at my ankles.

I gently picked up the book and recognized the Kenyan passport. I opened it up to find Nylie's new name sketched into the front in the same fine ink.

Name: Israel Noela Laiza
Birthdate: December 25, 1991
Ethnicity: Kenyan

The ink was perfect, un-smeared and delicate. The Kenyan coat of arms reflected back across the page. But my eyes slowly traced the book and landed on the bottom left corner that contained the photograph.

There was the problem Penn was referring to: the picture showed a scowling white woman, black hair severe and bangs cut too short over her eyebrows. Her pale eyes and face accentuated the red of her lips, the pink of her cheeks.

"Who the fuck is this?" I said, too loudly. A nun walking past threw a scowl in my direction.

"I don't know," Penn put his head in his hands, "Probably someone else who is trying to get a passport from these guys. I know they do Eastern European stuff, too. There must have been some sort of mistake."

I slammed the passport down. The tiny boy next to me looked startled and dropped the third *mandazi* back into the bowl.

"This is ridiculous. Who the hell thought that this girl's picture belonged in a Kenyan passport?" My anger and frustration seemed to aggravate the malaria. My head instantly became unfocused and my hands began to tingle.

175

My fingers curled into a ball and gently released, over and over again and I counted my breaths. One through eight. One through eight. There was a feeble attempt to regain control of my emotions in order to control the physical aspects of my body.

"How soon can we get a new passport?" I sighed, spoke in a whisper, resenting the beads of sweat caused by the interminable sun.

"Friday. My guy guaranteed we could get the new one, the right one, by Friday."

I slammed bare knuckles into the cement once, twice three times. I felt them instantly swell, turn pink, purple, felt the crack of skin give way to a small trickle of blood.

Penn grabbed my hands and held them. Blood leaked from my knuckles and a tear leaked from my eye. "You promised me this would work. You promised me that if I helped you there would be absolutely no problems. You promised me, Penn. You were desperate and I helped you because I thought that you could keep your promise. But those girls are leaving on Wednesday. Friday will be too late."

Penn squeezed my hands tighter and resisted my urge to slam my knuckles into the cement a few more times. "I know, Isabel, I know. This was a mistake, a stupid, unprofessional mistake. But we are going to get this figured out. I've already started. I've already got them fixing the issue. You've got to trust me."

"Why, Penn?" I felt myself getting worked up again. Blood rushed to my brain. I stood then I quickly sat back down to steady myself. My feet began to feel numb, my hands started to tingle. All my composure melted away with the color in my cheeks, "Why should I trust you? I'm tired. I'm so tired and I don't know what to do."

The tears came full force now. The small boy grabbed the remaining *mandazi* and scooted away, far from the undoing of the light-skinned girl. Penn grabbed my shoulders and kissed my forehead over and over again. He rocked me back and forth, back and forth, and let the world and the oceans between Africa and America pour out of my eyes.

I cried for the malaria, strange like ink staining my thoughts and emotions. I cried for Nylie, terrified to go home or even kiss her son goodbye for what her husband may do.

I cried for Loveness and the choices she could not make. I cried for Maya and the emotion she could not share. I cried for every woman who gave birth to a daughter and knew she would grow up with unavoidable pain and inequality. I cried for Penn's mother, and for the moment she decided whether to leave home and brave the unknown or risk the danger of growing up in a war-torn land. I cried for Theresa for having to love a child who was not her own. And I cried for Ivy and the daughter she never knew.

42

My eyes were swollen and my voice shaky. Penn gently pushed me upright to wash the snot from the shoulder of his tight shirt. The nuns placed a cold rag on my eyes and told me to lie down in my room in the convent.

"Your friend can wait outside and stay for lunch," Sapphira grinned.

I dreamt but I did not sleep. Textures crossed and split in my mind, creating colorful illusions and dramatic scenarios that were so complex, I could not sense if my eyes were open or closed. The tears had brought out a red in my cheeks, a green in my eyes, and the blue from the vein that slanted across my forehead. When the dreams finished coloring my body, the tears colored my mind, too.

I shuffled into the dining room after a fitful sleep with a blue cloth around my hips and a gray sweatshirt over my shoulders. Penn sat in the wooden chair. The nun was rattling on in Swahili and he nodded politely, unsure how to respond to the elderly woman who was feeding him for free.

"Good morning, beautiful," Penn laughed at my outfit and the confused look in my eyes.

"How are you feeling, dear?" The nun switched to English at the sight of me and put her fat hand across my forehead. "Malaria is such a strange disease. It plays tricks with your brain, makes your dreams feel true. I'm sorry you are having to suffer it." She squeezed my cheeks like a child. Nausea pulsed through me.

The food she brought out smelled thick and heavy, like the sister's hand on my forehead, or a night in the village, or Penn's body on mine. Chicken legs, fried in oil and salt. Fried bananas dusted in pepper, and carrots and peas mixed with chicken insides. The deep, fatty smell made my jaw tighten.

Penn ate eagerly, tearing meat from the bone with such precision I could not help but watch. He scooped up chicken intestines with a piece of banana, just as he had seen others do in the village. He ate happily and chewed loudly.

My eyes were transfixed on his long limbs, his big lips, his overwhelming hands.

"When we go back to America," he said, his mouth full of peas and meat and banana, "I am going to open up a chicken shop and cook it just like the chicken they cook here. The chicken here is always so fucking good. It's simple, you know? In America, we are always trying to make things complex. But chicken doesn't need any help, it's good all on its own." Penn leaned back in his chair and licked his fingers happily.

"Isabel, I can't tell you how much I think about going home," he prattled on. "I am going to show my mom my passport, and she is going to cry and scream with happiness. She is going to have a big party; I know she is. She's going to invite all the damn Africans to that damn fancy neighborhood she lives in and she's going to cook stew. And then I am going to get a real job, Isabel. I know I have had some questionable jobs and made some bad decisions, but it was all circumstantial. I would never do any of that if I had the opportunity to get a real job. So, who knows, I think I would like to go into law. Maybe I can get an internship at a law firm. I would even like to be the secretary or something, just so I can be around all of those people making the important decisions, before I start to make them."

He pulled his banana apart and thrust it into the chicken gravy. The sight simultaneously disgusted and intrigued me, "But maybe before that I will need to get another job, so I can start paying bills and going to school. I saw they are hiring a front desk manager at one of those hotels close by. I could work there in the evenings and go to community college during the day. So, with the money I am saving I can pay for school, and get Mama a little something extra. Maybe a new car or something? Oh my God, I can't even imagine her face when I tell her I am going to go to school. And then I will fly to New York and find my dad. He's going to ask how I got there, and I am going to tell him I flew on an airplane, because I got a passport, *motherfucker.*"

Penn placed a hand on my back, then a palm on my forehead. "And then do you know what I am going to do? I am going to fly home from visiting my dad in New York, drive to downtown Denver, look up your address and knock on your door. And I am going to buy you a red dress and red high heels, fully aware that you will be as tall as me when you put those high heels on, and I will take you out to eat steak. And lobster. Once a week I will do this. Oh yeah, I will also get you a manicure and a pedicure because, girl, your toes are looking gnarly."

I did not smile at his exuberance and excitement, and could not help but feeling nervous about his new big plans. I knew Denver and I knew Penn, but I had not yet decided if I wanted them together in the same world. I had yet to decide who I would be back in America. Would I be the success story, inspired and inspiring those through my work in Africa? The one that never quite made it, forever grieving a mother she never knew in a world where she never belonged? The businesswoman? The therapist? The restless one? Would I ever be that alive?

Guilt pricked at me for the mental shadow I had cast on Penn's optimistic plans. I reached for a banana and attempted to eat, "Before you go planning your wedding and children's names," I attempted to joke, "Can you please tell me how we are going to solve Nylie's passport issue?" The sleep had increased my patience but the nagging feeling that something was wrong poked and prodded at my ribs like the boys poked at their cattle. We weren't playing with fire, we were teasing it, taunting it, and I could not yet believe that we weren't going to get burned.

Penn stretched his arms overhead and smiled happily at me. "I talked to that poet dude, the one in Kenya, the one where the girls are staying. He's a weird guy, by the way, but I think you already knew that. He is going to pick up Maya and Loveness at the airport. They can stay at his safe house for two nights on their own, begin to get adjusted. I have already changed my flight to fly out late on Friday evening, with Nylie. She and I can hop that red eye into Nairobi Friday night, and I will be with her so she can get to that safe house, even though we are arriving after dark. In fact, this plan is even better because Maya and Loveness will have been there for a few days, so they can let me know how it is and if there are any problems we need to address. I can check everything out Friday and make sure it's legit. I will get Nylie settled in, and then I am on my way to America on Sunday. Foolproof."

I chewed thoughtfully on my banana. Wouldn't the village be suspicious when Maya and Loveness had already left? Would Nylie even survive until Friday? My face flashed red hot as I considered how Penn had decided to come here and play in the dirt and speak his plans when someone should be watching over the girls back home. I hated him for it. My wrists tingled and my head felt light.

Sapphira came in and placed two fat white pills in front of me. "Take them with food," she instructed. "I will be checking to make sure they made it all the way down, miss." The antiseptic smell of the pills instantly made my stomach churn. I clenched my jaw to control my gag.

I nodded obediently, and swallowed the pills quickly. They went down my throat heavily, hindered by the starchiness of the banana.

Sapphira clucked her tongue approvingly and took heavy steps out of the dining area.

"I guess that works," I said to Penn, but I could not look at him. I felt angry that he did not feel the stress I did or acknowledge the importance of the decisions we were making.

"Is Nylie going to be okay until Friday? Has she been home?" My thoughts were tired. I thought of moments ago, when I shattered like glass, and wished they had left me in tiny pieces inside of the pool. The stress seemed to heighten the effects of the malaria. I needed kind answers and definitive solutions that would not require my input.

Penn nodded slowly, "Yes. She has been home. She is not doing too great, and her husband is not happy. He's beating the crap out of her, Isabel. But he's not touching their son, and she will be out of there in less than a week. Just sucks. Everyone is acting like what is happening to Nylie is acceptable. They are acting like she did wrong, so she is going to pay for it."

The weight of the situation felt artificial, as if I were watching a movie in which I hoped one of the best characters survived. My body begged me to believe there was nothing I could do. I shook my head violently as to rid my mind of the image of returning to the school and discovering that Nylie's body had taken too much, that her husband had taken it one step too far.

"Can she come here, to the convent?"

Penn rubbed the back of my neck and lowered his voice, "I don't think we would be able to get her into the convent, and then also smuggle her into Kenya. That's too risky, we would have to pick one or the other."

Penn was right. The best course of action was to hold tight for just a few more days.

My mind spoke despite the pleas from my body, "I have to get back to school. I can make some plans so Nylie has to work until late night and early in the morning. I can say that she needs to work overtime hours for a special project. God, we are so fucking close, I'm not going to have a pissed off husband ruin this for us, for her. This is his wife we are talking about. How could he be that angry? Even if she had done something wrong. Say she had cheated on him; this reaction is so…destructive."

"When do you think you can get out of here?" asked Penn. "With all due respect, Isabel, you don't look great. I'm wondering about how well your brain is focusing. Your health is the priority here, so if you think you need to spend some time resting, they will understand…"

I shook my head enthusiastically side to side and felt my thoughts sway with the movement, "But that's the difference, Penn. I have literally been waiting twenty-six years for this exact moment: a chance to be part of something bigger than a confused and dysfunctional existence. Being present and in the village right now is worth more than a few days of being sick. Hell, it's worth ten thousand moments of malaria if it means I can use my life for some type of purpose. Penn, this moment is why I was brought here."

Tears welled up in my eyes. I could not seem to keep my thoughts clear, my eyes open or dry.

"Okay, Isabel, girl, do your thing. But if you need time to relax, it's all right. Either way, these girls will always remember you. And just so you know, your life is meaningful. Even without this…venture."

Penn kissed the top of my head and held my arm as he helped me stand and walked me back to my room. He tucked the covers in tight around my shivering body and pulled my mass of curls up off my neck.

He put my cell phone underneath my pillow and rubbed his nose on my forehead, "Your cell phone is charged," he said, motioning under my head. "And if you want to make it back and say goodbye to the girls, I am putting it here." He pulled a small square baggy of white powder out of his pocket and placed it in the toe of my tennis shoe.

"Just in case this helps you get out of bed. We love you, Isa." He kissed my lips, my breath hot against his cool skin. And then, he was gone.

43

Dear Mom-

Did you ever go to your prom? I was thinking about this the other day and I really wish I knew. What dress did you wear? I'm sure you looked beautiful; I hope you left your hair down. I know you think that we look different, but I am starting to think we look more and more the same. I think my hands look like yours. I think my arms do, too.

Were you and Dad ever in love? It's okay if you weren't, I'm just wondering. I think I fell in love! With that boy who went to my high school who had the African mother, remember him? I don't know if its lasting love, but it feels good right now.

I spent the night in the hospital last night; I think that is part of why I feel so disoriented and part of why I am writing to you. When I woke up this morning, I couldn't remember where I was. I felt sick with my eyes open, so I had to figure out where I had been sleeping with my eyes completely shut. I listened very, very carefully. I expected to hear your voice for a while: you humming into the air, or talking on the phone. But when I heard a voice, it wasn't your voice at all. The words were different; tumbling and rolling. They were Swahili words. I speak Swahili now, Mom! I forgot you didn't know that. There's a lot that I forget you don't know. I moved to Tanzania after you left, and I learned Swahili here.

I did a lot of things here, Mom, that I think may have surprised you. I may have your arms, but I can carry more. You should've called me when you found out about the rape. You should've called me on every single one of my birthdays. You should've asked me about my prom, and what I dreamt about and asked if I ever feel tired and heavy and hopeless like you. Because I do. You also should have ended every phone call with "I love you."

There are people who are waiting for me right now, Mom. They need me to get up even though I'm sick because they are in bad situations. There are bad situations no matter where you go, I found out. You can't really run away from them. Unless, you know, someone does what you did. You should've stayed here, Mom. I wanted you to stay. We weren't done learning each other yet. And now, there is no time.

I hope you found "uhuru". That's how they say "freedom" in Swahili. That's what you were looking for, right? I haven't found it yet either, but you know what? I kept on going anyway. Maybe that's what freedom is: making the choice to keep moving.

I love you. Despite it all. I'll always love you.

Isa

44

Nylie's husband was at the gate when I returned to the school, my body fevered and sweating and shivering despite the sticky heat of the night. He leaned up against the gate and talked quietly with the guard in their native language. Both men instantly quieted as the car pulled in the dusty driveway, Bob Marley singing on the taxi's radio. My head was cloudy, foggy, from the sickness; but my brain attempted time and time again to kick into overdrive, to solve the problems that ebbed and flowed with my thought process.

Her husband made eye contact with me in the backseat of the taxi. His eyes were yellowed and stood out across his shiny, unshaven skin. He readjusted his red wraps around his shoulders and held my gaze. Through the open window our eyes locked and I was certain that he knew everything I had planned and plotted. I believed his eyes judged my character, along with the intelligence of my scheme, the integrity in which I executed a drug trade in order to give girls a choice. The Swahili left my throat. I had no words for the man who stood outside my home late at night. He smiled, the bottom two teeth missing from his grin, but his eyes showed no joy. I smiled, wished him a good evening, and motioned to the taxi driver to pull forward into the gate. My neck felt hot where his gaze burned into the car.

"Why are you here?" I asked the man over and over in my head, "What are you talking with the guard about at this hour?"

Before I'd left the convent, I slid a wrapper around my waist and an *ngati* around my shoulders. I tried to press my foot into my tennis shoe, but was stopped by a thin plastic bag in the toe. I pulled the baggie out, dumped the contents in my palm, and inhaled deeply. The smell was like gasoline and the drug dripped down my throat until it was coated with a thick layer of numbness. My mind came alive with a cold blue fire. I dialed a taxi with cold blue fingers and waited outside in the cold blue light and gave him instructions on how to get to school.

The drugs did not permit sleep, and my cell phone began vibrating without stopping when I arrived at the Manor. Two days without Internet had prevented international communication and my family could not have been more anxious. Several missed calls from my father popped onto my cell phone screen, several text messages from Theresa begging me to call her back and let her know I was alright. I dialed her number and held the phone with shaky hands up to my ear.

"Thank God," she exclaimed into the phone, "We have been worried sick. So worried that I sent a Facebook message to Annie, and she told us you were safe and good, but were staying with the nuns for a few days. She said you were sick." I heard the relief in her voice and I felt a trickle of guilt for causing that type of pain to a woman who loved me.

"I'm sorry, Theresa, I really am. I got sick at the pool and the nuns wanted me to stay at the convent a few nights to rest. They gave me some medicine and I am back at the school safe and sound."

"What time is it there?" Theresa asked. I heard her shuffle her phone around in order to check the world clock app she had set to my time zone. "It's 4 a.m., why are you up so late? You should be resting!"

"I had a hard time sleeping at the convent," I said, "And I wanted to get back to let you guys know I was okay." I bit my lip at my lie, but it was a kind lie. Theresa would appreciate that.

"Is there anything you need? I am going to be honest with you, Isabel, I will finally get some sleep when you come back home. I am getting gray hair just imagining what kind of situation you could be in out there. I will be the happiest woman alive when you come home again."

I closed my eyes for a moment and thought of eating spicy chili with my dad in Theresa's kitchen. I thought of sitting on the hardwood floors near the fireplace and pulling fresh rolls out of the oven.

"Are you doing okay? You sound a little stuffy. I'm sure it's just because you have been sick, but promise me you will take it easy, okay?" As Theresa murmured into the phone, I instantly allowed myself to be homesick in the way that every human becomes when they are sick and vulnerable and far from home.

"I'm fine," I choked, bit my tongue to keep the tears from coming. I bit until I felt the metallic taste of blood. I needed to rest. "I'm going to lie down a little bit, Theresa. But I love you. Let the family know I am doing alright."

"I will, sweetheart. Take it easy. I love you." The dial tone buzzed in my ear. I wanted to call Ivy. I wanted to rest my head in her coconut oil lap and let her hum and twist my hair. I wanted to go home, and no matter how tightly I squeezed my eyes shut I could not determine where home was.

I rubbed my eyes with the palm of my hands, and sent a text to Penn and Nylie, telling them I was back at the school and I would see them in the morning. The rooster crowed out back, the first crow of the morning, and I determined it was time to pull myself together before making an appearance for the school day. I fished the baggie Penn had given me at the convent out of pocket and held the remainder of the contents up to my nose. I inhaled sharply in the dark office. My mind awakened, my body discovered strength.

With newfound energy, I allowed my mind to wander to the dark places that could be a reality. Where was Loveness, and had her mother kept her secret? Had she packed all of the things I instructed her to bring, like the poet's phone number in Nairobi and instructions on how to catch a taxi? Had Maya's father found out the truth about his daughter? Would Maya be responsible and show up on time? Where was Nylie now? Had the bruises distracted her from where she was going? Had she offered her husband information about our plan for a night of peace?

With my heart in overdrive, I did not waste time. I took advantage of my focused mind and walked to a cold shower behind the chicken coop. I left the lights off and watched the orange grapefruit sun seep into the cracks of the wooden door. Beetles scuttled on the shower floor. I gently kicked their crunchy bodies out of the way as I reached for my shampoo bottle.

Afterward, I intricately braided my hair, tight and new, and prayed my twisted hair would leave me fresh-faced. I pulled on my last clean skirt and white t-shirt tinged pink from the red dress that had shared the washing bucket. My sandals rinsed with the hose, I trekked to the chicken coop to find fresh eggs to cook. I boiled water and took down a precious packet of American coffee that I was saving for special occasions, and drank the too hot liquid before the students arrived.

Miriam was the first in my office, a construction paper heart in her hand. "I heard you fell sick, Madam," she whispered. She placed the paper heart on my desk, giggled, then ran out of the office, her skirt slipping down her thin hips.

I sifted through emails: requests from sponsors wanting to know how their student was doing. Emails from owners of other schools in the area, asking how we achieved donations. A note from the founder, detailing her trip out to her school in the next few months. I read them absentmindedly, making no plans to attend to any of the emails until the girls were out of the country safe and sound.

Loveness tapped me on the shoulder and I jumped with such surprise that she startled in her plastic sandals. "You scared me!" I breathed, but laid my head into her stomach as she stood over me with her hands on my shoulders. For a split second, I considered what would have happened if I had not said goodbye to these women. If I could not kiss their sweet foreheads one last time, allow them to cross long lean legs over my skirt. I imagined not being able to hear their quiet laughter again, sleepy yawns when Loveness lay her tired head on her bicep.

"I missed you so much!" I squealed. We held hands as she smiled. A big salty tear gathered at the lip of her eye, then rolled down her perfect coffee cheek. "Why are you crying, Loveness? I came back! I was able to see you before you had to leave! This is such good news!"

She wiped her tear away, embarrassed, and rolled her head in a giant circle. "There are other reasons I'm sad, Madam," she leaned closer to me and whispered in my ear, "I am sad to leave my country behind."

"Do you still want to do this, my dear?" I whispered to her, kept hold of her hands as I sat back down in the office chair. "I don't ever want to make decisions for you. I just want you to have the opportunity to live a different life, if that is what you want."

Loveness nodded eagerly. She gritted her teeth and turned her chin up towards the sky, "Oh, I am ready to go, Madam. I have packed one bag and I have kissed my son on his head and I have helped my mother in every way that I know how. There is nothing left for me to do. It's time."

"And you know what else? If you choose to do so, when you start making a little bit of money in Kenya, you can send it back to your baby and your mama. That would be pretty cool, wouldn't it?" I wondered if she and Theresa would get along. I pictured them exchanging jokes, puns on common English words. My heart burst in an immediate painful bubble that this fantasy would never come true.

Loveness choked back a fresh batch of tears, "My mother could buy new fabrics and maybe some new shoes for my baby. Maybe day shoes and church shoes, too. Maybe if I send back enough money, then they can have a celebration and buy an entire cow to share with the neighbors. Wouldn't that be amazing? If they were able to feast because of the money that I made?"

"That would be pretty awesome," I smiled at her optimism. A wave of nausea rushed over me like the dust that swirled around my ankles then tangled itself in my throat. "Let's go for a walk, shall we? Say goodbye to the Manor together?"

Loveness nodded and stood with me, linked her elbow into mine. I tried to imagine saying goodbye to every piece of life I had ever known. As I stepped foot off of that dusty plane all of those months ago, there was always the option to return home. That freedom would always be mine in a way others would not know. Privilege always rested in choices.

We walked past the driveway, lined with pink and scarlet begonias, hanging from wire that the gardeners had twisted together so the vines would climb. We walked past the bananas trees and the few blades of grass that had attempted to poke their heads through the dust and into the hot sun. I remembered throwing pounds of grass seed below those trees, certain that the area would be green and bountiful within a few months' time. I smiled at my misguided optimism. A prayer formed on my tongue that this unfounded hope would not rear its deceptive head as I prepared to send these women to another country.

We walked by the kitchen, where the big-busted cooks laughed and yelled and swatted naked babies with dishtowels. It was mid-morning and the kitchen smelled like burnt wood and smoke and the sweet spices of milky chai. We kept our arms linked as we walked into the garden down each row of tomatoes and watermelon and eggplant so purple and shiny that you could see your reflection in it if you held the vegetable up to the sun. We watched as a gardener freed a newborn goat from the thistles that surrounded the garden, and then gently tossed him to his mother on the other side of the thorny fence.

We walked past the classrooms where thin hipped girls and big breasted women and bright-eyed teenagers called out the national anthem, then their multiplication tables, then the prologue of the country's constitution. We passed a field close to the swings, where freshly shaved heads bounced up and down in a circle, tapping plastic shoes in rhythm with their song. We walked by Harriet's sewing room, the hum of her machine outlining a new powder blue shirt, her hair twisted with a lime green cloth the exact same way that Ivy used to do.

We passed the garage that once housed cocaine, hidden in tubs of self-proclaimed baby formula. We passed the room where Penn and I had made understanding. We walked by the awning where I would lie on my back, then look out and see the Acacia trees, unmoving despite the unrelenting wind. The breeze picked up and I held my skirt around my ankles. Loveness squeezed the cloths over her forearms and shoulders, and tucked her chin to her chest. We would never be able to walk past the dust.

Then, we saw Nylie. She was sitting on the wooden bench outside the office, her shoulders covered with a large sweater despite the heat. Her head was covered with a yellow and red cloth; she wore socks underneath her sandals and kept her head bowed. Loveness squeezed my hand and told me she had to go.

"You and Maya need to be here at 8 p.m. sharp," I told her, "None of this African time, either. You need to be here exactly then. Pass that information onto Maya." Loveness nodded and kept her head down, the thought of her leaving heavy on her heart once again. "And Loveness? Kiss that baby of yours one more time."

45

It was a face I did not recognize. It was purple and engorged and gave the impression that her entire head had been pumped full of water and not properly drained. Her eyelids were purple and swollen creating small crescent moons for eyes that peeked out from the eclipse of eyelids. Even her lips were swollen, pink and tender. I shuddered at what wounds her clothes were hiding.

"Hey, sister," I whispered, as if speaking loudly would injure her tattered body further. "Can I get you some tea?" I held Nylie's hand and led her shaking body into the office. She sat on the dusty purple cushions and shook silently. I stirred sugar into the chai and brought her a lukewarm mug. She held it in shaky hands and refused to match my gaze.

"Are you... alright?" I knew how ridiculous the question sounded coming out of my mouth but I did not know what else to say. "I mean..." I searched for words in a desert, "Has your husband cooled down at all?"

She shook her head slowly and brought the tea up to her swollen lips. I winced at the thought of the hot liquid hitting her battered mouth. "I don't know when he will stop being angry." She shook her head and attempted another sip of the tea.

"Do you think you will be able to hold on until Friday? I'm sure Penn told you the plan, didn't he?" I hated being factual, stating dates and plans instead of the comfort that I would have wanted at a time like this.

Nylie nodded, stayed silent. Her calmness scared me, I worried for a moment she had accepted defeat.

"Nylie, when you leave on Friday, your husband and his other wife, they won't... they wouldn't take that out on your son, would they?"

Nylie sat up instantly and opened her eyes as wide as her swollen purple eyelids would allow. "Isabel. I am a good mother. I would never leave if I thought my son would be harmed."

I looked down at my dusty feet and nodded solemnly. "Let me know if you need anything." I walked to the back and grabbed a few aspirin and swallowed them dry before squeezing two pills into Nylie's sweaty hand.

I thought about Theresa's panicked voice on the phone this morning. I believed Theresa would have left her country if it meant a better life for her children, like Penn's mother had done. Theresa was a brave woman. Braver than Ivy had ever been.

The day ebbed and flowed like my thoughts and coherent consciousness. Food tasted strange in my mouth, and I could not find warmth no matter how many sweaters from the donation room I wrapped myself in. I felt a strange combination of the sickness and sadness and excitement that the day held, and I could not divide my honest feelings from the drug induced way my body was behaving. My heart sped up when I heard Penn at the door. I blamed my thumping pulse on the malaria medication.

He kissed my forehead as he entered the office. Harriet clicked her tongue in disapproval as she left her sewing room keys on my desk.

"How are you feeling?" he asked, attempting to place his hand on my forehead, which I quickly swatted away.

"I'm fine. What news do you have for me?" I pulled my braids off of my neck. The breeze that hit my skin sent goose bumps up and down my legs.

"Well, apparently they have the passport in for printing. So far so good! Max is going to drop it off Friday morning," Penn looked at my chilled arms and his eyebrows knit together.

"Are you coming with us today?" I asked, as I pulled a fabric up over my shoulders. "To the airport, I mean?" I covered up the thermometer on my desk. I didn't want Penn worrying over my chilled state in ninety-four-degree weather.

"Do you want me to?" Penn rubbed the back of his hand on my bicep. It was hard to understand the origin of the goose bumps at this point. I wanted to know his lips again.

"Well, Loveness would probably like it if you said goodbye, and Maya probably would act like she doesn't care, but she may. You never know, she could have some soft spot behind all of that grit and resistance."

"And you?" Penn asked, looking up at me through long eyelashes. He smiled his crooked tooth smile and I knew he was trying to make a joke, but something in his eyes told me that he needed to know the answer.

"Yes, I would like you to come to the airport with me. I may need a little help getting back, saying goodbye to those two is going to be hard…"

Life had felt so much like facts lately: where to go, what the next move could be, that emotion had gotten stuffed way back into my chest. I placed this emotion right next to the space where I saw my dad cry and had my first heartbreak. These were the feelings you never wanted to relive, but also knew you should probably not forget.

"What time are you leaving for the airport?" Nylie stirred on the couch and placed her bare feet on the dusty floor. She yawned and stretched her arms overhead, and winced at something underneath her clothes. It was nearly six in the evening now. Her husband would be expecting her home soon.

"The girls are coming back to school in about two hours," I said, and slouched on the bench next to her long legs stretched painfully in front of her. "Do you think you can go to the airport with us?"

Nylie shook her head and rubbed her face with her hands, "No, I need to get home. I need to say goodbye to those girls, and then I need to hold my son for a while. I bought him something yesterday and I wanted to bring it to him." She reached under the couch and pulled out a plastic lid nailed to one end of a wooden stick. She rolled it around like a wheel on the ground. "It's a toy car," she explained, "It's good, isn't it?"

I laughed and rolled the toy car around myself. "It's very good. Greet your baby for me, okay? And if things get too crazy at home, or you need anything, call me." I pinched the place between my eyebrows and studied Nylie's swollen face. She cast her eyes down. "Just hang on. Just hang on two more days."

46

We were seaweed at the airport. Our arms flowed together and linked, and smoothly unhooked as we neared the security line. Maya and Loveness flowed in their Western skirts that came down past their knees, burgundy and white and clean. They flowed in their new bras and plastic sandals and they flowed as they handed their single backpack to the man in the security line. I had picked these clothes out just last week, demanding a discount if I purchased the skirts and shoes two at a time. I had been so proud of my Swahili then. The plan had seemed so simple.

The girls flowed as they watched everything worth keeping scanned through strange machines with strange beeps and buzzing. They flowed as they watched black men in white uniforms touch women who were not their wives to make sure they were not carrying anything they should not be carrying onto the plane. They flowed as their long black fingers covered small black ears when the planes took off overhead. They flowed as they ducked in order to avoid getting hit by the landing plane that seemed so, so close to their heads, and as tears leaked out of tired eyes and slid gently down perfect cheekbones. They flowed when I told them I loved them. And when I told them not to be scared. They flowed as I promised that I would never, ever forget about them and that we would find a way to communicate, especially since they would be working on computers so often.

Their lips flowed goodbyes. Their eyes rained. Loveness flowed her eyes up around Penn's neck and he told her that he would see her soon, just a few days when he came into Kenya with Nylie. Maya kept her head down. She bit her lip and pulled her socks up higher on her thick calves.

Maya's chest heaved and her eyes flickered and she pulled her sweater closer to her body. She reached down and squeezed my hand, harder, harder, until I felt the pulse in my palm and knew my knuckles were white. She leaned her head on my shoulder and I smelled the smoke from the fire in the home she would not return to. I breathed in her scent one more time.

When Maya let go, Loveness grabbed my shoulders. She pressed her face into my collarbone, wiped her dripping nose on my shirt and cried loudly. I placed my hands on the back of her head and let her melt into my hair.

Finally, Loveness spoke. "My mother told me to tell you," she leaned her head back and rubbed her eyes with the back of her hand, "That she is thankful you could help me in a way she couldn't. And she said to thank your own mother, for raising a brave woman."

47

"My clothes will never be dry again." That was what I told Penn as we lay together on my bed that night, "I will never stop sweating enough to wear dry clothes again. I must resign myself to the fact that I will be damp for the rest of my life." Penn laughed sleepily and squeezed my body, softly, too cautiously. He was hesitant to agitate my fevered body. I stared at his closed eyelids, the curly eyelashes that fluttered with the promise of dreams.

I envied his ability to sleep at a time like this. I wished he could breathe his exhaustion into my lips. My mind ran faster than ever in the midst of the exhaustion. I worried over Maya and Loveness's journey. I worried over their motion sickness on the plane, being followed out of the village, that their nerves would finally give out and would return with their heads down and defeat in their step. I felt the dread of not truly knowing the poet, his intentions blurred in my mind like the shapes outside the dimly lit window. Penn's naked chest looked big and cool, and I rubbed my burning forehead against it while he slept.

What if Nylie didn't make it two more days? What if I didn't? What if I got caught and sent to jail and this is what was left of Ivy's legacy: a woman who loved death more than her family and her drug dealer daughter. I placed my forehead on Penn's chest and I hoped it burned a little. I wanted him to be awake for this, to suffer with me.

My mind wandered to what these women would be in this next piece of life. I envisioned Nylie in high heels and a dress skirt. I imagined Maya arguing in a courtroom. Soon, I felt my mind shift to career day at my high school. Everyone was supposed to dress up as his or her chosen profession. There were lots of business suits, a fireman's hat. Penn had worn a basketball uniform; I remembered that now. What had I worn? What had I wanted to be?

One student had worn her mother's dress and claimed proudly she wanted to be a stay at home mother, just like her mother. Nothing terrified me more than that thought: growing up to become an adult in a world where I didn't fit in, a world I couldn't understand. Making impulsive decisions because of loneliness or to create meaning. Is this why Ivy had left in the way she did? To create meaning?

Panic dripped out of my pores and onto Penn's skin. Who had I planned on becoming?

I shook Penn awake, "Penn! Penn! You need to wake up right now."

His eyes opened lazily, "What's up, Isa?" He stretched his arms over head.

"Remember that time in high school when we had career day at school? Remember how you dressed up like a basketball player? Well what was I? What was my future like back then?"

Penn was caught off guard at my question. He wrinkled his forehead with sleepy eyes. "I don't remember, Isabel, go to sleep!" He rolled over and the small bed frame creaked.

"Penn! I need to know what I was then!" I sat in bed and felt curls sticking out in all directions. Curls that did not belong to Ivy or my father or Africa or America. My hands shook with sickness and stress.

Penn sat up in bed and pulled my hair off of my sweating neck. He put his chin on my naked shoulder, "I don't remember, Isabel. I don't remember who we were back then."

48

I stayed awake the entire night the girls left. I heard the car pull into the driveway sometime in the early hours of the morning. Penn lay awake next to me, pulled on long khaki pants and a white t-shirt over his head.

"That's Nylie's passport," he whispered. He kissed my forehead and told me to go back to sleep. I kicked the covers off my sweaty body and watched his dark figure disappear through the thin wooden door. The lights in the driveway shone through the window. I refused to be concerned about what the guard would think about a man staying late into the night at a single woman's apartment.

My body shivered with the breeze and shivered with the sound of the diesel engine. It shivered as I heard men's voices calling over the noise of the jeep. I rubbed my face into the pillow and prayed for Nylie, prayed for Loveness and Maya and prayed for forgiveness for the sins I was committing. The guard yelled outside and I winced, instantly concerned with his knowledge, the vague memory of him talking with Nylie's husband late in the dark hours of the morning. I recalled the gruff tone in her husband's voice and the suspicion in his eyes and the swollen bruises he had created on my friend.

Penn came in minutes later. I heard the diesel engine drive out of the dust we lived in. He took off his shirt and sat in bed with the khakis slicked to his legs. Penn held the small blue book in his large palms like a treasure, a jewel that had finally been uncovered. The light flicked on and I recovered my body in the blankets, feeling the malaria sink into my thoughts and limbs once again. "How does it look?" I whispered, nearly afraid of his response.

Penn opened the book slowly to the first page. Nylie's new name and date of birth were printed in the same neat blue ink. The picture showed the shaved head of a tribal girl, eyes wide, filled with fire. It was a picture of Nylie.

He turned to the second page, a stamp firmly stating she had visited other countries in the East African region, that she had returned home to Kenya a few times in the past.

"It's perfect," Penn whispered. Tears filled the lip of his eyes and I was taken aback at his emotion. "I can't believe we are actually getting away with all of this." We sat, wordless on the creaking bed, afraid that even one word would break our lives and our plans and the hope we held so preciously in our palms. We sat until the sun finished rising and our hearts slowed down and our cheeks dried. Then, we kept going.

I checked my phone so often in the morning after Maya and Loveness had left for Kenya, that the battery died. Around the same time, the electricity within the school grew stubborn and tired and flickered until the lights went out. I held a dead phone in my hand: my only link to the travels of the two young souls. In my panic, I called thin-hipped Miriam to the office, handed her a few shillings, and told her to find someone in the village to charge my phone. There were small pockets within the village of innovation and entrepreneurship: men in their twenties who'd purchased a solar panel and charged others a few shillings for the chance to charge their phone or their radio or the occasional laptop.

Miriam sprinted out of the school, eyes shining with the pleasant weight of her responsibility. When she returned thirty minutes later, I switched my phone on again, and no messages lit up my screen. The anxiety of the unknown dripped down my throat and into my arms, my thighs, and rested in the bottom of my feet until I felt too heavy to move or speak. This man was a fraud, a human trafficker, I was sure of it now. I should have had Penn go with these girls, and have Nylie get on the flight on her own. In my stress I pulled the soft pieces of skin that formed around my fingernails. I pulled until I felt blood and my head felt heavy.

The strangeness of the girls' absence had not yet sunk in. You don't realize you miss someone until they are not where you expect them to be. I would not know the deepness of our friendship until I could not see Loveness's curly eyelashes in the office Monday morning. I would not feel my loss until I yearned for Maya's laughter. Instead, I busied myself with thoughts of Nylie and Penn's nearing departure.

The day moved quickly despite my panicked state. The bell rang and the girls screamed with delight as they left school, just as they always did every day. I stayed in the office once everyone had left, and watched out the window as the sky melted from blue to pink to deep purple to black. I texted the poet, and my message read "undelivered." Perhaps Nairobi was experiencing similar power outages. My fingers moved mechanically to text Nylie, despite the late hour. I knew she would be awake. She told me she spent her nights staring at her son, watching his chest rise and fall with his breath, admiring his perfect fingers, the curve on the bridge of his nose.

The text read, "We got what we are waiting for. You are ready to go tomorrow."

She texted me back instantly, "I'm ready, my sister."

Nylie said her husband had been sleeping in the other wife's bed. She said he had not laid a hand on her son. She swore he was slowly calming down, and I wanted to believe her with every ounce of my soul. Yet, I remained unsettled.

Penn and I stayed awake for the rest of the night, divided between smoking cheap cigarettes and making lazy love. I cried when the sun came up. I was not ready to love him and I was not ready for him to leave this country. I was not ready to wake up alone at night. I was not ready for the fact the next time I would see his crooked smile would be on the American soil I had run from. What would my life look like out of this country, out of this dust, with tight jeans covering my legs instead of my orange and yellow and green skirts? My heart was not ready to accept the fact that this place would not be my home forever.

My face felt hot as I dressed for the workday. I pulled hair back too tightly in braids and my stomach felt thin and hungry but I could not imagine food in my mouth. Penn left before the students came. He understood the importance of anonymity in relationships within the cultural climate and promised he would be back with his bags at Amani Manor at 5 p.m. He held my hand for a long time before he left.

Nylie sang for the entirety of the workday. She said she sang to her baby boy before she left her home to keep from crying, and swore she would continue to sing to keep the tears away. She sang while the smooth faced students ate oatmeal and she sang while she filed papers from the end of term examinations. She sang loudest during the national anthem. And when the teacher asked her why she was singing so much, she said she was singing because she was happy.

In eighth grade I learned that a smart person does not fight the ocean waves when the current has taken them out too far; they swim parallel to the beach, they let the waves flow with them. So, I flowed with the anxieties of the plan. My heart fluttered and scraped against my ribcage at the thought that Nylie had told too many people the agenda. Or that Loveness's mother would grow tired of carrying the burden of her knowledge. That she would allow the truth of where her daughter was hiding to float from her mouth like the ash that floated from the fires where she boiled chai. I could pinch Nylie's arm; I could demand she be more silent. I could try and bribe Loveness's mother and beg her not to show what she knows. But in the end, that would be fighting the ocean waves.

After I greeted the students and bandaged scraped knees and talked with parents about uniforms and report cards and school fees, the phone rang. It was not the first call of the day. The mechanic had called earlier and explained the problem with the safari jeep's engine. Then, an unknown number from a young man wanting to interview for a music teaching position. "I am the best pianist in all of Tanzania!" the man had assured me. Then, a wrong number that created such anxiety in my chest and the soles of my feet that I hung up instantly. Why was the poet not calling?

My mood dipped with the stress of not knowing. The cook smiled as she brought rice and cabbage to the office.

"Are you going to eat with the girls in the cafeteria?" she asked in her usually friendly way. The staff seemed to find it hilarious that I was eating with the students. Harriet even offered, in that teasing tone of hers, to make me a school uniform so I could fit in more readily with the students.

But my mood was not one of jokes or small talk. I waved the cook away and mumbled that I would eat by myself today. She looked at my thin, bare arms. The bone on top of my shoulder protruded slightly and I knew she bit back her concern in big, tired cheeks.

Finally, around 3 p.m., the screen flashed a Nairobi area code, and my heart felt a little looser, a little calmer. I heard the strangely gaudy voice on the other line.

"Good afternoon! The girls have arrived safely. I just wanted to make sure I understood what your plan was for this evening." I wished he spoke more cautiously, less cheerfully. I wanted him to know the stress his delayed response had put on my body.

"I'm glad you called," I said to the poet, lowering my voice despite the fact no one in the vicinity spoke many English words. "Yes, we are all set for tonight." I explained the game plan. The flight left at 10 p.m. Nylie would be coming with Penn, and they would take a taxi to the safe house. We verified the address. Penn would stay that night in Nairobi but would have to leave the next day.

"How are the girls doing?" I asked, automatically switching to Swahili when I heard Penn walk into the office.

"They are well," he responded in English. "A little shy. They aren't eating very much yet. But it's new. They will come around. Their English is incredible."

My heart burst into tiny fragments between the homesickness for these women and pride for who they were.

"They are excited for Nylie to come," the poet said, "And they said they miss you."

I began singing silently in my head, determined to keep the tears from falling.

"Well, they will be able to see Nylie this evening," I said, my voice wavering, "Tell them I love them…"

The connection became fuzzy and the connection cut. Nylie stood in the doorway and glanced at her backpack she had intricately packed and placed in the corner of the office. Another life in a simple bag.

I hung up the phone and placed my face in my hands. My head was swarming, buzzing, the lack of rest and the malaria creating the loudest version of my brain possible. I stood up and watched my vision speckle to black. My head felt light. I allowed my tired body to fall back into my chair.

Nylie rushed to my side, and called out for Penn. My head did not stop spinning. I was reminded of the time Ivy took me to the amusement park in New Orleans. We climbed into the teacups and spun until all of the colors blended like a painting. Ivy told me to spin faster, faster! Our eyes watered because of the wind and we could not remember if we were crying or trying not to.

Penn came quickly and placed a paper towel under my nose, to my mouth. I hadn't realized my nose was bleeding. I felt it drip down my throat and down my chin. He put a big palm on my forehead. "I think this one has pushed it too hard with the malaria. She's burning up."

Nylie took a cloth and dipped it in the bucket reserved for student drinking water. She washed it across my face, on my palms and under my nose. She kept on singing.

Nylie and Penn said goodbye to me from my small, hot bedroom. They kissed my fevered forehead and stuck love notes in my sweaty palm. They told me they loved me.

My head swarmed with strange thoughts and ideas but the sleep that had evaded me for so long finally took over. I could not make the trip to the airport. I could not say goodbye.

At 10 p.m. I heard the plane overhead and I waved to a dust-covered ceiling. "Goodbye," I said aloud, alone in my room. "Goodbye, good luck, I love you!"

49

The phone rang in my dreams. It wouldn't stop ringing. In my dream, I was too tired to answer it. In my dream it was Ivy, she had something she wanted to tell me, but I was just too sleepy. But no matter how tired I was, it kept ringing. Then, I understood, it was not ringing in my dream, but in reality, in my bedroom, in my home, here in Tanzania.

"Hello?" I said, my voice heavy with sleep, sticky with sickness.

I expected to hear Nylie's voice on the other end, telling me she had arrived safely. Perhaps Penn would be the one to call: ensuring me that all of the girls were happy and safe. Maybe it would be Maya's voice on the phone: gritty and gruff in the only way she knew how to love. But I did not know the voice that spoke into my ear that morning. It was a female voice, who spoke in rushed and rapid Swahili. I asked her to repeat what she said, slowly this time. My brain was still awakening. It was tired from stress and malaria pills. It was tired of thinking in a language that was not its own. As the woman on the static line repeated in her hybrid English, I pieced together her message: "You friend is here, Penn Clemence. You must come to the airport now." My heart dropped. Had we been caught?

None of my clothes seemed right. I dressed in a mid-shin skirt and pulled a t-shirt over my head. Sticky reside from an Aloe plant had stained this skirt a few days ago; the stains looked like mucus and turned my stomach. I took the skirt off and pulled on loose cotton pants with elastic at the ankle. They hung low on my hips... too low. I pulled a skirt over top of the pants and looked in the mirror. It didn't feel right. I added a jacket and another T-shirt. If I were to go to jail tonight, I wanted to have plenty of clothing.

The urgency of the woman on the phone was apparent, yet my actions were too slow, too calculated for my usual haphazard demeanor. I was staving off news. I was basking in the eternal hope of not knowing. Anything is possible if you don't know better. Bliss came in all sorts of terrible forms.

But my bliss only lasted to the door of the safari jeep. My hands shook as I unlocked the car, and turned the key one, two, three times before the engine rumbled up to a start. Penn and I should have spoken about how to lie. What would we say if they asked about the drugs? Would we claim we had assumed it was just baby formula? We would of course leave Max out of this. Would they arrest the girls, too? Surely, they would not blame children for the careless mistakes of two people who were barely adults themselves. I pulled the jeep over to the side of the road and vomited in the red dirt. I reached down and put my hand on the ground.

"This could be the last time I feel this dust," I thought, "This could be the last time I gasp at the stars." I stood there, at the side of the road, and tried to sink it all in.

What was it that I could smell? The smoke from burning rubbish? Perhaps cooked meat? I marveled at the hot wind, how it still inspired goose bumps on my skin. I turned my face at the stars right there by the side of the road and screamed. Not out of anger or frustration. But just to hear my voice and remind myself that I was alive. And at that moment, being alive was the most beautiful thing I could be.

I tried to drive the speed limit. I had moved several kilos of cocaine, sped away from a convent and sent runaway girls out of their country with fake passports, yet I pressed on the brake of the old safari jeep so I could slow down to match the suggested speed sign. My brain did not register the criminal I had become.

The dusty brown skirt fell to my ankles, grazing the silver chains that Nylie had tied to my feet just weeks before. I wrapped a scarf around my shoulders and parked the safari jeep illegally at the front of the small, tired airport. My body couldn't take the walk across the parking lot through thorns and needles. There were never many cars here anyway. Not in this land.

My eyes were drawn to a flash of red that stood big and immovable in the corner of the airport, underneath the street lamp. I knew that red fabric, the same steely stare and crossed arms over a big wide chest on short, stout legs. This was Nylie's husband, eyes full of fresh anger and perhaps something else? I searched his face and my heart pounded as I considered all of the reasons he may be here. He shifted his gaze and did not meet my eyes. Shame. That was what I sensed in the man. Shame looks the same in every language.

An airport employee wearing a crisp white shirt and blue slacks waved me over. She had smoothed her black hair into a bun that was tied at the base of her neck and her lips were serious. My mind was frantic; I could not remember the language: hers or my own. My eyes were burning.

"Penn Clemence," I whispered. I hated how fragile my voice sounded. The employee understood and led me through the empty room that was occasionally filled with tired travelers. She opened the door to a side room and motioned for me to go inside.

Penn and Nylie sat side-by-side, wrists bounds with handcuffs made from zip ties. A police officer sat with them and sipped a soda. Penn kept his head down. He didn't raise his chin when I walked into the room.

I greeted the police officer formally and reached out to touch Penn's shoulder. Penn raised his head at my touch. His eyes were different: brighter, clearer. They did not look tired or brimmed with tears, but younger. More naïve. They reminded me of the water in the pool I had dove into just a week before: chilling. Shattering.

Penn stood when he saw me. The officer yelled in Swahili to stay sitting down. In his brown uniform, he paced back and forth tapping his baton in his hand. The officer seemed nervous; he had never had criminals in his custody before. And that's what we were. Criminals.

I squatted down next to Penn and put my head down, clasped my fingers around his knee.

Nylie shook and did not stop shaking, "Madam, you saw my husband is there?" Nylie whispered. She was convulsing now, a tired, brown leaf.

"Yes, I saw him. What is he doing here? How did he find out...?" I didn't recognize my voice. It sounded swollen and purple like Nylie's eyes.

"He told the man at the security that he knows, Isabel," Nylie muttered. She exhaled her words like smoke. "He said he knows about the passports. I didn't know what to do, so we told them to call you."

Another security guard walked in, wearing starched clothes and smooth, ironed hair. She carried a baton and held in her hand two passports: an American passport for Penn and a Kenyan passport for Nylie. She closed the door behind her.

"Israel?" the security guard asked. Penn and Nylie looked up curiously at the woman. There had to be some mistake, there was no Israel here. Nylie suddenly stood. She looked different in her Western clothes, the black skirt that hit her shins and the white sleeves that covered her slim shoulders. She seemed bigger, curvier, compared to the enveloping fabric she usually wore.

"It's me, Madam!" Nylie shrieked like a bird, "I am Israel."

The security guard looked bored. She casually handed the passport over to the pathetic tall woman with the black eyes that came in two different colors and the cracked voice.

"Go." The security guard commanded her. She pulled a letter opener from her pocked and cut the zip ties that bound her hands.

Nylie, Penn, and I exchanged confused glances. The intercom spoke about the flight to Kenya leaving soon. It screamed out last call and Nylie grabbed her backpack.

My heart rose from my stomach to my chest. "Go!" I shouted to Nylie. "Go, you are going to be late!"

Sometimes bravery and fear look the same.

The woman in the starched uniform searched Penn's face. "Penn Clemence?" she asked. Penn nodded solemnly. He kept his head down; I still had not seen his eyes. "You are not an American citizen, are you?"

Penn stayed silent. No one knew what to say.

"Let me help you," the starched woman sighed, "We know you are not an American citizen. We contacted the embassy." She seemed sad and tired.

Penn stayed silent and continued to nod. I wanted to put my face in the back of his neck.

"We tracked down your birth certificate, Penn. You are a Congolese citizen with no record of ever having a home in the United States."

A sound escaped Penn's mouth. It was not an argument, not an explanation. It was pain.

The security guard softened. I pictured her at home with her own children. She would've done exactly what Penn's mother did in her situation, I was certain of it. She would've hidden her own child to her chest and insisted they find safety. I waited for her words to calm my raging soul. I waited for Penn to find a solution like he always did. But we did not speak. Words dried up in our throats and floated out of our nostrils in a long exhale.

"I'm sorry," the security guard whispered in English.

We floated above our bodies for a moment and watched the scene play out. The security guard left and Penn reached out to embrace me as best he could with his wrists tied. My arms felt thin under the sweatshirt and his embrace. I placed my hands behind my neck. I hummed gently the song the students would sing, "Your mother may let you down, your brother may let you down, your sister may let you down but Jesus never fails." It was a strange song to be running through my body now. But I wanted words, and they were the only ones I knew in that moment.

Penn bent his head down so close to my neck I could feel his exhales on my skin. His breath prickled and sent goose bumps up my cold arms, my tired legs.

The humming continued and I felt something wet on the back of my neck. It's strange, to be able to feel the salt in a teardrop.

I continued to hum. I gently rocked and I felt Penn rain. His muscles relaxed as he slowly came undone.

We felt that moment: the heaviness of the air and the deepness of our thoughts. It was the last moment before he said truths that both of us knew but did not want to speak out loud. We tried to relish that space between knowing and naivety. We pulled off the Band-Aid as slowly as possible and left behind the sticky residue. I no longer controlled my mind. I allowed myself to think of every potential desire that I had willed out of my thoughts all of these months. Penn and I could live nearby in Denver. He could pick me up in his new car and we could go to brunch on Sundays. I would sit with his mom when I went over to visit and allow her to tell me stories about my own mother. I would let Penn come to my father's house and I would watch him talk about football. When I felt scared or misunderstood back in the place that I thought was my home, I would press my face into Penn's brown chest, and he would understand. I would let him tell me he loved me. I would tell him that I loved him, too. My body shivered at the prospects of what could be, held my breath, and watched Penn do the same.

When we could not hold our breaths any longer, Penn spoke. It was too soon; I was not done imagining. I wanted to dream for a moment more, about what we could tell everyone about our adventures in Africa. About what people would say when they saw us hold hands. I wanted to know what we would look like in a photograph together.

"Fix this!" I hissed to Penn between blurry eyes and wet cheeks, "Fix this so you can go home!"

And then, there was that look. The look Penn saved for moments like this where nothing in the whole world could touch him. That the worst news was nothing compared to the strength of his shoulders or the focus inside him. "I am going home, Isabel. Africa is my home."

50

My body did not return to Africa for five years. I returned often in my thoughts, my dreams, the way I attempted to roll my r's and click my tongue to signify disappointment. My dreams were flighty and confusing, but a few images remained engrained in my thoughts and mind for the rest of my life: an orange grapefruit sun melting into the horizon; the thin ankles of girls decorated with silver chains retrieving water from the well, laughing black eyes with skin so smooth it did not crease at the corners. I often found myself absentmindedly shielding my eyes from the dust that no longer encompassed my life when the breeze picked up. I still twisted fabric around my waist as a more efficient alternative to finding pants when the mailman was at the door. The bright fabrics holding babies to backs, breasts to chests, tomatoes close to the body carried in from the garden filled my head when my eyes were closed.

Three months after I returned to the states I went to New Orleans and laid pink begonias at the ridgeline where I had refused to attend Ivy's funeral a year before. I told my mother I had gone to Tanzania, and I was sorry I hadn't come to tell her sooner. I told her I loved her, and promised that I forgave her. I told her that there was a headstrong, stubborn girl I had met in Tanzania, and she needed a new name so we called her Ivy Supeet. I told her that I needed to move on now that those words were spoken. That day, as sticky and sweet as her funeral, I prayed for the first time in a long time. I prayed that heaven existed.

The day I came home from visiting the gravesite in New Orleans I pulled Theresa alone into the bedroom she shared with my father and asked her to formally adopt me. She cried but I stood steady. I knew pain and this wasn't it.

My life adjusted. I held a job in the corporate office for the public-school system, and instinctively brushed dust from the chair every morning. Annie had moved to New York and we talked about returning to Tanzania one day. We texted occasionally about strange thoughts and memories, and allowed the other to assure us that we were not crazy, that those things actually did happen. I lived alone and fell in love and out of love a million times in those five years. But I never would know love the way I did with Nylie, Maya and Loveness. Eventually, I stopped looking.

My arms and legs that knew the sweat and my eyes that knew tears in Africa, they did not make the journey back until five years later. I did not return to Amani Manor on this journey. That structure of yellow walls permanently creased with dust was not what made Africa my home. Instead, I booked my ticket into Nairobi to see the women who had changed me.

I walked up stone steps painted bright blue and I noticed handprints in the cement near the staircase. One had a curly "L" drawn in the center, the other an "N" carefully drawn below the handprint. My heart pounded faster.

Nylie and Loveness lived together. They shared a one-bedroom apartment in a quiet part of town surrounded by red and purple Jacaranda trees. Their courtyard had avocado trees and lemon trees and the girls told me they could take the fruit whenever they felt like it. The smell had been familiar as I flew into the Nairobi airport: burning rubbish. Sweet chai. Fresh milk. I'd closed my eyes and remembered a place I had not been before. Kenya was new to me, but the memories overtook me: the orange sun and brown skin that warmed up my insides like coffee with sugar. My head pounded when I arrived; the bizarre combination of memories mixed with wonder at the new.

I raised my fist up to the wooden door and held my knuckles inches away from the peeling paint. I wondered if I would recognize them. I wondered if they would recognize me. My hair was shorter now. I had cut the length almost entirely off upon arriving home, convinced the dust and the memories were stuck within the curls somewhere. Perhaps I looked a bit older. I noticed a line permanently etched into my forehead, vertical between my eyebrows. Theresa told me it made me look distinguished, some maturity between big eyes and curly hair. The line was a road on the map of my face, formed from the furrowing of my brow when I thought of the miles I had travelled.

The door creaked open without my knuckles ever touching the wood. There, in the doorway, a woman stood, tall and proud, shoulders pressed down her back. Her arms were toned and defined, but her eyes were the same: milky brown and soft in contrast to the inky black of her perfect face and shoulders. I cried when I saw Loveness. She squealed with delight and we embraced until five years of distance and culture and fear and memories dissolved into nothing more than pure and unshakable love between women.

Loveness had not yet been back to the village. Her mother had come to visit three times. She brought her baby along, a chubby preschooler with wispy hair like his mother. Loveness led me to the couch and sat me down on the familiar dusty furniture. She handed me a warm orange soda and looked at my eyes expectantly, awaiting my reaction to a home she and Nylie had maintained on their own.

"This is absolutely wonderful," I said in a whisper, and wiped the dust from the mouthpiece of the glass soda bottle. Loveness beamed with the approval.

She told me that she had excelled in teaching English through the computer. She was still at the company, and had the title of manager now.

"No other woman has had the title of manager at work except me," she said shyly.

Loveness handed me a photo she had tucked into the pocket of the same burgundy and white skirt we had bought for her all of those years ago. In the photo stood her son, smiling in a school uniform, complete with black patent shoes and the same shy smile as his mother.

"The extra money I make," Loveness explained, she kept her eyes down to the cement floor, "I send back home. My mother built a cement house. And my son goes to school. He's just in those young grades now, but he's top of his class."

I smiled and squeezed her hand. We heard the door creak, and the same bubbling soul I had last seen with two black eyes and a bleeding heart stood at the door, in a full skirt suit and black high heels. She had grown her hair long enough for braids. Nylie screamed like a child when she saw me. She looked beautiful.

Loveness sat on the couch and held my hand while Nylie bustled inside and started cooking rice on the first gas lit stove I had seen in Africa. Nylie rattled on about her job as a secretary and all of the people she had met, and how they could not believe that she had come from a tribal village and possessed such good English, that she had undoubtedly learned at Amani Manor. She told me that she worked at the office during the day, and in the evenings, she took classes at the teacher's college down the street.

"Do you want to become a teacher here in Nairobi?" I asked, as I watched Nylie spice the rice in the exact same way she used to over the open fire. I wondered if she remembered how hectic it had been to collect wood every evening to boil their water. I wondered if she missed those long dusty walks to the well. I wondered if she thought of that struggle fondly.

Nylie looked up and smiled. "No, my dear sister, I am returning home to the village to teach." A sharp inhale entered through my chest, a burst of excitement like stars. She told me she had been talking with her husband. They had spoken in a way she never had before, with honesty. He had taken another wife, even younger than Nylie, but he seemed to respect the move Nylie had made. She sent money home and her son was growing, tall and long with curly eyelashes like his mother. Apparently, her son even asked about "the light skin lady that was friends with my mama."

"I plan to return to the village by the time by son is in grade one, so I can be the teacher. He will have to call me "mama" at home and "madam" at school." Nylie squealed with excitement at this prospect.

Nylie told me years before I arrived in Kenya that Maya had not liked the rules of the safe house: the hours that the lights were to be turned down and the chores required of the girls or the work that was expected of a brilliant nineteen-year-old who had only made it through grade five. Maya had left the safe house two months after arriving in Nairobi. The poet and the other girls had seen her working as a sex worker on the main road of the city: she had high heels and long nails and the long hair she could have never been able to keep in the village where she was born.

I instantly balked at the news, nauseated that so much work and struggle had been met by the stubbornness of a girl who needed to make her own decisions. Was this better than being married to a man and creating a family with someone she did not love? Better than watching her father's cattle? My mind flashed to Maya's powerful voice and adamant "no's." I thought of her unwavering desire to make her own choices, whether it be remaining in fifth grade for five years or becoming a prostitute on bright Nairobi streets. Could she live that life and be happy? I held on to the idea that her choice and her voice allowed something like happiness. Maybe a choice is as close to happiness as anyone can get.

51

The Congo did not feel familiar the way Nairobi did. The trees were greener and the language was smoother, bubblier, spoken more quickly like the cars that drove down rain-soaked pavement. I felt cold and shivered, then hailed a pink taxi and showed the driver the address scrolled on a scrap of paper. He smiled and gave thumbs up towards my teal and coffee fabric, a gift from Nylie and Loveness as we cried and kissed goodbye.

I smiled nervously. "Merci," I whispered.

The house was further out in the country than I expected, surrounded by a wooden gate with goats and chickens milling around the courtyard. I was surprised at the greenness and freshness. Banana trees stood outside and waved large wet branches like triumphant fists. I stepped sandaled feet through rain puddles as I tiptoed my way to the front door. In the garden, eggplants hung heavy from vines and mangoes burned yellow on shiny green branches.

A child ran out from behind the front door, tall and thin with a wide crooked smile and flaming brown eyes. She grabbed my legs and hugged me, and looked up with a glittering face. The child wore a blue and orange dress, made out of silky material that reflected every raindrop as it fell from the graying sky.

A man appeared in the doorway: strong, firm. His muscles rippled beneath his shirt and he stretched his arms up behind his head, revealing the familiar trail of hair from his navel to his belt.

"Who is this?" I asked, and scooped the small child up in my arms. She twisted her legs together behind my back and beamed.

Penn looked down at his bare feet, perhaps embarrassed at the vulnerability of the situation. I had felt that vulnerability during the drive over. He looked well: happy and strong. He had written me that he had started a garden and begun some construction work on the side. He told me he had loved speaking French again, just the way his mother used to do when he was a child. He said he had his own child now, and that he loved another woman. It was only in that letter that he had failed to sign "I love you" at the end. But we continued to write. Penn wrote me that he was happy and his mother came to visit at least once a year. He said that now that he had a family, he didn't need to return back to the States, at least not yet. I cried when I read that letter; I was thankful for his peace.

I set the small child down and she kept hold of my hand.

"What is your name?" I asked softly and slowly, bending down to look into her bright eyes. I wondered if Penn had taught his daughter English in the way he had promised in his letters.

The little girl blushed and brought her shoulder to her cheek, "My name is Isabel."

My eyes flickered toward Penn, who remained smiling in the doorway. He shrugged and looked up at me shyly, "I wanted her to be brave."

ABOUT THE AUTHOR

Ella Rachel Kerr was born and raised near Denver, Colorado, and has spent time in the rural village at the base of Mt. Kilimanjaro. Her passions include advocating for women's education all over the world and running through the mountains. You can read more about her life in Tanzania, as well as her current adventures at www.ellakerr.com.

SUGAR AND DUST

Made in the USA
Monee, IL
05 November 2020